THE PUNISHMENTS

JB WINSOR
AUTHOR OF RIVER STONE

THE PUNISHMENTS

A NOVEL BY

JB WINSOR

BOULDER DIGITAL PUBLISHING, LLC
Boulder, Colorado USA

THE PUNISHMENTS
by
John B Winsor

Copyright © 2016 John B Winsor

All rights reserved.

Boulder Digital Publishing
568 Marine Street
Boulder, CO 80302

Cover design by Ben Wright, bwrightimages
Interior layout by Nick Zelinger, NZ Graphics

ISBN: 978-0-9829194-4-6 (soft cover)
ISBN: 978-0-9829194-5-3 (hard cover)
ISBN: 978-0-9829194-3-9 (e-book)

Library of Congress Cataloging-in-Publication Data

First Edition June 2016

Printed in the United States of America

*"Men never do evil so completely and so cheerfully
as when they do it from religious conviction."*
—Blaise Pascal
17th-century French mathematician and philosopher

*" . . . an authoritarian state church . . . a fascist ideology . . .
could replace the liberal polity of the Enlightenment."*
—Karen Armstrong
The Battle for God

CHAPTER 1

Washington

Senator William Thatcher

TEN DAYS BEFORE THE KIDNAPPING, Thatcher dropped the unemployment crisis report on his desk in the Hart Senate Office Building. He leaned back in his chair, irritated by the rich tones of the electronic bell striking fourteen o'clock.

The bell had been installed high in the Capitol's Dome after the last election. On Sundays the bell ordered four hundred forty-eight selectmen to church services in the chamber of the House of Representatives. There was historic precedent—the chamber had been used for worship during the Jefferson and Madison presidencies. Back then, of course, the services were nondiscriminatory and voluntary.

Now the Director of Virtue conducted Sunday prayers, resplendent in his red robes, standing below the stainless steel neo-cross clinging to the wall behind the Speaker's rostrum.

Now the bell called Thatcher to Virtue's unveiling ceremony.

Thatcher checked his neo-cross lapel pin and touched his wall-hung wooden crucifix for good luck as he walked past. He had made the cross when he had been a kid. He strode past his staff in the office and walked into the hallway. He joined a group of senators waiting for the elevators. He nodded a greeting at Senator Dupré, who had voted with Thatcher against giving the Department of Virtue the power to enforce Biblical Law. Their action had formed the type of warrior respect created during Afghan war fire-fights. They had lost the vote—Virtue now had enforcement power. Dupré slipped into an elevator and the door closed. Thatcher rode the next elevator down to the subway platform where other senators waited silently for a ride to the Capitol. Virtue's opto-screens plastered the walls:

FREEDOM   SECURITY   FOOD

He boarded the train and sat next to his mentor, Alan Long, the senior senator from his home state of Montana. They remained silent during the trip. There was a chance their conversation would be recorded. They got off at the station under the Capitol Building, walked through long corridors, hurried past more opto-screens, rode up an elevator, and emerged into bright September sunshine at the top of the Capitol's west stairs over-looking the National Mall. Thatcher squinted in the bright September sunshine. When his eyes adjusted, he stopped, awed by the sight.

A solid mass of men jammed the Mall between the Lincoln Memorial, Washington Monument and Capitol Building. The hum of voices sounded like a swarm of angry hornets.

"How many would you guess?" Long asked.

"Virtue estimated a million men," Thatcher said.

"Always a million. Doesn't look half that to me. What do you think?"

"I believe whatever Virtue tells me."

"Stop being cynical, Thatcher."

Thatcher and Senator Long queued up in one of twenty dignitary-only seating lines. They shuffled forward like a line of ants toward a security checkpoint.

Senator Long pointed to the Capitol Dome draped by a thin opaque material. "So what's Virtue hidden under that shroud?"

"I've got an idea."

"Gonna tell me?" Senator Long asked.

"Nope."

In 1863 former slaves hoisted the 15,000-pound, 19-foot-tall Statue of Freedom to the top of the Capitol Dome. Last week, in secrecy of night, Virtue removed Freedom.

Thatcher looked at an armed security guard, wearing body armor, helmet and black plastic face shield. Robot or human? Hard to tell the difference, unless you could see the eyes. He decided it was human. Perhaps that was wishful thinking.

The guard motioned Thatcher into a circular glass booth. The door hissed shut. He spotted the ceiling vent tubes that could spray poison. Trapped. He wiped his damp hands against his trousers.

Others had died inside the booths when the facial identification system identified them as terrorists. Rumors said some innocents died when the system failed. The technology wasn't perfect. Virtue proclaimed the gas caused immediate death. Humane. Instant justice. Thatcher's breathing quickened as he inserted his National ID card into a wall slot. He placed his hand on a graphite pad. He looked into a facecam and held his breath. He shouldn't have voted against Virtue's Supreme Biblical Law and Moral Court legislation.

The scanning process would have been faster if he had an ID chip, the size of a grain of rice, implanted under his skin. The embedding technology, called "CertiChip," had been used for the past ten years for personnel in high-security facilities.

Implantations would be mandatory for all citizens by the end of the year. Virtue promoted CertiChips as an anti-terrorism security program.

Even though the embedded chip allowed satellite tracking of every movement, there had been no public outcry. People gave up freedom to feel safe from terrorists. Soon everyone would be tracked, movements and motivations analyzed, their future predicted for potential intervention.

Thatcher felt a rivulet of sweat course down from his armpit. He waited as computers compared his face and DNA to the card's data and the dignitary database. His ID popped up. Rumors said the poison was released the moment an identified terrorist pulled his card from the machine. He prayed there had not been a deadly mistake. He held his breath and jerked out the card. The front barrier hissed open. He exhaled. He stepped out and waited for Senator Long. Nearby, a line of twenty Force members stood at frozen attention, awaiting orders. Obviously robots.

Startled by noise from the security booth on his left, he watched Senator Dupré claw at the door and bang on the glass as mist poured from ceiling vents. His eyes bulged, face contorted with grotesque fear and pain. He coughed, spraying droplets of blood against the glass before collapsing out of sight.

Two robot Force members moved to the security booth, waited for vents to clear the poison, opened the door, and dragged Senator Dupré by his feet across the lawn, then behind a cloth-draped fence bearing Virtue's slogan, 'Security'. Struggling not to show emotion, Thatcher quickly looked away. Perhaps the rumor that Virtue had an "enemies" list was true.

If so, why had Virtue killed Dupré and not him? He kept his face frozen. He was watched. All were watched. Senator Long stepped out of his booth and joined him, face expressionless.

They walked past black-clad Metro Force members, armed with machine guns, scanning an open field of fire between the bleachers and the fence that separated the masses from dignitaries. Other officers, humans, watched through the scopes of .50-caliber Barrett sniper rifles, scrutinizing the crowd from various positions on the scaffolding of opto-screens first seen in football stadiums. A fence of two-inch thick Plexiglas, strong enough to stop a hand-held rocket, protected the senators' bleachers.

They found their assigned seats high on the stands facing the Capitol Building with its shroud-covered dome. Opto-screens pictured men crowding the Mall. Men. Only men. They would watch the unveiling ceremony on four-story-high screens flanking the Mall.

The screens went black. Virtue's official music, Wagner's *Meistersinger* overture, Hitler's favorite, blared out. The music echoed off the Capitol Building, merging with the refrain, mixing the two refrains into reverberating dissonant sound.

The screens snapped back to life. A Virtue cameraman panned from the Reflecting Pool to the US Capitol Building, and zoomed in on the hooded dome. Black words appeared under the image:

Unveiling Ceremony
Honoring those who died
during the September 11th
World Trade Center
Terrorist Attack

The image of the veiled dome melted into a picture of the World Trade Center's twin towers.

"Not again." Thatcher moaned to himself. He had been in the grade school cafeteria during the attack. Hearing shouts, he had turned to watch other students point to the wall-mounted TV.

When the opto-screens showed the second plane crashing into the second tower, a bestial growl rose from the men in the Mall. The first structure began to implode, raining tons of steel and glass and desks and computers and water coolers and toilets and telephones and papers and bodies. Men and women ran down the street, fleeing a wall of thick gray smoke rolling over them like a lava flow. Mouths open, gasping for air, faces masks of death.

A chant, beginning somewhere in the middle of the Mall, spread through the crowd. Anger grew in vehemence and volume. The mob's sound waves hammered Thatcher's body. He smelled their rage.

"New—York! NEW—YORK!! **NEW—YORK!!!**"

The dignitaries in the bleachers picked up the chant.

Thatcher listened to the chants of the mob. He remained silent, remembering the many years of relative peace between major terrorist events against America. And then there was Chicago.

The images of the World Trade Center rubble faded into a picture of John Hancock Building. A security camera had captured grainy pictures of a wholesale food semi-trailer truck turning off Michigan Avenue onto Delaware Street. Hijacked four hours earlier, it had been loaded with explosives. Committing suicide, its driver detonated a blast four times as powerful as the one that destroyed the Murrah Federal Building in Oklahoma City. The blast destroyed the Hancock building's north superstructure. The 100 story skyscraper tipped at a precarious twenty-degree angle, trapping tourists in 360° Chicago, the building's observatory on the 94th floor, 1,030 feet above the sidewalk. Fires trapped residents.

Image quality improved after TV crews from WMAQ-TV, located a few blocks away, began filming the disaster. Flames engulfed buildings across the street from the Hancock Building, including the Westin Hotel. South, across Chestnut Street, Water Tower Place, Chicago's upscale shopping mall, received fatal collateral damage. Over 6,000 people died.

Unlike the World Trade Center buildings, the Hancock Building stood for eight days, giving ample time for close-ups of trapped residents suffocating, burning to death, one by one, floor by floor by floor.

"Chi—ca—go! CHI—CA- GO!! **CHI—CA—GO!!!**"

The chanting began slowly, over and over. The sound of feet stamping on pavement increased, the combined force hammering Thatcher with a body shaking rhythm.

Thatcher felt disoriented. He tried to tune out the mob's chants by recalling other problems that had shaken America: the imperceptible rise of robotics throwing millions out of work, the financial meltdown, and the anger and frustration created by the disappearance of the middle class. Baby Boomers died off, forcing the sale of their real estate and equities, depressing the economy even further.

The standard of living continued to fall. Society split: the minority—the highly educated scientists, technologists, business people and academics were doing well economically.

The others, the vast majority, had no hope of improving themselves. Their anger drove them to elect demagogues and fundamentalists—men who promised a return to a better life, a return to prosperity and Christian values.

The rise of ISIS and other terrorist groups created more enemies, but it proved to be difficult to bomb an ideology. Terrorists popped up everywhere—it was like playing Whack-A-Mole. That conflict, Thatcher thought, would go on for a hundred years or more. They would always be fighting terrorists of one belief or another.

The images of the John Hancock Building attack faded, replaced by pictures of a five-year-old girl, body covered with festering black sores. The pandemic had been blamed on terrorists. The little girl writhed in agony as she died. The men in the Mall began another chant:

"A—mer—i -ca! A—MER- I—CA!!
A—MER—I—CA!!!"

Overpowered by the reek of the mob's sweat, Thatcher watched the images change to other gruesome scenes of the victims of the bioterrorist attack that killed over five hundred thousand Americans before the doctors from the Centers for Disease Control contained the scourge.

"A—mer—i -ca! A—MER- I—CA!!
A—MER—I—CA!!!"

Next, appeared the pictures of the hacker attack that destroyed the electrical grid. Parts of the country had been thrown back into the Middle Ages. No heat, no light, no gas, no ability to transport food. Within a week there was no food in grocery stores. No one kept more than several weeks of food in their cabinets—food in the refrigerators and freezers rotted.

Pharmacies, reliant on just-in-time deliveries, ran out. There were no deliveries. Older people, dependent on medicines, died soon after swallowing their last pill. It had been a grisly triage.

Some areas of the country, primarily in the warmer climates of the South and West, managed to survive better than others.

The Mormons survived because of their family food storage policy, but millions of others died. It took five years to restore the grid. After martial law was lifted, men with strong, uncompromising, fundamental ideals had been swept into office.

"A—mer—i -ca! A—MER- I—CA!!

A—MER—I—CA!!!"

The opto-screens faded to black. Chanting slowed until an eerie silence blanketed the Mall. A robin chirped displeasure at someone standing under its nest.

An image formed on the screens: an unblinking obsidian eye. The Eye, uncaring, human yet mechanical, was the tip of a drill bit auguring into Thatcher's soul. Probing for impurities. He wanted to confess sins, real or imagined. Everyone had personal secrets. He did. Those dead school kids in Afghanistan. Thatcher shook his head and shivered.

The president, senators, congressmen, dignitaries and men in the Mall avoided the glower of the Eye. Heads lowered as the Director's voice boomed, "Bow thy heads for prayer!"

Senator Long elbowed him. He lowered his head, but still watched the screen. The close-up of the Eye receded, revealing the face of Reverend John, the Director of the Department of Virtue. He began talking,

"Today we commemorate the anniversary of the cowardly terrorist attack on the World Trade Center.

"Today we celebrate our return to the wisdom of our Founding Fathers to create a Christian Nation.

"Today we affirm the imminence of the Rapture and Second Coming.

"The Lord hath spoken unto me. '*It is time*'!

"It is time to raise our heads to be blessed by God. It is time to celebrate His wisdom to replace the temporal with the spiritual.

"LET THE UNVEILING CEREMONY BEGIN!"

The Director's image faded from the screens. Virtue's cameramen panned toward the Lincoln Memorial at the west end of the Mall. Five black helicopters rose like specters behind the Memorial. They hovered in a tight diamond formation. Dipping low, they swooped over the long reflecting pool. Their rotors' wash roiled the water into whitecaps before they rose vertically to hover over the five-hundred-fifty-five-foot-high Washington Monument. Plunging down, they skimmed the World War II Memorial, and then charged toward the nation's Capitol Building, buzzing the spectators on the Mall. Thumping rotors smothered their cheers.

The helicopters roared overhead. Thatcher covered his ears and shut his eyes from swirling dust. When he looked again, they hovered over the Capitol Building's veiled dome. A cable snaked out of the belly of each helicopter toward the dome's cover, lowering a scarlet-shirted Virtue agent balancing on a steel hook. Each man wore a safety harness attached to a winch inside the craft.

Each man guided his hook through a metal ring that protruded from the bottom of the dome's white veil. Once the hook had been attached, the men were pulled into the safety of the fuselage. Now connected to the shroud, the helicopters hovered stationary over the Capitol Dome.

Reverend John began a blessing for the unveiling, beginning as always with the fact that the National Council of Churches and the Congress of the United States had voted to adopt the fundamental tenets of the Old and New Testaments as Biblical Law for the nation during the War on Terrorism, yet still abide by the Constitution to respect the rights of all religions.

Rotor blades thumped louder. The helicopters inched upward and outward, lifting the corners of the cover to expose more of the dome. They gained altitude faster, removing the shroud like a strip-teaser raising her white gown. Male voices roared approval.

From the top of the Capitol Dome, a giant silver neo-cross rose toward Heaven. The neo-cross was fifteen feet higher than the cupola: the spiritual symbol taller than its temporal base. Its pointed base was a dagger about to thrust into the Capital Building. The supporting feet of the neo-cross that imprisoned the Dome were like the talons of a hawk.

Dignitaries jumped to their feet. Thatcher cheered along with the mob, stomping his feet against the metal bleacher. The rhythmic noise washed over him like waves, smothering reason. Chest quivering, he chanted with the rest. Men clapped him on the back. The bleachers shook. The sound rose to a climax of frenzy. He glanced at Senator Long. Their eyes met. He quickly looked away, embarrassed that he'd been swept up by the mob's emotions.

Later, walking back up the Capitol's west stairs, thinking about Senator Dupré, Thatcher asked Senator Long, "Think we made a mistake backing the lawsuit against the formation of Virtue's Supreme Moral Court?"

Long shook his head, "The road to Hell is paved with good intentions."

Thatcher walked into his office. His chief aide, Richard Bowman rushed to greet him. "Virtue agents installed a neo-cross in your office. I tried to stop them, but they showed me their orders: a neo-cross in every office. They took your wooden cross."

He stared at the five-foot-tall neo-cross on the far wall. He wanted to rip it down, but that would be a criminal act of aggression against Virtue. Constructed of highly polished stainless steel, the arms radiated from a flat-mirrored middle. His reflection from the beveled centerline of the upper arm split his face: his right side normal, his left drawn into anguished scream. He looked like a man trapped in Hell.

Thatcher sucked in a ragged breath. There were rumors of a camera embedded behind the mirror in the center of the neo-cross. He forced a grave nod at the cross—for Virtue's sake.

CHAPTER 2

Washington, DC

Felix

FELIX LIMPED ALONG A DESERTED forest trail in the Rock Creek Park. A distant church bell chimed fifteen o'clock.

She wore a Redskins ball cap covered by a hood, a ragged overcoat and a backpack with a soiled blanket strapped on top. A bottle of vodka nestled in the left coat pocket. It was a good disguise, but still she searched for signs of danger. She listened to the hum of distant traffic. Her fingers caressed the comfort of the .45 caliber derringer in her coat pocket.

Crows flew into a tree and cawed.

She inhaled scents: the stink of her filthy cloths, decaying leaves, the sharp fragrance of cedar trees reminding her of the hillsides of Morocco, and then a sudden pungent odor of feces. She glanced down in time to avoid a pile of dog shit.

Her forefinger traced the five-inch double-barreled derringer. Her father had given it to her years ago in Marrakesh—"A gift for you, Princess—the only defense you'll ever need."

The gun had looked small in his massive palm, like a toy, harmless.

She knew about his charming 'gifts'.

"I don't want it. I won't kill anyone."

"Simply for defense. Just in case. You are beautiful and you now know how men are. You'll feel better having it."

She didn't know how men were, but she knew him.

"I'll never use it."

"That's up to you, but I'd feel terrible if someone hurt you."

Because losing her would cost him money.

"Then teach me how to shoot."

"Abdul will teach you."

"Are you afraid?"

He laughed. "I know better than to be nearby if you had a loaded gun."

A gust of wind swayed tree branches. The sun cast darting shadows, making her edgy, pumping adrenaline. She loved the rush, this heightened awareness.

Still . . .

He'd forced her into a double life of innocence and evil. She'd used the derringer seven times. Seven kills. Clean kills. They hadn't suffered. She saw herself as an angel of mercy. Stamped out evil. She'd killed because she had to. Killed without joy. Killed without hatred.

Never had the chance to kill him. Wanted to. Given the opportunity, killing him would help cleanse the world of evil. Perhaps purify her soul as well. Or had evil genes passed to her through his sperm? Was she infected? Was Sara?

She had to think of something else. She hobbled along the trail trying to ignore the pain she was causing herself by dragging her foot. It had been a last-minute idea: a damaged limb to go along with the disguise of a damaged life. But it did no good, her willful attempts at oblivion. This mission didn't involve one life, or two. This was about a 'clean' nuclear weapon. The radiation wouldn't be as bad, as if anyone would care if the bomb were 'clean' or 'dirty'. This was about hundreds of thousands of lives. Anonymous lives. Innocent lives. All to save another innocent. A single innocent. Her daughter.

How could she balance one life against all those others? It was a simple question that wasn't at all simple. It was a small question that loomed large as the Atlas Mountains of her far-away Morocco.

A homeless man—a real one—sprawled under a tree, arms and legs stiff, eyes staring at the sky. He looked dead. It might be a trap. If so, she'd rather know sooner than later. She picked her way through fallen branches and leaves until she stood over him.

"Hello?"

Nothing.

"Are you asleep?"

She bent into the stench of death. Covering her nose, she used the first two fingers of her right hand to close his eyes. Even the homeless deserved dignity in death.

They died by the thousands these days, on streets, in alleys, and in parks. Sometimes city crews picked them up, sometimes not. Millions of homeless, careers eliminated by robots and artificial intelligence, roamed the country. The old government, frozen by partisanship, had been unable or unwilling to find a solution. *The bastards!*

She patted the dead man's pockets and discovered a wad of cash—hundred dollar bills. *Strange.* The government discouraged the use of money—it wanted the ability to track all purchases through smart-cards. *How could he have all this money?* She didn't want to think about that. Pocketing the cash, she returned to the trail.

Wary of an ambush, Felix studied islands of overgrown brush. She had chosen this path toward the dead drop because an earlier reconnaissance had revealed no Eyes watching.

The government had installed millions of surveillance cameras to elevate civility: if people knew they were being watched, their behavior would improve. Advanced facial recognition cameras would force them to behave as God commanded. That was the idea, anyway.

Felix hoped her heavy dark makeup; cotton stuffed between her teeth and lips, up her nostrils, and in her cheeks would fool the cameras. Vertical snake-like slits in bright blue contact lenses would help distort her eyes. Still, she didn't dare look at the sky. There might be drones.

Two crows sitting on a tree branch took flight, cawing raucously. Footsteps sprinted from behind. She jerked the bottle from her pocket and raised it toward her lips. Stumbling as if drunk, knees bent to receive an impact, she turned to face her attacker. She brought up the derringer.

A young woman wearing a tight black top, black Spandex shorts, and florescent red running shoes skidded to a halt, flinging her arms across her chest, mouth agape. A jogger.

Felix slipped the gun back into her pocket and offered the vodka bottle. The cotton balls in her cheeks slurred her words. "Want a little drink, honey?"

The runner looked like she'd seen a rattlesnake.

"You're stupid to run out here alone."

"What . . . ?"

"Stupid, I said." Felix hooked her thumbs under the backpack straps.

"I run here every day." She glanced at her watch and began jogging in place.

"You're asking for trouble."

"Uh-huh." The jogger stared, repulsed. She sidestepped around Felix, avoiding eye contact, and sprinted away. Felix inhaled a scent of healthy sweat and perfume, a combination that hinted at the gardenias in the entrance to her father's Marrakesh compound. She exhaled, slipped the bottle into her pocket, and watched the woman glance back, and then slow from a sprint to a jog.

The jogger's ponytail, lit by a sunbeam, swung in an undulating rhythm. Why didn't it bounce up and down? That side-to-side motion—a blond ponytail reflecting sunlight—was a lovely sight. On the other hand, the fool was asking for trouble, seeking an endorphin high on a deserted trail. Despite the homeless hordes, the plagues of despair and exposure, many were arrogant about safety, unaware of evil.

Felix knew evil. She watched the woman's round hips pump, tight and firm, under the stretch shorts, her smooth body a contrast against the gnarled oaks and maples. Felix envied and resented her indifference.

An arm lashed out from behind a tree trunk hooking the jogger's neck. Her head snapped back. Her feet kept pumping, red sneakers swinging off the ground like a pendulum. For an instant, her body froze horizontally. Then she crashed to the ground, a confused mass of arms, legs, and blond hair.

Warned the fool. Felix slipped behind a tree. The woman's moans sparked terrible memories—her father's eyes, his searing weight forcing breath from her lungs.

Felix shook her head to concentrate. The white face of a huge man peered up and down the trail. He bent over the woman, and dragged her by the feet into thick brush. *A trap?* Felix scanned the canopy overhead, wondering if drone watchers had picked up the attack.

The woman screamed.

Felix waited for a mini-missile strike. No retribution came tearing from the sky. Nothing.

This was none of her business. She had to get past them to reach the dead drop. She shuffled up the trail, trying to ignore the thrashing and moaning. The jogger's black running shorts were cast aside. The man's left forearm pinned the woman's throat, choking off her moans. He unbuckled his belt, pulled down his pants, his ass white against dark shadows.

A crow cawed.

The man forced the woman's legs apart. The woman screamed a ragged sharp yelp.

Still no drone strike. Perhaps the trail was not being scanned. Perhaps the ethical decision-making algorithm on the drone's computer had slowed uselessly in its attempt to identify the victim, analyze her worth—Single? Mother? Education? Job importance? Perhaps the computer had given up and referred the question to a human at Virtue.

Can't let this happen. Felix pulled the derringer from her pocket, thumbed back the hammer. The man would not rape the jogger. He would not rape any woman again. Ever. The derringer's hollow-point bullet would expand inside his skull and literally blow his brains out.

Later, Felix wondered what, at that precise moment, made her dive and flatten on the trail. A change in air pressure? A faint swoosh? She covered her head with her arms, opened her mouth wide to relieve explosive pressure. She pressed her cheek hard into the earth an instant before the tearing of leaves, the breaking of branches, the blast of skin and bone and guts.

Ears ringing, Felix staggered up, listening for footsteps. The forest was silent, smelled of charred flesh and stomach gas. She had no choice but to hobble through the clearing toward the dead drop, glancing at bits of clothing, skin, and hair, ropes of pink intestines impaled on bushes. The mini-missile had shredded the bodies. Virtue punished guilty and innocent alike.

Told her. She wouldn't listen.

Twenty minutes later, nearing the edge of the park, Felix walked through a homeless camp. She'd seen places like this all over the world. The sights and smells had been unbearable at first. Now? Just another camp. New for America, though.

Tarps covered cardboard refrigerator boxes and weathered plywood to form shelters. Men and women sat on lawn chairs and wooden stumps. They stood in small groups, staring through vacant eyes, watching their lethargic children. Judging by their clothes they had been middle class. *A long, hard fall. There but for the grace of god . . .*

Felix approached a woman who sat with her arm around a girl that reminded her of Sara.

"How old is your daughter?" Felix asked.

"Eleven and hungry" the woman said in a listless voice without looking up.

At least Sara was well fed. On the other hand . . .

"What happened?" Felix asked.

"Job taken by the robots and immigrants, like all the rest." She turned her head and coughed into her fist.

"Your husband . . .?"

"Who the hell are you? Why is it any of your business?"

"Another widow," Felix lied.

"He thought the life insurance would see us through. Good plan, but the money didn't last."

The daughter seemed not to have heard. Perhaps the girl was beyond caring.

"I'm sorry." Felix moved close to the woman, glanced around to be certain others were not watching, and slipped her the wad of cash.

The woman looked at the money and quickly hid it in her pocket. Her eyes teared. "Why?"

"I have a daughter."

The woman stared at her face. Her defeated eyes widened.

"Virtue agents around?" Felix asked.

"Not now. But they come and tell us faith will get us through tough times. Can't eat faith."

Felix limped away, nodding. Her hip hurt from her dragging foot.

"Wait," the woman called out.

She turned back. "What?"

The woman pointed with her chin to Felix's leg. "What happened?"

"Car accident," she lied, again.

"Good luck," the woman said.

Felix emerged from the park, stepped onto a cracked sidewalk and studied the cars, the pedestrians, and the homeless, looking for anything out of place. She spotted the dead drop across the street—a bench at a bus stop. She squatted, pretending to pick at her nails.

A piece of chewing gum had been pressed on a lamppost on the other side of the park: her signal that the information was taped to the bottom of the bench. Hundreds and thousands of innocent lives and she was working with the enemy to end them. She chuckled grimly: look on the bright side, she told herself. At least she wasn't sleeping with them.

It was ironic, survival in a high-tech world meant adopting the old way, low-tech ways. She shuffled past the bench and joined a group of three homeless men huddled by a windowless building. Were they the trap?

She nodded to them. "Got anything?"

"Go fuck yourself, chipmunk face," said a man stinking of booze.

They resumed their opaque conversation. She watched their eyes, listening to them argue about which church gave the best meals—ruling them out as Virtue agents attempting to identify her. She moved to study the drop zone. Leaning against the building, hands deep in pockets, she watched from under the visor of her cap as respectable people strolled past, giving the homeless nervous glances and wide berth.

Nothing spooked her, though she noted an Eye atop a pole on the corner. The Eye program—"If you have nothing to hide, you have nothing to fear!"—had been in place so long that most people either forgot they were being watched or no longer cared.

She shuffled on, into an alley where a red-bearded homeless man, wrapped in a blanket, sat in a doorway. Scanning the area to make certain no Eye watched, she moved into the doorway to avoid drone detection. She showed the man the vodka bottle. He grinned. She told him what she wanted. He nodded and stood up, dropping his blanket. He stumbled down the alley toward the bus stop, rounded the corner of the building, and disappeared.

She limped across the broken pavement toward another doorway, but turned away at the smell: a dead woman claimed it.

She moved back across the alley, burrowed inside a deep door recess, and waited. Her fingers wrapped around the derringer as she focused on the end of the alley away from the bus stop, ignoring a blowing piece of paper and the flutter of pigeon wings close overhead.

She took deep breaths to calm her breathing. Waited. Finally, the red-bearded man stumbled back into the alley looking for her. He swore and spat, perplexed, then plopped down in his doorway and covered himself with the blanket. When she was certain he had not been followed, she strode across the alley, gave him the bottle of vodka in exchange for the envelope, and returned to her doorway.

Crouching, she tore open the envelope, pulled out a three-by-five card, and memorized the numbers for a Swiss bank account.

The number that would save Sara.

She pulled out a lighter, lit the card, dropped it on the concrete, and watched the paper curl on itself in flames. She ground the black flakes of ash under her shoe, shuffled out of the alley, and turned left.

Three blocks later, after doubling back twice looking for tails, she paused under a low-hanging roof, removed her contact lenses, and spat out the cotton balls. She discarded her homeless clothes in a dumpster, smoothed the dress she had worn under the overcoat, and walked away without a limp.

She would return to the boutique shop where she'd seen the off-the-shoulder long red dress. He would be at the French Embassy reception. She was eager to meet him again after all these years.

CHAPTER 3

Five miles southeast of Washington

Reverend John

THE REVEREND JOHN THOMAS waited for them on the sunlit flagstone patio of his colonial-style house. He wore grey flannel pants and a double-breasted blue blazer. His fingers played with the brass buttons, which strained against the buttonholes. He resolved, once again, to lose weight. But good Lord, he loved eating. It was one of the few pleasures he still enjoyed, a respite from his growing responsibilities as lifetime director of The Department of Virtue.

He absorbed the peaceful surroundings of his estate: a forested five acres full of wildlife: rabbits, raccoons, quail, deer, and turkeys. A light breeze carried an acrid scent of urine. Deer droppings, small piles of black pellets, marred his perfect lawn. His property was simply overrun with white-tails. They were destroying his flowers and shrubs.

He loved watching the deer, but he loved his flowers more. There was only one solution, yet he hated the thought of killing any innocent creature.

When he'd been a child, his daddy shot deer for their table. Venison steaks, venison chops, venison hamburger—even venison tongue. Only meat they could afford, scraping out life on a patch of South Carolina dirt next to the national forest. Put on their best rags for church every Sunday. Learned that God gave authority to the man as head of the household, women and children subordinate. God gave man dominion over the earth. The Good Book was the inerrant Truth—the answer for any question man could conceive. Biblical Laws trumped man-made laws. Learned to ignore man-made laws that violated Biblical principles. Learned his obligation was to make Christianity dominate throughout the world.

The church congregation had jumped to their feet and cheered at the announcement that he'd won a scholarship to major in Christian Leadership Management and Communications at Liberty University in Lynchburg, Virginia.

Four years later, walking across campus on a crisp fall day under a canopy of bright leaves, he spotted Linda, books held across her chest, hiding God's finest creations, laughing with his friend Ted Wilson. Linda's breathtaking smile forced him to strong-arm Wilson for an introduction. Three years later, with God's help and blessing, they were married in the chapel of his first rural ministry.

Linda had wanted children. Couldn't. A doctor of their congregation had tested them. Infertile. Wasn't his fault. She wanted to adopt. He refused to accept a child created in sin.

One day several years later, he walked through several inches of fresh snow on the sidewalk next to the creek behind his church, thinking about a subject for Sunday's sermon. Something made him stop, turn and look back at his tracks, fading shadows blemishing the purity of the snow. His footprints, like life, were ephemeral.

At that moment, he was swept, unprepared, into a state of searing, otherworldly awareness. He experienced a cataclysmic personal event, a mystical occurrence. He heard the Voice of God.

"It is time to do more for the Glory of God!"

Yes! Yes of course. But what could he do? He remembered being hungry and poor. A sea of humanity flooded the planet. He would help the world's most desperate children. His chosen few would crawl to high ground to take leadership positions throughout our culture and spread the Word.

When he realized he'd actually heard the Voice of God ordering him to create a Save-a-Child Foundation, he fell to his knees, ignoring the cold snow wetting his trousers. He prayed for forgiveness at his hubris at believing his thoughts had ever been directed by anything other than the Word of the Lord.

God listened to his humility and gave him a national TV audience who flooded the Foundation with donations—millions upon millions of dollars. More money than he used saving kids. He began feeling guilty about hoarding tens of millions, hundreds of millions.

The Voice spoke again: use that extra money to help returning veterans who helped make the country safe by fighting terrorists in far off, God-forsaken places. He would provide jobs and give vets a sense of purpose by bringing the nation back to its Christian roots. He started the *Vets for a Christian Nation Foundation.*

Fundamentalists had been successful in using the Tea Party to change the grass roots political landscape of counties, states and Congress. The Voice told him it was time to use his *VCNF* manpower and money to promote candidates for national offices. He used his core group of vets to get out the vote for favored Christian fundamentalist candidates for the Senate and Congress, to intimidate and threaten political opposition. No one knew how to threaten like battle-hardened vets. As a result, his foundation's money quietly influenced elections on the state and national level.

After America's long economic malaise caused by globalization, the price-cost depressive power of the Internet, and job-killing rise of Artificial Intelligence and robotics, the Voice ordered him to back a wealthy New Mexico businessman to run for President.

Lopez-Chin was a demagogue, like several other unfortunate examples in America's political history. He gained power and popularity by arousing the emotions, anger and prejudices of the people.

He was a narcissist with no center, no principles, and no political knowledge. He had no skills other than self-aggrandizement and an uncanny ability to articulate the fears and fading hopes of economically disenfranchised voters who had lost faith in the future of America, who had watched the ties of their communities and families dissolve, watched their culture lose its meaning and hope. And they watched their jobs taken by others. By immigrants.

Reverend John knew how to manipulate the man's ego and had gone all-in to support Lopez-Chin's campaign. He poured hundreds of millions of dollars and focused his vet's organization toward the campaign.

The demagogue and fundamentalists swept into power by a landslide.

After winning the election, he called in his debt from President Lopez-Chin, and all the other congressmen and senators he had helped into office, to create the Department of Virtue. Virtue's mission was to protect the homeland through a smaller but much more efficient FBI, CIA and NSA, to replace the hated IRS with a simple flat-tax system, and to spread the Judeo-Christian belief system throughout the world: to spread Christian values. He had been named lifetime director of Virtue.

Nearly a year later, he'd had a crisis of faith after the Voice told him it was time to trigger the Rapture—just prior to the Second Coming of Jesus Christ, both dead and living believers would be caught up into the clouds to meet the Lord in the air, followed by a seven-year period of suffering in which the Antichrist would conquer the world and persecute those who refused to worship him. At the end of this period of tribulation, Christ would return to defeat the Antichrist and establish the age of peace.

Reverend John had not believed in the Rapture. His eschatology had been based on end-times theology, post-millennialism, believing Christ would come again only after the majority of the global population was converted to Christianity as a result of evangelization.

That issue of the Rapture, the method and timing of the second coming, had been disputed for as long as he could remember. In fact, the argument originated in the nineteenth century by a preacher by the name of John Nelson Darby. The argument had been caused by different interpretations of the Bible. Man-made interpretations.

After agonizing about what to do, Reverend John decided to pick and choose what he needed from both beliefs in order to obey God. After all, it was His Voice that ordered him to trigger the Rapture.

That's why he'd ordered the nuke from a shadowy character named Felix. What were a hundred thousand lives, compared with hundreds of millions who would be saved?

Now, standing on the patio of his mansion, feeling truly blessed, he watched a gentle breeze rustle oak leaves. The Voice whispered to him. He fought an impulse to fall to his knees.

There had been a time early on when he wasn't certain he listened to the voice of God. Perhaps the words had been his own thoughts. There had been so many competing voices, but the Voice revealed the truth and led to success. He now obeyed the Voice with certainty, resolve and humility.

Powerful words coursed through his mind. He listened carefully and nodded. The Voice faded with the breeze, leaving him feeling hollow and lonely, but that's how He worked. God had chosen him to demonstrate the power of Biblical Law to the world before triggering the Rapture. When His plan succeeded, Reverend John would be filled with power and glory for eternity. Still, he felt ambivalent about going up at the Rapture—he so enjoyed his earthly work for the Lord. But how could he disobey God Himself?

Filled with the Spirit, he watched two cameramen from his studio arrive, set up cameras, and attend to last minute details. After making certain his blazer collar lay smooth and flat, he smiled and waved. The cameramen waved back with obvious fondness and respect. Everyone loved and admired him. He had been blessed.

Reverend Ted Wilson, his old college friend and now director of Save-A-Child orphanage, stood on the far side of the gate talking to Linda. Their heads were close together. She laughed, face alive, flirtatious. Smiling like that first time he had spotted her on campus. Nothing unusual. Linda and Reverend Ted had been childhood friends. Reverend John was happy they had a chance to visit. He pulled a comb from his breast pocket, stroked his long white hair, pocketed the comb, and nodded to the assistant, who opened the gate.

A flood of smiling orphans rushed in, young girls and boys wearing black shorts and crisp white shirts, a mix of Blacks, Whites, Hispanics and Asians. They ran toward him across the lawn, arms outstretched to touch their savior.

The waist-length black hair of a budding girl reflected sunrays as she raced toward him. The boy running next to her was an Asian-black mix, with smooth skin, almond eyes and brilliant teeth framed by sensuous full lips. Both would have been forced into sexual slavery and would have died early. His foundation's scouts chose the children for their beauty and native intelligence, plucking more than five hundred from the millions of orphans in the world's worst slums. It wasn't quantity, but quality they selected. Besides, millions of dollars annually diverted to the Vets foundation were a better investment in the Lord's work.

The children surrounded him, fingering the fabric of his pants, the hem of his blazer. Sweat and unidentifiable child smells pricked his nostrils. Jostled by little bodies, fingers explored his pockets. He didn't mind. The children were street smart. They had learned to steal to survive. Years ago, he learned to carry nothing during such public relations events.

He considered these kids, and those that had come before, his children. God had decided that his wife Linda would be fruitless. And He had been all-wise, because Reverend John would have been a terrible father. He did not know how Linda felt—they avoided the subject. Being childless did not bother him—this greeting session and his annual inspection of the orphanage fulfilled his parental needs. God had bigger plans for him—much bigger. He felt the pacemaker implanted under his collarbone. *Just grant me the time to complete your plans, merciful God.*

He forced his lips into an avuncular smile and patted heads for the cameras. He imagined lice crawling from their hair onto his hands, creeping up his arms, swarming across his neck into his thick white hair, scrabbling across his scalp, seeking nesting sites.

Reverend Ted lined up the children on the patio. Reverend John helped straighten up the line. He hated uneven lines. He told the children to tuck in their shirts and smooth them down so they did not look messy. Kids could look untidy without trying. Turning his best angle to the cameras, he addressed them.

"God and I welcome you to your new life here in the United States of America, a Christian nation. By the grace of Jesus Christ, you have been selected for salvation and redemption. Many children just like you have been selected for our teaching orphanage. They have learned how to live a life of Christian values. Many have gone on to accomplish great things. All had an opportunity to live a better life. Study hard and obey Reverend Ted, for he is now your father. I will come to visit you and hear about your progress. Good luck and God bless!"

Reverend Ted waved his arms for the children to cheer. After the kids quieted, he said, "Stand tall to receive a cross from Reverend John—a symbol of your new life."

As he pinned a silver neo-cross on each child's shirt, he imagined lice burrowing into his skin, sucking his blood, propagating. He used all his will power to keep smiling, not scratch his head and run screaming for a shower.

After the last pinning, Reverend Ted twirled his forefinger in the air, ordering the cameramen to capture more footage of the happy gathering.

Reverend John sighed and looked up for deliverance. He spied Pearl watching from the window of her attic bedroom, her face framed by a white curtain. He remembered when Pearl had run across the lawn to him for the first time. There had been something about her that drew him besides her beauty. Perhaps he witnessed a conflict between shyness and boldness. Now, three years later, her youthful body raced toward puberty, and he was fighting a different type of attraction.

Perhaps now she wished she were back in the slums, free. But how could she possibly understand? The young simply do not have enough experience to understand. How could she appreciate her fortune to have been chosen as his servant? Someday she would look back at her time with him with fondness and longing.

He waved at her. The white curtain swung back into place.

At last, Reverend Ted gathered up the children, herded them out the gate, toward the bus for the drive back to Manhattan. Linda stood next to Reverend Ted, talking, as the kids climbed the bus stairs. Cameramen gathered their equipment. Reverend John rushed into the house and, rounding the corner from the hall to the stairs, practically bumped into Pearl.

"Wait five minutes, then come to the master bathroom and take a bag of used garments to the incinerator."

Pearl nodded. He hated the way she stared at the floor, avoiding his eyes.

He hurried to the bathroom, stripped off his clothes, stuffed them into a large plastic garbage sack, tied off the neck, folded it back upon itself, and tied it again so that nothing could crawl out. He stepped into a scalding shower and lathered himself with an astringent anti-bacterial, anti-parasitic soap. He stepped out and stowed the soap container in the medicine chest, carefully aligning it with other plastic jars and bottles, then stepped back under the shower.

As hot water streamed over his head, he tried to ignore images of Pearl's pubescent figure. He rinsed thoroughly, concentrating on the bitter smell of the soap, then rubbed a lavender scented shampoo all over his body. His fingertips slipped through the delicious foam, slid down his belly toward a growing erection. He loved the feeling, a minor miracle, even if it was Satan's miracle.

The bathroom door opened, and Pearl slipped in. Fully erect, he turned toward her. Through the foggy shower glass, he saw her eyes widen, and glance away. Cheeks blushing, she picked up the plastic sack and rushed out.

Satan controlled him fully now, providing lurid images, forcing his hand to stroke faster and faster. He shuddered and groaned, leaning against the shower, moaning in ecstasy and disgust at his weakness.

CHAPTER 4

Arlington National Cemetery

Thatcher

SENATOR WILLIAM THATCHER STOOD WITH his wife Carol in the Arlington National Cemetery, facing a flag-draped coffin lying on a brass frame above a carpet of Astroturf. The coffin held the only son of Ralph Thompson, a Montana carpenter and Thatcher's best friend from boyhood. Ralph and his wife Martha sat in green cloth-covered chairs, heads bent for the boy who had given his life to protect America. Thatcher draped a hand on Ralph's shoulder. The worn sport coat must have been twenty-years old. He'd probably borrowed it from a friend.

Dried-out leaves tumbled across the rolling green landscape like children racing through a graveyard.

Fifty yards to the south, on a hillside of white crosses, a tall man wearing a black suit stood in the shade of a maple tree.

Carol sucked in her breath, her usual sign of alarm—real or imagined. Mostly imagined. He leaned against her, nose brushing her black hair. "What?"

She nodded at the man under the tree. "Virtue."

"At a graveside service?" he whispered.

"Watching you."

He sighed, "It's just a curious citizen."

"Uh-huh." She shook her head like a pit bull with a bone.

Four Marine honor guards stood at attention on either side of the casket. A bugler waited, rigid, at the head of the grave, the tail of his jacket flapping in the wind.

Thatcher had met the Thompson boy twice, once when he was a child in Montana, the last time about a year ago here in Washington. Handsome and proud of his uniform, Jim would have made his folks proud. Now he was joining the nation's fallen in the black earth of Arlington. Other than a few words carved on the headstone, his grave would be indistinguishable from 350,000 others in the nation's hallowed ground. These were the lucky ones. Many survivors wore scars both visible and invisible. Thatcher should know.

Thatcher's son Billy would be eligible for military service in seven years. At eleven, Billy had already asked him about joining the Reserve Officer's Training Corps. What could he say? ROTC had been his own path—to Afghanistan and onward, to the Senate. He wouldn't wish war on anyone, and yet couldn't warn Billy against following his path.

The honor guard raised the flag from the casket, snapped it straight, folded it slowly into a triangle, and handed it to the chaplain. In the distance, a seven-man rifle squad fired a three-shot salute. The chaplain knelt and handed Martha the flag, his condolences smothered by the roar of a jet departing Ronald Reagan National Airport.

Ralph, husky and gray-haired, pressed an arm around heavy-set Martha as they hobbled to the casket to say good-bye. Martha put a single white rose on the coffin. They turned and walked away. A gust of wind blew the flower away.

Thatcher and Carol accompanied the dead hero's parents across the lawn toward a waiting limo. Martha, who looked so much like Jim, with wide-set blue eyes and curly dark hair, looked up and touched Thatcher's arm.

"Thanks for sending us the plane tickets, Senator. We couldn't have afford . . . ."

Thatcher shook his head, almost harshly, took her hand and squeezed it. He thought about, once again, asking them to stay over a few days. He knew it would do no good. These were proud people, and felt, he knew, they had accepted enough charity to last a lifetime. The whole scene was hopeless.

"Thank you again. We'll never forget your generosity." Martha pulled on Ralph's arm, led him to the limo.

Thatcher put his arm around Carol and watched the limo drive away.

"I can't imagine how parents survive the loss of a child."

Carol leaned into him. "Maybe it'll be a different world when Billy comes of age."

Thatcher shrugged. "We'll make it better."

"The world's greatest optimist." Carol laughed. "That's why I love you."

"Realist."

"If you say so." She smiled, looked at her watch. "I have to pick up some groceries."

"How about a steak?" Thatcher looked forward to a quiet night at home.

"Remember, Frank and Betty are coming for dinner."

Another peaceful night shot in the ass.

"Don't roll your eyes! She's my sister; you'll just have to put up with him."

"I don't want Billy exposed to him."

"Already taken care of it. He's doing an overnight with a friend."

He smiled. Just like an attorney: anticipating problems and taking action. He walked her to her SUV, put his arms around her and kissed her.

She pinched his butt and grinned. "Get back to saving the world, big boy."

He watched her climb behind the steering wheel. The years had made her figure softer, more beautiful, rounding the angles of youth into sensuous curves. She smiled, waved, and drove off, and he felt a surge of love, a mix of lust, pride, and admiration.

Thatcher's chief aide, Richard Bowman, leaned against the front fender of a black sedan, parked a few spaces in front of the spot Carol had left. As Thatcher approached, Bowman pushed off to open the passenger door. His left leg collapsed. Swearing, he caught himself, grabbing the door handle. He used his left hand to swing the leg under him for balance.

Thatcher grinned. "Smooth move."

"You'd think I could learn to walk without falling down." Bowman opened the passenger door, limped to the driver's side, and slid behind the wheel. His right leg was fine, at least, so he could drive. He pulled away from the curb, heading for Memorial Drive.

Afghanistan hadn't been all-bad. That's where he'd met Bowman.

Thatcher's sergeant had told him to discipline a private first class for causing morale problems. Bowman entered the tent and stood at attention in front of his desk. Skinny, skin-headed, a protruding Adam's apple, he looked like a lot of the other young kids whose lives had been disrupted by the war.

"Sarge tells me you're causing discipline problems."

"Yes, Sir!"

"How are you causing problems?"

"Singing, Sir."

"Singing?"

"The Sarge doesn't like my songs. Says they're anti-war."

"Are they?"

"They're popular at home."

"What do the rest of the guys think about your songs?"

"They ask me to sing, Sir."

"Were you singing in a band before you were drafted?"

Bowman grinned. "I was finishing Georgetown law school when I got my notice. Had a college deferment before that. The machine needed more cannon fodder."

"It's hard enough for all of us to be over here. Tough to keep up morale. So cut it out, Private. I don't want to see you again."

"Yes, Sir!"

"Dismissed." Thatcher picked up some paperwork and then noticed Bowman still stood at attention in front of his desk.

"What?"

Bowman began tapping his left foot against the plywood floor in a slow rhythm. He sang in a rich voice.

Thatcher shook his head to keep from choking up. "Bob Dylan."

"Yes, Sir!"

"Get the hell out of here and keep your singing to yourself."

Bowman struggled to keep disappointment from his face. As Bowman neared the door, Thatcher said, "I play a guitar."

In their off moments, Thatcher risked being accused of fraternizing with enlisted men by playing his guitar while Bowman sang, stomping out the rhythm with his left foot.

After singing one night, heading off to their bunks, Bowman said he missed his wife; he would do a better job if she were here.

Thatcher said, "Private, if the army wanted you to have a wife, it would have issued you one."

They lost track of each other after the grenade intended for Thatcher blew off Bowman's leg. He was evacuated Stateside. Bowman would never tap out a rhythm with his left foot again.

After Thatcher's tour of duty was over and he was mustered out of the army, he found Bowman, down and out. Disillusioned, he had become a longhaired, drugged out, divorced protester. Thatcher helped him dry out, clean up, and gave him a job as his assistant where he was a vice president at Moral America. They had become like brothers—without the usual sibling rivalry.

At the Lincoln Memorial Circle, clumps of homeless people spotted the sidewalks like measles. Independence Avenue was lined with banners:

"FREEDOM, SECURITY, FOOD"

"I'm getting tired of those Virtue slogans," Thatcher said.

"Reverend John is obsessed with slogans."

"So was Hitler."

"So was the army."

They stopped for a construction crew bolting a stanchion —an obese, golden, light pole—into the sidewalk. Its horizontal arm arched across the street to another pillar. Crews of government workers were putting up gold stanchions on Constitution Avenue as well, twelve stanchions in all, like huge staples intended to keep cars from fleeing into the sky.

"What do you think they are for?" Bowman asked.

"Who knows? It's a Virtue project."

"For a senator, you don't know shit."

"Thanks," he said, laughing. A flagman waved them on and Bowman drove toward the Hart Senate Office Building. Homeless people lined the sidewalks.

A young woman, holding a child, jumped off the curb in front of an oncoming bus.

"Oh my God!" Thatcher grabbed the dashboard.

The onboard computer simultaneously hit the brakes and served around the bus.

Bodies flew.

Thatcher looked out the back window. What had been a woman, wearing a tattered once-fashionable dress, lay shapeless on the asphalt. Her smashed child sprawled nearby.

The image that stuck with Thatcher was of the woman spinning just before the moment of impact so that the bus smashed her baby first.

Thatcher fought acid refluxing into his mouth. He swallowed hard and tried to take deep breaths to stop gagging.

The woman's final thrust, making certain the baby would die even if she did not, had been a sick act of love. The child would not suffer, would not grow up to face a hopeless life. The new reality sucked.

Suicide by automobile "accident" was the newest grass roots solution to the hopelessness of unemployment and hunger and slow death. It had replaced suicide by cop shooting months ago. There had been so many. The newspapers? Television? No longer even reported.

Bowman glanced at Thatcher, his shades throwing broken reflections of car and sky.

"Don't," Thatcher said.

"Don't what?"

"Look at me without looking at me, wondering what I'm going to do? Why don't you just ask me about the new public works program the Senate is working on?"

"Okay, what about . . ."

"It's a sham. Window dressing. It won't put a dent in unemployment."

They'd had this conversation before. Bowman would say that robots might get the job done quicker and cheaper for a corporation, but robots didn't buy things. And making products that nobody could buy because they had no money . . .

And Thatcher would say that things were only going to get worse. And he would add, he was speaking as an optimist.

And Bowman would shake his head slowing, sadly, and Thatcher would join him.

Trapped in an uncomfortable silence, they passed the Korean War Veterans Memorial and the Holocaust Museum. War had changed since Korea, Viet Nam, Iraq, and Afghanistan.

Now, constant "terrorism," cyber hacking, and special-forces wars unfolded on ever-shifting landscapes, including American landscapes. The separatists—the secessionists—were a relatively new threat. The public no longer knew the face of the enemy. Cynics claimed the "enemy" was a political invention, a method to hold power. They could be right. So much was classified, even to senators.

Bowman stopped for a traffic light and Thatcher watched a two-story opto-screen projecting a desert scene—American special forces, riding new combat mini-tanks, weaving through a line of burning enemy Toyota pickups with their ever present bed-mounted .50 caliber machine guns. The mini-tanks sprinted across flat desert, computerized 20mm cannons firing, killing dirty, bearded fanatics.

The screens, located in all public spaces, announced victory after victory in a never-ending battle. Yesterday's enemies became today's allies and would become tomorrow's enemies. The constant shifting of alliances did not worry voters. As long as their government fought an enemy called "terrorist," they felt safe.

Fear had motivated voters to sweep into office strong candidates who promised prosperity and to lead the country back to its moral roots—back to Christian fundamentals.

That wave of nervous faith had catapulted Thatcher from a post as vice president of Moral America, a Christian lobbying organization, to a Senate seat. Surfing a wave of euphoria, within the first 100 days Congress had proposed the *Citizens Security and Justice Act.*

Swallowing his reservations and believing it was necessary to quell anarchy, he had agreed that a radical reorganization of the government that spawned the Department of Virtue might eliminate bureaucracy and corruption. He had been wrong. And now, after watching Virtue begin to eliminate its opposition, he wondered if his vote against the lifetime directorship provision put him on an enemies list.

Certainly Reverend John knew by now that Thatcher and Senator Long had motivated the Americans for Separation of Church and State to file suit against the creators of Virtue's Supreme Moral Court.

Bowman swung into the Hart Building parking garage and parked in the senator's reserved spot. They rode the elevator up and walked to the office in silence, appalled at the accident they'd witnessed. Accident? Or a suicide and murder?

In his office, Thatcher looked at the neo-cross. Maybe it would help him communicate with God. The old cross never had the power to do so. Over time, Thatcher's relationship with God had waxed and waned.

One day after Sunday school, maybe when he'd been six or seven, he found several thick branches fallen from an oak tree. He used the handsaw from his father's workbench to trim off smaller branches, and then he cut a long and a shorter piece. He nailed the limbs together, but the nail heads showed. Rummaging around his father's stuff, he found thick, long, dark leather shoelaces, which he wrapped around the center of the cross to hide the nails. He'd been proud to show his Mom and Dad. Even prouder at the praise of his Sunday school teacher, Miss . . . he couldn't now remember her name, but she'd been pretty and kind. His dad hung the cross at the foot of his bed and he clasped his little hands together every night, thanking God for all his blessings. God was kind and loving and protected him. And it was good.

Then one late winter day after school at the pond, his very best friend, Joey, fell though the ice and drowned. He prayed to his wooden cross and asked why God had killed a little kid. God didn't answer. He didn't pray to the cross much after that.

Not until he was in high school. One night a group of his football buddies and their dates drove out to the gravel pit to swim and hang out. Ralph Thompson brought a case of Shlitz. There was music and dancing and laughing. Trevor Johnson and George Mellon got drunk. The beer ran out. They jumped into George's car to get another case of beer. Thatcher and Ralph tried to stop them, but they laughed and peeled down the highway.

That was the first funeral he attended. He couldn't make sense of people staring at the embalmed faces of his friends and saying things like, "He looks so natural." He thought those comments were bullshit—his buddies were dead.

After the funeral, some of the kids started on drugs, others joined the Fellowship of Christian Athletes to associate with a 'clean' group. He joined FCA and once again began his nightly ritual of praying to his wooden cross. Members voted him president of their local FCA chapter and, while attending the annual conference he met Caleb Gates, head of Moral America, a Christian political lobbying group from Washington.

He left his wooden cross at home when he left for college, where he'd sit around his room arguing both sides, usually coming down in a pseudo-sophisticated denial and rejection of the Almighty.

That changed during his first firefight in Afghanistan. Bullets screamed past him. One blew the head off of his friend crouched next to him. Thatcher called for God's help. He watched more of his buddies die.

Afterward, he wanted to think his prayers had been answered. After all, he had lived through the war.

But his enemies, Muslims trying to kill him, had also prayed to God. He believed it was the same God.

After the war, Thatcher returned and joined Caleb Gates at Moral America to promote conservative Christian candidates but, unlike many of his Evangelical friends, who claimed to hold personal conversations with God, he had never connected. Was God too busy for him? Were his pleas for forgiveness unworthy?

Bowman knocked timidly on his office door, and when Thatcher grunted a welcome, slipped in and handed him a printout.

"This just came over the Congressional Wire—a new bill to clean up missing pieces of the *Citizen Security and Justice Act*. I thought you'd want to see it."

You've read it. I can see," Thatcher said.

Bowman nodded.

"Any surprises?"

Bowman shook his head.

"The United Theocracy of America."

"For starters."

Bowman stood on his right leg, resting his prosthesis. Thatcher went to the cupboard, pulled out a bottle of Canadian Club, and poured them each a short drink.

"I swear to God, Dick . . ." Thatcher found himself reading the pages of the new bill, despite knowing what they contained.

"This might, emphasis on the might, give us a chance to limit the term of the Director of Virtue. But this increased enforcement of Biblical Law . . . I'll talk to Senator Long. I'll . . . I'll raise this glass to you, Dick. We've got to keep trying." Bowman nodded and left.

A few minutes later the bells struck seventeen. Thatcher rose from his desk to follow his daily ritual. Only now, he would no longer bow his head to a kid's rough wooden cross. He would kneel to Virtue's neo-cross. He would fold his hands and pray for forgiveness. That, at least would remain the same. Always asking forgiveness.

As always, his prayer evoked an image of two buildings; one, where the CIA station chief and his associates met with a Taliban chief, and next door a children's hospital. The suicide bomber's explosion. Children screaming, pieces of little arms and legs twitching in pooling blood. Children crying, moaning, begging, pleading to God. Innocent kids wounded, dying, dead.

The stink of burning flesh.

It was his fault.

CHAPTER 5

Washington

Carol

SEVERAL HOURS AFTER THE FUNERAL, Carol met Teri Johnson at a coffee shop in the La Quinta Inn in Vienna, Virginia. Thatcher had worked on the Johnsons' Montana ranch during high school summers. After an auto accident killed Thatcher's mother and father, Teri and her husband had become like second parents to him.

Carol had met the Johnsons at her wedding and fell in love with them. She never understood why Teri lived in that godforsaken landscape, especially after her husband died. But Teri loved working the ranch, riding horses and herding cattle with her hired hands. In spite of the distance, Teri and Carol—the rancher and the Planned Parenthood attorney—had become close friends. Teri was in Washington visiting her son.

Teri rose from the table to greet Carol. She was tanned, lean and energetic in spite of—what was she?—mid-eighties? Looked like the same outfit she wore last time they met five years ago. Teri could afford to be fashionable, but she was most comfortable in ranch clothes.

They ordered tea and scones.

Teri nodded at the silver neo-cross pinned to Carol's crisp blue dress. "Are you required to wear that?

"Not when I'm naked."

The waiter returned with their tea and scones.

Teri spread a bit of English clotted cream, took a bite, and beamed. "Delicious! I tried to bake scones once, but added too much sugar. They burned and made a mess."

"Try again."

Teri laughed. "I do horses better than ovens." She took another bite and then turned serious. "How are you coping?"

Carol stared into her tea, silent. How could she answer a question like that, a good question, from an old friend, without crying? How *was* she coping?

Not well. Her career, as an attorney for Planned Parenthood, representing surrogate egg and uterus donors for in-vitro fertilizations, had been destroyed when Virtue outlawed the organization and blacklisted its employees.

Other employees had no way to survive without the generosity of family members. It had been especially devastating for fellow attorney Mary Lee, who had used scholarships and education to climb out of Washington's ghetto. With no job alternatives for a blacklisted single black mother, even one with education, Mary Lee, and her son had been forced to return to the ghetto to live with her mother who survived on meager Social Security checks. Then Mary Lee's mother died. The Social Security checks stopped.

Early on, Carol had sent several checks, which had been returned without a message. Carol had wanted to communicate with Mary Lee, but she could not bring herself to call. Perhaps she suffered from survivor's guilt.

It wasn't that she didn't love her own son, Billy, but he was in school most of the day and Carol simply didn't feel fulfilled. She used to make a positive difference in people's lives.

Carol looked at Teri. "I'm exhausted. Defeated. Sick to my soul, but I'm not giving up."

"Are you safe?"

"Wives of U.S. Senators are safe."

"Will you be tomorrow? Next week? Next year? Don't answer. Remember this: I live forty dirt-road miles from pavement and another seventy-five to a grocery store. A store I don't really need. I'm self-sufficient. I have loads of room. And, I know I can whip you into shape to hold up your part of the chores. I'll start you out mucking out the horse pens. The invitation is open."

"I hope it never comes to that," Carol said.

After they parted, Carol stood at the hotel's entrance waiting for the valet to retrieve her car, feeling lonely and exposed. She looked at her watch. Frank and Betty were coming for dinner. She tipped the valet, and headed for Eagan's, the closest grocer.

She hadn't been to Eagan's in ages. Old man Eagan gained notoriety when he filed suit against Virtue's Seal of Approval Retailers Program. Stores could apply for an expensive official seal of approval. Virtue promoted shopping at only approved stores. While not illegal, Christians were encouraged not to do business at non-approved establishments.

Carol rankled at the pressure to shop exclusively at such businesses. She admired old man Eagan's defiance and courage to stand up to Virtue. Of course, Eagan lost, but he still refused to knuckle under.

On the other hand, she suspected she'd be hassled in the store, because she was a Christian. She would not be intimidated. She would not take off her neo-cross pin. After all, she was in a hurry and she only needed four filets and a head of lettuce. She could handle it.

The store, once upscale, had fallen into neglect, merchandise old and sparse. It was obvious that business had been hurt. Other customers stared at her, eyeing her neo-cross pin. She stopped at the meat display counter. The case was almost bare, the few poor cuts of grayish meat. A middle-aged butcher wiped his hands on a stained apron, scowled across the counter at her neo-cross pin. "You lost, lady?"

"I'd like four small filets," she said.

"You gotta be kidding."

She felt the heat rise to her face. "What?"

The butcher's eyes hardened. "Our customers can't afford filets. Try one of your Virtue-approved stores."

She didn't deserve that rudeness. But, putting herself in the butcher's position, suffering from poor business on account of Virtue, she understood his attitude. Perhaps, if she were in his shoes, she'd react the same way.

Carol jerked the cart around and headed for the produce section. Another customer, a thin woman wearing a blue blouse and black slacks with a torn knee, pushed a cart down the middle of the aisle. Carol moved to the left. The customer banged her cart into Carol's.

Carol didn't want a confrontation and murmured, "Sorry". She avoided the woman's eyes and looked at the floor. The woman's dirty slacks were frayed at the hem. At least the woman could have worn clean clothes. Carol wished she'd left her neo-cross in the glove compartment.

The woman hissed, "Why don't you shop where you belong?"

Carol turned her cart, retraced her steps, and found the produce department. The lettuce was wilted, but she refused to be intimidated. She placed two heads in her cart, and on the way to checkout, picked up a loaf of bread she didn't need. It felt hard and stale.

The clerk was a pockmarked kid in his early twenties, fingers tobacco-stained yellow. He scanned the price on the bread, and slid it across the narrow counter. It fell to the floor before Carol could catch it. She picked it up, and avoided his eyes.

"Sure you want to buy this stuff, lady?" he said loudly. "It's not Virtue-approved. This isn't an approved store."

She felt the glare of other shoppers, and the Eye mounted above the checkout counter swung to focus on her. She rummaged in her wallet for some old twenties she'd stashed for emergencies. It was a habit from the old days, before cash was discouraged.

The clerk peered at her wallet. "Don't you have your smart card?"

"Lost it," she lied.

"Yeah, sure," he smirked and tipped his chin toward the Eye. "You don't want Virtue to know you shopped here, but it knows." He took her cash and rung her up.

The parking lot was full of older model cars. She sensed someone followed her and glanced over her shoulder. She was alone. She threw her groceries in the passenger seat, climbed behind the wheel, shut and locked the door, leaned back and exhaled.

A few minutes later, she found a Virtue-approved grocery store to buy steaks—and fresh lettuce. She drove home the back way, through residential neighborhoods of unkempt yards, rotting wooden play structures, and leafy sycamore canopies.

She couldn't wait to get back to her gated community, her sheltered cocoon, and her shield against contact with commoners, their difficulties and resentments. She was a political Christian living a privileged life

She turned the corner toward the guardhouse, squinting at the sun's reflection off whorls of razor wire topping the electric fence protecting her neighborhood. She'd be safe inside. She felt grateful. The next moment she hated herself.

CHAPTER 6

Thatcher home—Washington

Thatcher

THATCHER ARRIVED HOME FROM THE office, far beyond tense: burying the Thompson boy, watching the mother kill her baby while committing suicide, finding Virtue's neo-cross hanging in his office, losing his hand-made cross, learning about the crazy *Voting Act*, enduring yet another fruitless prayer session pleading for God's forgiveness.

He needed a quiet night with Carol, but he'd have to endure his boring sister-in-law and that arrogant, holier-than-thou, son of a bitch brother-in-law.

He found Carol in the kitchen. "Good day, Hon?"

"So-so," she said. "You can help—wash that head of lettuce."

"Just so-so?" He tossed the lettuce into the sink with more force than he'd intended.

She told him about Eagan's. "I didn't realize how much hostility your *Security Act* causes."

"Hey! That wasn't—isn't—*my* act!"

"You voted for it, Bill. Take some responsibility." She picked up a tenderizing mallet and started pounding the steaks.

"Hey, you don't need to tenderize fillets."

"I feel like it! Besides, that's not the point. You voted for it."

In the end, after protesting, he had voted for the *Security Act*, which passed on the 96th day after the new Congress took over.

Voters had demanded a radical change in their government after cyber hackers destroyed much of the electrical grid: voting in the first election after martial law had been lifted.

There had been years of warnings, but politicians ignored the problem, refusing to spend the billions necessary to protect the system with Faraday cages and giant surge protectors. There had been sexier issues: spending billions on stealth bombers, aircraft carriers, subs—weapons designed to fight the last wars with big easily defined targets—weapons represented by lobbyists and easily sold to voters as investments to keep them 'safe.' Voters and politicians had trouble wrapping their minds around spending billions to defend against an anonymous third-world cyber hacker who could destroy America's electrical grid.

Thatcher picked up a knife and began chopping the lettuce into quarters.

"You know I tried," he said.

Inevitable Congressional studies shifted blame to the intelligence agencies, the FBI, CIA and NSA, who should have picked up the signals and stopped the attack. Additional studies blamed the IRS for corruption, a problem that had existed since the 2008 "too large to fail" banking system meltdown. The latest scandal, involving five of the country's billionaires, had been just the last evidence of a corrupt IRS catering to special interests. So, the idea was: get rid of these bureaucratic fiefdoms, dissolve them, and roll them into one organization: start afresh.

"Yes. And I think, now, you were naïve. Just say: I helped create Virtue," Carol said.

"But . . ."

"Don't 'but' me. And chop that lettuce. Quarters remind me of the Golden Corral."

He chopped, angrily, silently. He had fought against the provisions that allowed Virtue to define and enforce Biblical Law. He had voted against naming Virtue's director to a lifetime term.

After a long half-minute, he said, "I didn't have the votes, we didn't, to defeat the bill, to even amend those sections."

"I know. You extended unemployment benefits."

"Yes. Crumbs from the table. God help us."

"He seems to be helping himself."

"Carol!"

They'd been through this before. Many times. But he'd never seen her so angry with him before. No not angry, disappointed.

"I'm sorry, Bill."

"We'll move things back toward center."

"Good luck. The time for playing it safe, for moving in increments, inching along . . ."

"No. It isn't passed. And another thing . . ."

The doorbell rang. Thatcher jerked at the sound.

"I told security we were expecting them, so they didn't need to alert us," Carol said.

"I'll go."

Betty, in a shapeless gray dress, and Frank, in a black suit and tie, stood stiffly, reminding him of Grant Wood's *American Gothic*. Mary's mouse-like and wet eyes stared through wire-rim glasses. Her shoulders slumped. She kneaded her hands as though wiping off something filthy. Frank reminded Thatcher of a medieval monk: a fringe of dark hair ringed a large bald skull, a body at once erect and sunken.

Carol came up behind Thatcher, took her sister's hand, pulled her inside, and gave her a hug. Frank offered a dry hand to Thatcher. He pulled away from Carol's attempt to kiss his cheek. They walked toward the kitchen. Frank's eyes scanned the living room—the abstract paintings, the Scandinavian couch.

"Where's Billy?" Betty asked.

"A sleepover with a friend," Carol said.

"Good Christians?" Frank's gave a thin-lipped smile, as though to defang the question.

"Of course." Thatcher's stomach tensed.

"Fundamentalists or evangelicals like you?" Frank asked.

Thatcher ignored Carol's warning look. "Not your type, Frank," he said. "Evangelicals believe in compassion."

Carol handed Thatcher a platter.

"You boys cook the steaks while Betty and I get the rest on the table."

Frank followed Thatcher out to the patio and watched Thatcher fork the steaks onto the grill.

"Frank, there's lemonade in the fridge. I'm going to have a drink. I know better than to ask you. Watch these for a second."

Thatcher returned, handed Frank his lemonade. The two men lifted their glasses, a foot apart from each other, in a parody of a toast.

"How's Billy enjoying school? Seventh grade now?"

Here it comes again, the same old argument, Thatcher thought. He stabbed a steak, flipped it, decided it was too rare, and flipped it back over. Betty, no doubt at Frank's command, kept pushing Carol to send Billy to the Virtue-approved

Christian Academy that taught fundamentalist curriculum and values. Betty pleaded with Carol—"All knowledge derives from God and Biblical law makes the head of the family responsible for education. Not the state. Please don't expose Billy to a state-sponsored humanist agenda!"

They'd had three choices for Billy's schooling: public, private or Virtue-approved Christian.

Public schools were a disaster, especially since federal funding had been cut. The best teachers and students fled public schools, which soon devolved into war zones.

Federal funding had been diverted to Virtue-approved Christian schools through a program called "Faith Based Education", and enrollment at those schools was skyrocketing.

Parents who felt religion was a private family matter and should be kept out of schools, and others who, for example, didn't believe their child should be taught that the earth was only 6,000 years old, when scientific evidence proved it was over 3 billion years old, opted for private school education— if they could afford the tuition. Carol and Thatcher sent Billy to the Dawson School, an expensive private school with an outstanding reputation.

"Frank, let's not start. Billy's doing fine. He's happy. This week they're doing a class project on how to shoot heroin and worship the devil."

"That's not funny. I don't appreciate your sarcasm."

"It's what you wanted to hear. And while we're clearing the air, I don't want Betty sending brochures about the Christian Academy, or bombarding Carol about the subject."

Frank's lips twisted into a sarcastic smile. "Carol makes the decisions, doesn't she?"

"WE make the decisions."

"'WE' undercuts your authority. God gave the man authority . . ."

"Frank, I'm this close to throwing you out of this house. Let's talk Redskins. Or Nationals, or roses. But we are on two sides of damn near everything else and I don't think, even if we spoke a million words, we are going to agree."

"But you want me to agree with you to not talk about . . ."

"Yes. At least that."

Thatcher went back to the steaks, but not before he took a long drink. He should have brought the bottle out, rattle Frank's cage with some force.

He forked the steaks onto the platter and took them into the dining room. He sat at the head of the table, Carol to his right, Betty to the left and Frank at the opposite end. He reached out to hold hands and cleared his throat, "Shall we pray?"

Frank interrupted, "Dear God, bless this food for our use. Help the Thatchers understand and accept your God ordained authority to the man as head of the household. Show Bill the path of righteousness in teaching his wife and son to be subordinate to Your authority and Your truth. Amen."

Thatcher felt Carol's foot hit his ankle, warning him not to rise to Frank's bait.

"Virtue installed a large neo-cross in my office today. The curious thing is Carol hasn't been able to buy a house-size one. I'm sure you noticed there aren't any here."

"I had."

"I guess since Virtue selected—what's his name? Ralph Huntington—his design, they are running way behind, production-wise. At least some models. Huntington must be making billions."

"It isn't right."

Thatcher looked at Frank. Were they going to actually agree on something?

"The profits," Frank said, "should go to improving the country's morality."

"Huntington should give his profits to Virtue?"

"Of course."

Thatcher knew how hard this was for Carol to hold her tongue. He took another sip of his bourbon. It made him feel loose. He was ready for a little scrap. To hell with being polite.

"What do you think, Frank," Thatcher asked, passing the basket of French bread to his brother-in-law, "of these rumors about every neo-cross containing spying equipment?"

"How would I know? But let me ask you something, Thatcher. You evangelicals claim to talk directly to God. Has God talked to you lately?"

Carol said, "Let's talk . . ."

Thatcher interrupted her. "He has better things to do than talk to me, Frank."

"Oh!" Betty beamed. "Have you heard the good news about Frank?"

"Betty." Frank pointed his fork at her.

She didn't hear her husband, so proud of him. "Reverend John promoted Frank to . . ."

"Betty!" Frank glared at her.

Betty looked down, about to cry. "I'm sorry. I forgot. I'm so sorry."

What promotion? Why was Frank so secretive? After law school, he began his career representing fundamentalist Christian organizations. Later, he was elected a judge on the State of Virginia Court of Appeals, and after that was appointed as a judge for the U.S. District Court of the District of Columbia. What now?

"No need to apologize, Betty," Thatcher said, "These conversations between God and his upper-level fundamentalists sometimes leak out. God speaks loudly, doesn't He, Frank?"

"Salad?" Carol asked.

"I'd love some. It looks delicious," Betty said.

Both Betty and Carol shot their husbands murderous looks. Cease and desist. Now!

Frank leaned forward, put his forearms on the table and looked at Thatcher. "I understand you and Senator Long are behind the law suit to declare Virtue's enforcement of Biblical Laws illegal."

Thatcher put down his fork and took a sip of water. "Senator Long and I are not plaintiffs on that suit, nor are we financially backing it."

"Details. We know you two are behind it. We'll tie that case up for years. In the meantime Virtue, through its Supreme Moral Court, will be the judge and jury on all moral issues. Let me give you a bit of advice. I'd be very careful when you think about opposing Reverend John and Virtue."

Ignoring Frank, Thatcher turned to Carol. "Speaking of opposing Virtue, I haven't had time to tell you what's happening with the *American Citizens' Voting Act*. I guess we were hoping to head off the worst provisions. One is that only qualified Christians would be able to vote."

Carol sat back as though slapped. "I can't believe what I'm hearing. Who decides who 'qualifies' as a Christian? What about the Jews, Muslims, and Buddhists? What about the seculars and atheists?" She looked around the room, and realized she was standing. She shook her head.

"If you liked that provision, you'll love the second," Thatcher said, reaching for Carol's hand.

"I'm holding my breath," she said.

"It temporarily suspends Amendment Nineteen."

Carol dropped Thatcher's hand. "Women's right to vote? You're kidding, right?"

Frank grinned. "There is a precedent. Roosevelt suspended Habeas Corpus during World War Two when he put Japanese-Americans in relocation camps."

"That was a disaster." Carol folded her napkin. She looked at her sister. "What do you think, Betty?"

Betty's eyes darted around the room. She lowered her head. "I leave politics to Frank."

Carol closed her eyes.

Frank stood up and dropped his napkin on top of the half eaten food on his plate. "We'll pass on dessert. We'll be leaving now."

Betty used her napkin to wipe tears from her eyes.

Carol asked, "Are you giving us an example of God's authority, Frank?"

Her barb went over Betty's head . . . or she chose to ignore it.

Betty followed Frank to the front door. He did not offer to shake hands. He stepped out onto the porch and turned. "You two should be very careful, Thatcher."

They stood at the door, watching them walk toward their car. Frank was gesturing angrily, Betty nodding agreement.

Thatcher felt his face flush. He didn't like the sour taste in his mouth.

CHAPTER 7

Reverend John Thomas' Home

Reverend John

AT DINNER, REVEREND JOHN SAT at the end of their long dining table, adjusting his silverware into perfect alignment. Linda sat at the far end. As always, the table was set with their formal tableware, silver water pitcher, flickering candles and best china, accoutrements that had been foreign to him. He loved the smell of scented candles. He stood up and moved one of the candles a half inch to the right. Linda had taught him table manners and the finer graces. He remained deeply appreciative of her efforts.

"Tell me about your day," he asked, half listening to her babble on about insignificant details of her life. He noted that she had aged with a rare elegance. Of course, the small fortune she spent on clothes helped. Plus the hours with her hairdresser and those weekly fingernail sessions she called "my Mani-Pedi time". And there was the weekly facial appointment to fight the wrinkles. She considered those paid service people to be her best friends. Every night during dinner, she prattled on about their personal travails as if they were family. He pretended to be interested.

But that was unfair. Even though sometimes she seemed bitter, she also spent hours each week on volunteer work, doing good for others. She had been an uncomplaining companion, had not whined about sleeping in separate rooms, and had never questioned his apparent loss of libido. Being a good Christian woman, she never nagged, but accepted her lot in life with quiet acceptance. She ran the household and took those burdensome life details off his shoulders, allowing him to concentrate on God's work.

She did not question him about his work, which was just as well, since he suspected she had never been fully caught up in the Holy Spirit. All in all, it was a satisfactory arrangement. An arrangement directed by Him, so Reverend John would not be distracted from doing His will as commanded by His Voice.

When they finished their soup, Linda picked up a small silver bell and rang it three times. The kitchen door swung open and Pearl cleared their bowls. She returned with dinner plates; lamb chops, rice and asparagus. The lamb issued a rich, juicy smell, his favorite. The girl served Linda first.

He smiled at Pearl when she placed the plate in front of him, inhaling her scent of soap and innocence. She blushed and averted her eyes. He watched her walk through the swinging door. A bitter, clouded look shadowed Linda's face. They ate in silence.

After being beckoned again by the bell, Pearl returned to clear the dinner plates. She walked behind him heading toward the kitchen and brushed the back of his shoulder. He was shocked. An accident? Pearl had never before physically acknowledged him.

She carried his plate out. He heard the scrape of a chair at the far end of the table. Linda rushed after the girl, using both hands to shove the door open. It swung back and forth, giving him an old-time movie view, one jerky frame at a time.

Linda knocked the plate from Pearl's hand. It shattered against the floor, garbage scattering, the knife and fork clattering.

"How dare you touch my husband," Linda screamed.

Shocked by the scene, he remained motionless.

Pearl stood silent, head bent, eyes down cast.

"Now look what you've done! You've ruined my best china."

The girl didn't move. Tears ran down her cheeks.

"You're just like the rest. You're nothing but a little whore!" She slapped Pearl's face.

He put his hands on the table to rise, but stopped. He wasn't about to step into this firestorm.

"Do you know what happened to the first Pearl?" Linda asked in a shrill voice

"No." Pearl's voice trembled.

"She was just like you. I held her passport, like I hold yours. She had no money and didn't speak English well. If she ran away, the police would catch her and throw her in prison. They'd do terrible things to her. Unspeakable things. Is that what you want?"

Pearl's body shook, but she remained silent.

"Well, is it? Is that what you want?"

"N-no. Please, no," Pearl sobbed.

He rose, but his interference could inflame the situation, so he walked toward the living room. He paused at the doorway to listen.

"When she got uppity like you, I drove her to the slums of New York and dumped her on the street. She had nothing. She knew no one. And that was the end of her. Is that what you want?"

"Please. No." The girl wiped her eyes with the back of her hand.

"Clean up this mess and then get to your room. Think about it. I'll have to do the dishes."

He heard Pearl's footsteps rush up the stairway leading from the kitchen to her bedroom. Linda pushed back through the swinging door and spotted him standing in the dining room entrance.

"And as far as you are concerned, you can go to your room."

"I'm sorry." He had never seen her lose her temper like this before. Her outburst embarrassed him. On the other hand, he had not realized she cared. Or maybe this incident triggered her anger at what the first Pearl had given him, and how his infection had altered their relationship. They had never discussed it.

He put on his pajamas and robe, sat on the edge of his bed and thought about the incident. His fingers traced the heart pacemaker. A foreign lump implanted under the collarbone. He prayed it would continue to work until he could trigger the Rapture.

He could not believe Linda had abandoned the first Pearl in a big city slum. Linda was not the type of person to do such a cruel thing to an innocent young girl.

But how could have the first Pearl been innocent if she gave him venereal disease? Perhaps she had been innocent. Perhaps she had been raped before his Save-a-Child organization had plucked her from a slum. He would never know. He regretted not talking with the first Pearl about the situation. He thought about this new girl. She had been sent to her room, scared to death, alone with no one to talk to.

At that moment, the Voice told him to show compassion, console her, and ease her suffering. Her room was just down the hall and around the corner. He heard Linda downstairs in the kitchen, cleaning dinner dishes, banging pots and pans. She would never know.

He tiptoed down the hallway to Pearl's door, just across from the stairs leading to the kitchen. He dared not knock. He opened the door. Pearl stood next to the bed. She seemed startled. He closed the door softly, opened his arms wide and walked toward her. She backed up, trapped by the bed.

"I'm so sorry. It wasn't your fault, Pearl. Let me give you the Lord's forgiveness."

He wrapped his arms around her and smelled the salt of her tears. He recognized other, more primitive scents the soap fragrance could no longer hide. The heat of her body inflamed him. He felt the Evil One breathing life into his penis. It slithered from his robe.

He tried to kiss her. She jerked her head side to side. He could not find her lips. She fell back on the bed. His fingers tore her blouse, exposing delicious small breasts. He fell on her, kissing her rosebud nipple. She squirmed away, scooted across the bed. His robe fell off as he rushed around the bed and trapped her again in his arms.

"No. Please leave me alone!" The girl sobbed.

A door crashed open behind him. An avenging angel from God flew through the door, eyes wild, lips snarling, swinging a frying pan against his skull.

And the world plunged into darkness.

CHAPTER 8

Washington Chapter of Meals on Wheels

Karen Huntington

PLEASANTLY SURPRISED THAT TWO BOARD members mentioned how much they liked her new dress, Karen Huntington called the board meeting to order. She sat at the head of a rectangular table used for training volunteers. The offices, kitchen and packing room were no-frill, unlike the old days. Two years ago, pressured by increased demand for food and financial pressures, she convinced the board to sell its building and rent cheap space in a defunct strip mall in the center of their service area.

She watched board members take their seats, thankful that Virtue had not demanded she step down to stay home as a submissive, obedient wife. Perhaps that was because Ralph had designed and manufactured the neo-cross Reverend John had declared the official symbol of Virtue, and, of course, she no longer had young children.

She waited for the board members to settle. They were a good board. They should be. She had picked most of them. An even split between women and men, they were wealthy, influential and philanthropic. Besides that, they followed her example of not only leading, but taking direct action by delivering meals. Personal contact with the indigent and elderly reinforced their passion for service. Service made them humble, thankful for what they had in their own lives.

The Executive Director, Tony White, presented the report: an exploding population of elderly poor, more demand for food services and fewer resources. His monthly reports seemed like an endless loop of bad news.

"We have another problem," White said. "The returns from our investment portfolio were killed by the financial markets meltdown. We're facing an immediate one-hundred-thousand-dollar shortfall."

Karen led a discussion of alternatives, all bad.

"We can't cut off food to those in need. This is both a short and long-term problem. We need to allocate some think-time to solve the long-term situation." She would appoint a committee and charge them with presenting alternatives at the next meeting.

"What about the shortfall?" White asked.

"You're right. So let's fix it. I'll gift fifty thousand."

As usual, several board members shifted in their chairs, several others crossed their arms over their chests, one looked at the ceiling.

"What we are doing here makes a difference. A positive difference in the lives of hungry elderly, but it also allows each of us to know we're making a difference. We can feel good about the sacrifice of our own time and money." She paused to let that settle. "So we need fifty more. I'd like each of you to chip in a share of the remainder." She looked at the man on her left. "What about you, Ed?"

Ed coughed into his fist. "I'm in."

The rest joined them to solve the crisis.

After the meeting she changed into a white shirt and lightweight khaki slacks before helping pack meals. It had been a good meeting. She loaded her allotment into her SUV and began delivering her route.

Her first stop was for Mr. Folsum, a ninety-year-old man suffering from age-related illnesses. He lived in a seedy apartment in a run-down mixed neighborhood controlled by a gang. She found a parking place near the apartment, took out a warm box containing a meal of meatloaf, mashed potatoes, and broccoli.

A gangbanger sat on the hood of a parked car, talking to two wannabes. He looked up and greeted her.

"Hi, Noah. Keep an eye on my car, okay?"

"Betcha, Momma." He grinned and flashed her the sign.

She smiled at him, wondering how she might provide him a better future . . . if he wanted one. Perhaps he couldn't imagine any other life. Noah was probably the reason no one had given her trouble. Or perhaps they reacted because she acted with confidence, or they respected her mission. She could do her task without fear of being hassled. But she wouldn't want to walk this neighborhood after dark.

She picked her way up crumbling concrete stairs to the three-story apartment building and opened the front door. A rat scuttled across the hall. She waited a beat before walking down a long corridor toward his apartment, through smells of boiling cabbage, cigarette smoke, marijuana, stale beer, and garbage.

Before she could knock twice, the door opened. Mr. Folsum gave her a toothless grin. He peered down the hallway and waved her in. Shutting the door, he struggled with three sliding locks before shuffling his walker to a small table. He backed into a chair and settled with a moan.

"How are you today, Mr. Folsum?"

"How'd you feel if you were my age, darlin'?"

She was touched by the endearment. "If I were as good looking as you, Mr. Folsum, I'd be feeling just fine." She pulled a dirty plate from the sink, washed it and put the meatloaf and the other food on it. She placed the plate in front of him.

"You didn't wash your dishes," she said in a gentle mocking tone.

"Arthritis flared again."

"I'll wash the rest while you eat, but I can't stay to chat. I have other hungry clients."

"I'd starve to death if it weren't for you."

"It's purely selfish on my part. I need you around to tease."

"Gonna see my son real soon."

She stopped drying a dish and closed her eyes. His son had died years ago. She had once reminded him his boy was gone. He had sobbed. Not wanting to cause pain, she played along. "You must be eager to see him."

"Yes I am. It'll be nicelike. I remember what he looks like, you know. It'll be soon now." Gumming the meat loaf, tears flooded his eyes.

She shivered. "I have to deliver other meals, so I have to go now, Mr. Folsum. Is there anything else I can do for you?"

"You're about the only person I see and you've been real sweet to me, Darlin'. I might not be here next time you come, cuz I'm gonna visit my son. So thank you for your kindness."

She fought tears and kissed him on the cheek. "Have a good visit, Mr. Folsum." She walked to the door and unlocked the locks before turning back. "Don't forget to lock up after me."

Mattie Johnson lived several blocks away. The neighborhood was better. In spite of being in her late eighties, wheelchair bound and impoverished, Mattie carried an air of refinement. Even though the furniture, light fixtures, pealing wallpaper and worn carpet were from a bygone era, the apartment was spotless. Mattie was usually cheerful. Today her thin lips worried, her usual sparkling eyes dull.

"What's wrong, Mattie?" Karen pushed the old lady up to the table and locked the wheels of the chair.

"Oh nothing," she waved a blue-veined hand as if to shoo away a pesky fly.

Karen put a meal in front of her. "Well, something is bothering you."

Mattie looked at her with moist eyes. "My grandson is coming tomorrow to introduce me to his fiancée."

"That's wonderful! You must be so proud."

"I'm embarrassed."

"About what? You have nothing to be embarrassed about."

"I look a mess. I can't wash my hair and my nails are atrocious."

The old woman was right. She looked terrible. Her dress was old and thin. Her white hair was dull and lifeless. She needed a makeover.

"Okay, Mattie. Tell you what. After I deliver the rest of my meals, I'm coming back and we'll fix you up so your grandson will be proud of you."

Back in her SUV, she called her friend Annie Bratton. "I'm sorry Annie, but something important has come up. I'll have to cancel tonight."

"But . . . I've been looking forward to visiting over dinner. I have something important to tell you."

Annie's important news was usually gossip. "I'll call you tomorrow and we'll reschedule another time."

She envied Mattie Johnson's excitement about meeting her grandson's fiancée. Would her Susan ever settle on a Mr. Right? Must have gotten the 'perfection' genes from her father. Thirty-two years old and still looking for the right man. No one was perfect.

It would be fun to be a grandmother, especially if they lived in the same town. There was no way she could convince her daughter to move back to Washington. Perhaps, if Susan was expecting, she could persuade Ralph to move his office to San Diego near one of his manufacturing plants so they could be a close family. When it was all said and done, family was the most important thing in life.

After delivering the rest of the meals, she stopped at a department store to look for a new dress for Mattie. It took longer than planned. She wanted something just right. She found a blue dress with a white collar and buttons that would bring Mattie up to date.

She returned to Mattie's apartment. After washing and blow-drying the old woman's hair, she painted her nails. She handed Mattie a mirror.

"What do you think?"

"Oh it's just wonderful, dear. Now I'm presentable. Thank you so much."

She stood back and looked at Mattie, sitting in the wheel-chair, barefooted. She couldn't remember her wearing shoes. She suspected Mattie wouldn't be able to put on shoes for her grandson's visit. "Let's do your toenails."

"You needn't bother, dear."

"It's no trouble." Karen knelt in front of the wheelchair. A splinter jabbed her left knee. She opened the nail polish bottle and balanced it on the floor. She picked up Mattie's right foot. It was cold. Blue veins bulged.

Karen shivered. Maybe her feet would become as ugly. Maybe she would live as long as Mattie. She didn't want to live that long. Illness and loneliness were the companions of old age. But that's the thing about life—you can't cherry pick the best parts.

She empathized with those who, faced with an incurable painful illness, decided to end it. But she'd face all that later. For now she was thankful she could bring food and a little companionship to the less fortunate like Mattie.

She balanced Mattie's foot on her thigh and began to paint the big toenail. "You have beautiful feet."

"You are such a sweet liar, Karen. My feet are ugly and you know it. I hate those big blue veins. When I was young, my husband loved to kiss my feet when we . . . well, you know," she giggled.

She finished painting Mattie's toenails and stood up and felt stabbing pain in her knee.

"Oh my! You're bleeding." Mattie pointed to her knee.

"It doesn't hurt. These slacks were worn out, so it doesn't matter. Now close your eyes. I have a surprise for you."

"A surprise? Oh, I love surprises."

She gave Mattie a red box wrapped with a white ribbon.

Mattie's hands trembled when she opened the box. "What in the world?"

"A new dress for you to wear for your grandson's visit."

Mattie cried.

Karen brought her a tissue and then kissed her on the forehead before saying goodbye.

She drove home, walked through the kitchen door and stopped. Her kitchen was twice as big as the apartments she had visited this afternoon. She fought a wave of guilt, even though she realized inequity was part of life. It had been for the history of mankind. There was no Biblical rule commanding everything be fair.

She checked the phone for messages. Susan had called from San Diego. Her voice carried the joyful exuberance of youth. She ended most of her sentences with a high pitch, as though they were questions, a habit that bugged Karen. She had never mentioned it; criticism simply wasn't that important.

"Just wanted to check in, Mom. Everything is fine out here. Joe invited me out to a fancy place for dinner tomorrow night. It's a dress-up place. He said it was something special. Maybe this is it. I'm really excited. Talk to you later. Love you."

She dialed back, determined not to act too curious about the date. Susan had been disappointed so many times, unlucky with love. Getting older.

Susan so wanted to get married and have a family. She wondered if Susan cast an aura of desperation off-putting to potential husbands. In any event, she didn't want to add pressure by asking directly. She listened to the phone ring and then heard Susan's cheery answering machine voice, "Leave a message."

Karen sent her love and asked her to call back.

She grabbed a bite of cheese and crackers. In the bathroom, she used a pair of tweezers to pluck several splinters embedded in her knee before soaking in a scented hot bath. She heard the garage door open and looked at the clock. Ralph must have caught an earlier flight home. She toweled off, dabbed a bit of perfume behind her ears, between her breasts and thighs, and then selected a diaphanous robe.

At the head of the stairs, she greeted him with a kiss. He lacked the usual passion. She followed him into the bedroom. The muscles in his neck were tense.

"Good trip?"

"OK." He placed the contents of his pockets on the dresser. His hand shook as he fumbled to unbutton his shirt. "Damn buttons."

"You're troubled."

"Reverend John wants a larger part of the business."

"You have a contract. He'd be immoral to not honor it. You have a patent. You made the right decision by holding firm and not giving him more. The neo-cross was your idea, your design. You've supported him forever. He needs to grow up."

"Still . . ."

"He's bluffing."

She turned him around and kissed him and led him to bed.

Later, after making love, she listened to his soft snoring. Her finger slipped between her legs. She imagined she was the main attraction of an orgy sparking delightful needles of sensation. Her body arched. She held her breath. She moaned in the ecstasy of an exquisite orgasm.

Tension released, she watched shadows dance across the ceiling. She loved Ralph with all her heart. Always had. Always would. She had never been unfaithful. Never would.

CHAPTER 9

Virtue Headquarters

Reverend John

A FIFTEEN-FOOT TALL NEO-CROSS dominated the far wall of Reverend John's cavernous office. Its gleaming stainless steel arms, suspended in front of a black velvet curtain, created a surreal effect.

Unfinished concrete walls, high ceiling, pools of light and shadows cast an impression of a medieval monk's lair. Plush leather couches in front of flickering opto-screens covering the opposite wall created a conflicted sensual impression. A large stainless steel desk, matching small round conference table and chairs completed the décor. The visual mixture produced an uneasy feeling of stark purpose and hedonistic comfort. Reverend John loved his office, even though he felt dizzy from the bruise on his head. When he had roused himself out of bed Linda and Pearl had been gone. There had been no note, but he assumed they would be back for dinner.

Reverend John rose from his desk to greet the Mitchell brothers, Ted and George. They looked as if they'd been formed in the same mold, old, tall, ascetic men, as if their father's sperm had been strained through a sheet during conception. Conservatively dressed in tailored suits and bow ties, their appearance screamed old establishment money. In fact, they controlled one of the largest industrial empires in America. Libertarians, they had been early, secret financial supporters of Reverend John's *Vets for a Christian Nation*

Foundation. They had given billions to assure the election of the new president, as well as winning governorships, senate and congressional seats. They were circling back for a payback.

"Gentlemen, before we discuss business, I'd like to show you what we're doing here at Virtue." He led the Mitchell brothers through a hall to a glass-enclosed booth overlooking a vast room where hundreds of Virtue employees worked in front of screens.

"This is the heart of Virtue. Three shifts, a thousand workers each shift, plus over a hundred thousand computers that you can't see, work to bring the country back to its moral center."

"What are they doing?"

"They are divided into departments concentrating on various aspects of our culture. For example, the one to our left concentrates on the registration and approval of Christian musicians. We are officially approving all music our citizens listen to—country, rock, classic and jazz—you name it. There will no longer be filthy words, no more filthy gyrations, like twerking or disgusting hip-hop and rap. We are disrupting all major non-Christian music events and concerts. We're driving them underground, away from mass audiences. Our approval and promotion of Christian musicians and music to control the emotions of the masses have worked well."

George Mitchell noted a subtle difference in the alignment of the workers toward the right. "And over there?"

"That's the writers department. All writers will have to join Virtue's Christian writer's guilds. Most will never be approved, because they're heretics. There is another department for censoring and approving TV programs, movies, the Internet.

"I'll cleanse this nation of all heretical artists, as well as others in the media, arts and entertainment business. We'll return to a Christian nation that would make our forefathers proud."

Reverend John spread his palms. "I want to go back to the early 1950s when the population only had a handful of information sources, when everyone watched the same thing and had the same opinions and same moral values. How can we mold opinions and have a peaceful population when everyone is exposed to something different, forming their own tribes? The faster we bring back a monoculture based on Biblical Law, the better."

"I had no idea you were this far along," Ted Mitchell said, obviously eager to get to their business agenda.

"I'm cleansing the country in preparation for the Second Coming, so the majority of our citizens can rise bodily whole at the Rapture, rise into His arms before Armageddon."

The brothers glanced at each other and nodded.

Reverend John continued, "That's not all. There's a special department that gathers real-time information on suspects. We use satellites, drones, the Eye system, the Internet as well as human resources."

Reverend John led them back to his office. They sat at the small round conference table. He enjoyed their furtive glances when he told them to hold his hands.

"Oh Lord, we give our thanks to you for guiding the Mitchell brothers in their untiring efforts to rid our nation of corruption and vice. We give thanks for their help to elect those who share Your values. I ask You to guide these great American citizens, true believers, toward the path of making our Christian nation economically prosperous. Amen!"

George cleared his throat, put his elbows on the table and leaned forward. "Our great Christian nation was built on private and public investments in infrastructure; the railroads in the nineteenth century, the interstate highway system in the twentieth century. Past administrations, through stupid regulations, have blocked our entrepreneurial attempts to invest in major projects, like refineries and power plants. Environmental terrorists blocked water projects and dams.

"The result is that the country has severe power and water shortages. The West Coast desperately needs more water. Its agricultural base, which feeds much of the nation, is hurting for agricultural irrigation water to replace water allocated to its populated cities."

Reverend John spread his arms and nodded. "Water is fundamental for life."

Ted smiled. "That's an amazing insight, Reverend. This country has a major problem and we can solve it."

His brother agreed. "As the Good Book demands in Genesis when it says 'And ye shall have dominion over all . . . .' We have a specific proposal to tap God-given natural resources to alleviate those problems and help our Christian nation become economically prosperous. However, in spite of staff approval, Secretary of Interior Zeller is blocking it."

"Tell me about your proposal."

"We'll tap the world's greatest hydrothermal basin and water source to provide power and water for the West Coast."

Reverend John rubbed his chin. "You're talking about Yellowstone National Park?"

Ted leaned back in his chair. "That's right. The Yellowstone's so-called 'hot-spot' is building pressure. It blew up 70,000 years ago. Erupted a number of times. Geologists predict if it erupts again, our entire country could be destroyed."

Reverend John had seen the satellite images showing the outline of the Yellowstone caldera to be 34 by 45 miles.

George added, "As well as destroy much of the rest of the world as we know it. Our plan is an environmental win-win. We siphon off a bit of the pressure to lessen the danger of a catastrophic explosion and, at the same time, create much needed power for a third of the nation's citizens."

Reverend John understood the logic and felt surging excitement. "And you mentioned water?"

"We would dam the Yellowstone River above the Falls, in a way tourists couldn't see the infrastructure, and then divert a portion of its water to the West."

"But that river flows north, not west," Reverend John said.

"That's no problem. Denver diverted water from the western slope back east over the Continental Divide for over a hundred years. We wouldn't use all of the Yellowstone River's water. Our dam would control the flow to make it a better year-around attraction. Tourists would benefit as well."

"You'd be providing the nation with greatly needed services and at the same time you will create a profit bonanza for yourself," Reverend John said.

The other brother added, "We had hoped this administration would be more far sighted. But sadly, that's not the case."

Reverend John stood up and walked toward the neo-cross. "So you're saying Interior Secretary Zeller is blocking your proposal?"

"He refuses to consider our plan."

"Have you approached him directly?"

"Of course."

"And you've offered him a personal incentive?"

The brothers looked at each other. The older one, George, said, "He simply doesn't understand capitalism. However, the Assistant Secretary shares our belief in the free market system."

"And if, for instance, Secretary Zeller were to, say, retire, we are certain the Assistant Secretary would be named to the position and support our proposal," Ted added.

Reverend John strode to the neo-cross, turned and spread his arms. "I believe in the free market system. I could help make your plan come to fruition. Making your dream come true could happen quickly, but it would require a great deal of investment on my part, and a great deal of risk."

The brothers looked at each other. George nodded. Ted said, "It would be worth five percent of the profits of the new company."

"You know it's worth twenty percent, but in respect for your past support, let's donate fifteen percent of the new company into my *Vets for a Christian Nation* to further the works of God." Reverend John smiled. He did not think any of them would be around by the time the project came on line and profits flowed, but it never hurt to be cautious. It would be good to have additional resources if God delayed His plan to call all Christians unto His bosom.

They sealed the deal by shaking hands below the neo-cross.

After the Mitchell brothers left, Reverend John's Assistant for Special Projects arrived. Reverend John thought of Deverence as his asp, his own venomous snake.

A man of medium height and build, Deverence sported a stylish cut, brown hair looping close to his left eyebrow. His eyes were remarkable, each a bright blue iris, floating in an impossibly white cornea. Those eyes drew people, communicating honesty, warmth and kindness. He cuddled Bebe, a white and tan Shih Tzu against his chest, perhaps to hide deformed hands—each forefinger missing. Reverend John shuddered as he remembered the story about how Deverence lost those fingers. Bebe squirmed and licked Deverence's face.

"News?" Reverend John pointed to a chair across his desk.

"What happened to your head?"

"Fell in the bathroom last night. Hit my head on the door. Should have turned on the light."

"Sorry." Deverence sat and put the Bebe on the floor. It trotted across the room, sniffing chair legs. He was happy she was a bitch. A male dog, peeing on everything, would have infuriated Reverend John.

Deverence said, "Senator Thatcher is upset about our placing a neo-cross in his office. He also plans to fight the *Voting Act*. Thatcher and Senator Long are trying to get an appointment with the President to convince him to pull the bill. And now there's no question that he and Long are behind the lawsuit questioning the legality of our enforcement of Biblical Law under the *Citizens Security and Justice Act*."

Reverend John stood, fist slamming into his hand, jugular vein throbbing. "God commanded *me* to write that act. God talked to *me*. The Almighty blesses *my* actions. He speaks to *me*. Breathes His Word through me. Only through *me*." He took short steps behind the desk, turning back and forth, touching his pacemaker.

"They are enemies," Deverence said.

"God has many enemies." Reverend John sat down. "We

need creative content for The Punishments. It's time to make a list and take action."

"Let's start with Long and Thatcher," Deverence said, picking up Bebe and cradling her on his lap.

"Long's too stubborn to be redeemed. We'll make Senator Long a symbol of the futility of opposing Virtue. On the other hand, Thatcher might be a useful tool to push our agenda through Congress. His eleven-year-old son, Billy, makes him vulnerable," Reverend John said.

"Pick up the kid?"

"Send Thatcher a signal first."

Deverence nodded. "The military could cause us a problem. The President, as Commander-In-Chief, could order Chairman of the Chiefs of Staff to take us over."

"Thought about that. General Slater believes man-made law trumps Biblical Law. All the other Chiefs know better. The President would have to appoint one of ours. We'd be safe if Slater was out of the way."

"He has a wife with MS, a son dying of colon cancer and a bunch of grandchildren," Deverence said.

"Lord's work comes first."

"Want Slater for The Punishments?"

"Sooner than that. An accident or something."

Deverence nodded. Bebe squirmed. He put her on the floor.

"Interior Secretary Zeller is a crypto-pagan pretending to be a Catholic," Reverend John said. The Mitchell brothers would be pleased.

"Zeller sounds like a Jewish name."

"Whatever. He worships false idols. We would send a strong message that not even Cabinet members are above Biblical Law."

Deverence looked for Bebe. Sprawled on a couch, she licked a paw. "We'll need a high profile adulteress and a homosexual."

"Ralph Huntington needs to be persuaded to share his neo-cross manufacturing profits with our Vets Foundation. His wife, Karen, is a nationally known community leader. She's being honored for her civic work."

Deverence nodded. "Mack Bradley has been tracking Steve Brooks of Network Two. Brooks is almost finished shooting his so-called investigative report on Virtue. It's scheduled to air the day before the Senate vote on the *Voting Act*. Bradley has video evidence that Brook's assistant is his lover."

Reverend John shook his head. "Isn't it ironic that we used Mack Bradley, a homo, to out the country's most respected newsman? Takes one to know one."

"So, our list covers high profile representatives of the Congress, the Cabinet, the LGBT and women's movements."

"Plus business, when you factor in how our actions will affect Ralph Huntington." Reverend John rose from his desk. Bebe jumped off the couch and trotted to Deverence. "Let's talk to Oliver and set this in motion."

They walked into a special room built next to the cavernous area housing the computers and robots of Virtue's Propgan Department. The room, jammed with computers and screens had been constructed for twenty-six year old Tim Oliver, the world's most notorious computer hacker.

The day after he had been named Director of Virtue, Reverend John plucked Oliver from prison, where he had served two years of a forty-year sentence without parole for hacking into the government's most sensitive computers.

Arrogant and sure that he could never be caught, Oliver had left a signature in each hack: a Shakespearian literary quote.

Oliver had lost more than fifty pounds in prison. Without his beloved computers, he endured severe depression. But it was something other that computer-loss which had caused him to twice attempt suicide. He had been raped. More than once.

Oliver was a genius. Reverend John gave him an enormous budget, even indulged the man's insistence that his basic research be located in a separate restricted room that no one, not even Reverend John had been allowed to enter. Oliver had said he was researching human-like robots. It didn't bother him, so long as Oliver created what he was told. On the other hand, the man seemed to be prescient and had few moral boundaries.

Reverend John learned early on that fear makes a man malleable. He played to Oliver's dread of being sent back to prison.

Oliver, tall, fit, sporting a bright bow tie and pinstriped suit, defied the clichéd image of computer geeks. He greeted them with civility, as if he had expected them.

Oliver agreed to produce what Reverend John wanted, but made it evident he did so only because of the threat of returning to prison.

At the end of the meeting, Oliver asked, "That's all I'll have to do?"

"For now," Reverend John said.

"I won't do kids," Oliver said.

Deverence, holding Bebe against his chest, looked up sharply. "Who said anything about kids?"

"I'm just saying. We're starting down a slippery slope here. That's a line I won't cross."

Deverence tensed. Reverend John touched his elbow and turned him toward the door. "Just remember, Oliver, you are doing God's work—don't anger a wrathful God."

CHAPTER 10

Billy's School

Thatcher

THATCHER DROVE TO THE ATHLETIC fields at Billy's school. He circled the parking lot three times in vain and fought growing impatience. Someone finally vacated a space. He strode down a gravel path splitting four game fields filled with lacrosse players. The boys chased up and down the grass like a confused ocean surf. He scanned the players, but couldn't find Billy's team.

Carol sat on the top of the farthest bleacher. He hurried toward her, checking the players on her field. Billy stood with other teammates on the sideline. Billy waved. Thatcher gave him their 'thumbs-up' sign. He climbed the bench, weaving up between other parents, saying hello and shaking hands. He sat next to Carol and gave her a hug.

She pointed to the field. "Billy's going in."

They watched Billy catch the ball. Rotating his lacrosse stick back and forth to keep the ball from falling out, he spun and ran toward the wrong goal, dodging teammates who shouted at him to stop.

"No. Wrong way, Billy!" Even as the scream flew from his lips, Thatcher regretted the words. He hoped some nearby parent would not brand his son "Wrong way Billy".

Billy stumbled. The ball fell out of his stick and rolled along the field. He fought two opponents for the ball. It spun between slashing aluminum sticks. An attacker for the other team scooped it up, ran past Billy's goalie and then spun and slammed the ball into the net.

"Oh no!" Carol moaned.

Thatcher hoped the coach would not take his boy out of the game for making a beginner's mistake.

Surrounded by cheering opponents, Billy hung his head. One of his teammates ran up to him and patted him on the shoulder. Billy avoided the coach's eyes when he jogged back to form up for the face off.

"Don't worry, he's still learning the game," he said as much to himself as Carol. The coach did the right thing not to bench Billy.

Billy stood behind his restraining line while the face-off players laid their sticks horizontally next to the ball, the head of each stick inches from the ball and the butt end pointing down the midfield line. The referee blew his whistle.

The face-off-men scrapped for the ball. Billy's man clamped the ball under his stick and then flicked it out toward Billy. He scooped it up with the head of his stick and ran toward the goal. Two defenders rushed him. One swung his stick, whacking Billy on the thigh. The bigger kid body-slammed Billy in the chest, knocking him to the ground. He lay on his back, dazed.

"How can they get away with that?" Carol asked.

"It's part of the game. Billy's tough. Look, he's getting up."

Billy ran after the kid who had knocked him down, slapped the ball out of his stick, picked it up and ran toward the goal. Thatcher jumped up, cheering, thrilled Billy ran the correct way. Billy dodged a defender and then took a shot. Thatcher held his breath. The ball slammed into the ground near the goalie's feet and bounced up into the net.

"One for the good guys!" Thatcher shouted.

Teammates crowded around Billy, slapping him on the shoulders. Billy grinned at his dad and gave him their 'thumbs-up' signal.

The game seesawed back and forth during the next three quarters. Billy's team tied the score. And then, in a wild last two minutes, Billy shot the winning goal. Thatcher laughed and hugged Carol.

The team rushed from the sideline to congratulate their teammates, screaming, jumping up and down, slapping shoulders, and hugging each other. Finally the coach lined them up, facing their opponents and the two lines moved forward, shaking each other's hands. Each team formed a circle and knelt in prayer.

Both teams had prayed for victory before the game. God, having nothing better to do than watch this eleven-year-old boy's game, in His omniscience, had picked Billy's team to be the victor. Thatcher suspected the losing coach spent little time wondering why his boys had been less deserving than thinking about how he could help his goalie gain better hand-eye coordination. If the coach thought about God's choice at all, he would more than likely chalk up His displeasure to some unspoken moral sin committed by one of his players, masturbation, maybe.

It wasn't that Thatcher didn't believe in God, it's just that he didn't believe in a God who watched every human's move. Shouldn't God be working on alleviating human suffering instead of guiding sports games? It seemed unreasonable, and mind numbingly boring.

They climbed down from the bleachers and talked with other parents while the boys walked toward the gym. Thatcher watched Billy stop to pet a little brown and white dog. The owner talked to Billy. The boy looked at the man and then pointed at Thatcher. Billy and the dog owner waved at him. He waved back, uneasy.

He excused himself and began striding toward Billy and the man with the Shih Tzu. Billy ran toward the gym. The man smiled and waved at Thatcher once again before walking swiftly toward the parking lot. Thatcher wanted to talk to him. Even with the innocence the little dog gave to the scene, something did not feel right. By the time he got to the parking lot, the man was gone.

They waited for Billy in the courtyard outside the locker room.

Carol said. "We have two cars here. Why don't I drive home to get a start on dinner?"

He watched her walk toward the car and realized how lucky he was to have her in his life.

He understood her frustration about losing her career at Planned Parenthood when Virtue declared it an immoral organization, shut it down and blacklisted its employees. Carol had been lucky to be married to a U.S. Senator. He had shared the brunt of her bitterness. He reminded himself, once again, to show forgiveness and patience.

Billy walked out of the gym with other teammates. He carried his lacrosse stick in his left hand, body bent from the weight of the huge black bag that held his shoulder pads, helmet, shoes, jersey and pants. His hair was wet from the shower. A huge grin split his face.

"Nice work, Billy." Thatcher touched his son's shoulder, shaking it a bit, feeling his son's mass, noting he was becoming something all his own. Billy carried the bag to the car, tossed it in the back seat and they drove toward home. Soon the car reeked of sweat-soaked athletic stink.

"Great goal, Billy. I was so proud of you."

"That kid knocked me down, but I got up, chased him down and slapped the ball out of his stick. And then I ran through their defenders and took the shot."

"It was a great shot. Their goalie didn't have a chance."

"I was really embarrassed when I got the ball and ran the wrong way. I was so excited I didn't think about which way to run."

Billy continued with his account of the game. It was great to listen to his son's enthusiastic conversation. He compared Billy's interpretation of his performance to what he had witnessed. The two versions were pretty close. That pleased him. His son was gaining the ability to view events objectively.

"I saw you petting a little dog after the game."

"The man who owned the dog wanted me to tell you something, but I don't understand."

"Oh?"

"He said, "Don't fight Virtue. Or something like that."

Thatcher's fingers strangled the steering wheel. "Really? What else did he say?"

"He asked me to point you out and to wave at you."

"Billy, I don't want you to ever talk to that man again. I don't want you to talk to any strangers. Be careful."

"Why?"

"We've talked about that before. There are bad people who prey on kids. Don't go near him or his dog."

"He didn't seem to be a bad man."

"Maybe not, but I want you to be careful. Whether we like it or not, there is evil in this world. Most people are good, but there are a few who are pure evil. Some of those like to hurt children. Stay with the other kids. If you sense trouble pick out a woman with kids and run to her for help."

"Okay."

At dinner, he listened to Billy again recount every detail of the game for his mother. The kid's going to grow up to be a sports announcer.

For dessert, Carol served bowls of vanilla iced cream topped with melted fudge sauce.

"Hey Dad. Guess what? I'm building a fort in the bushes in our backyard between the Smith's and us. You can't see it from either yard. It's really cool. I want to show it to you."

"That's great! I want to see it. How about tomorrow after school, when it's light?"

Carol picked up the dishes. "You put Billy to bed while I clean up the kitchen."

Billy concentrated on finishing his ice cream.

"You get ready for bed. I'll be up in a minute. I have a surprise for you."

"What is it?"

Thatcher grinned. "You'll find out soon enough."

A few minutes later, he walked into the bedroom. Billy, wearing red striped pajamas, leaned against the headboard.

"What do you have in your hand?" Billy asked.

"A surprise." He walked to the edge of the bed.

Grinning, Billy rose to his knees, reaching for his dad's hand.

Thatcher raised his hand above Billy's reach. The boy stood on the bed and grabbed his arm and pulled him down on the bed. Laughing, they wrestled for the surprise. They tickled and rolled around and giggled. Thatcher loved these rare intimate times with his son. Finally, Billy sat on his arm and pried his fingers apart and snatched the prize. He rolled off and held it up and looked at a gold medal embossed with a figure of a Greek athlete.

"What is it?" Billy asked.

"It's a gold medal I won at our college track championships."

Billy pointed to the figure. "What's he doing?"

"He's throwing the discus."

"What's a discus?"

"It's an event that began in ancient times. An athlete throws a heavy disc as far as he can. The farthest throw wins. I used be a pretty good discus thrower in high school and college. That medal was my reward when I won the conference championship. I watched you today and you showed the potential of a champion. So I wanted you to have this reminder to work hard and be honorable."

Billy threw his arms around his dad's neck.

They hugged each other, lay back and looked at the ceiling. A few minutes later, Billy broke the silence.

"Can I ask you something, Dad?"

"Anything."

"One of the kids at school, Johnny Franklin, his dad had a heart attack and died. Are you going to die?"

He pulled Billy's head into the crook of his elbow and squeezed gently. "No, I'm not going to die—soon. But everyone and everything dies someday. That's just one part of the circle of life, first you are born, then you grow up, then you get old and then you die. Then life starts all over again."

"But Johnny's Dad wasn't older than you."

"Some people get sick or get in an accident and die. God calls them home early. I'll try real hard not to go early."

"Where did he go?"

"If he'd been good, God sent him to heaven."

"But if he'd been bad, would've he been sent to hell?"

"I don't believe in hell, but we'll never know."

"Why not?"

"Because God works in mysterious ways," he said. God didn't answer his daily prayers. Maybe He doesn't care. Maybe He's too busy. Or maybe . . . He doesn't exist. He'd never before questioned God's existence. He was ashamed as if he'd lost something good and pure.

"Is there really a God?" Billy asked.

It was as if the boy had read his mind. "What?"

"I mean, why can't I see God?"

"Well, God is like the wind. You can't see God or the wind, but you can feel Him, and you can hear His voice whispering through the leaves in the trees."

"Oh . . . I don't want you to die, Dad."

"I'll never leave you, Billy. No matter what happens, I'll always be watching over you."

"Even from heaven?"

"Especially from heaven."

Thatcher tucked Billy under the covers and kissed his cheek. He tousled his son's hair, turned out the light and tiptoed downstairs to the den. He closed the door so Carol could not hear, pulled his iCom from his pocket and dialed a number.

A man answered on the third ring with a simple, "Yes?"

"I need help."

"Name it."

"Protection."

"I'm not surprised. Tell me what you need."

CHAPTER 11

Thatcher Home—Washington

Carol

THE NEXT MORNING, STANDING IN the bedroom, Thatcher said, "Yesterday, after the game, while you and I were talking with other parents, Billy talked to a man with a little dog."

"Billy's always wanted a dog."

"The man told him that I should stop fighting Virtue."

"What?"

"It was a warning. Unless I back off, something could happen to Billy."

"Oh my God! Maybe Billy didn't understand."

"Billy told me the guy was missing a couple fingers. Reverend John's assistant for special projects is missing both of his forefingers. There's no question: it was a warning from Virtue."

She folded her arms across her chest and shook her head.

"Hope I'm paranoid." Thatcher rubbed his face and pulled away from the stoplight. "In any case, we can't take a risk. I called Bob Roberts at Moral America. He's sending a retired security guard to watch our house and follow you when you take Billy to and from school."

"I can't believe this is happening."

"The school has a lock-down policy. Nobody can get at him there," he said. "We're safe in our gated community. No one can get past the guard without our permission. But, just in case, there will be a guard outside our house when I'm not here."

She shook her head. "I might have made our situation worse."

He glanced at her.

She said, "After our dinner with Frank, I decided to stop Virtue from suspending women's right to vote."

He shook his head. "You what?"

"I'm going to gut your so-called *American Citizen's Voting Act.*"

"That's not *my* act. I'm going to fight it through the legislative process."

"Virtue will have the votes to stop you," she said.

"So how will you fight it?"

"Through woman-power. I'm organizing the wives of legislators to persuade their husbands to vote against the bill."

"How?"

"By using the oldest method . . . cut them off until after the bill is defeated."

"Withhold sex?" He laughed and turned serious. "Some women could get hurt."

"The causalities of war. I've organized a stealth campaign: word-of-mouth, nothing in writing, nothing over the phone or Internet, nothing attributable to anyone else, just private girl-to-girl pledges. Congress has five hundred thirty-five voting members: one hundred Senators and the remainder Representatives. I'll ask each of ten wives to solicit ten more women, and they ask ten more. I only needed one cohort of ten wives to cover the House. One more and we'll cover the Senate."

"Meeting ten women at once will be noticed."

"I met with them individually. None know the names of the others, unless they approach someone who has already committed. I know more than ten wives who agree. Each of them knows others."

"It's risky. Have you thought about Billy?"

"I'd rather die than have our son grow up in a country where women are not allowed vote."

"It's a good thing we'll have some security. I think it would be wise for you to put cash and your passport in the locked bedside table with your gun."

She stopped buttoning her blouse. "Why?"

"I'm probably being paranoid, but have them handy in case we have to leave. Virtue is probably monitoring our calls. We also need a code word in case we have to split without them knowing our plan."

"Code word?"

"Red Wings. If I call and say I'll meet you at Red Wings for dinner, drop everything, grab Billy and meet me where we were engaged . . . at Captain Charlie's."

"You are being paranoid."

"Say it: Red Wings."

"If you call and say Red Wings, I'm to get Billy and meet you at Captain Charlie's. Sounds theatrical."

"Plan for the worst, hope for the best." He kissed her on the cheek. Gotta go to a meeting."

An hour later, once again late for her daily Women's Prayer Group, Carol drove out of her driveway and spotted a brown Toyota sedan parked in front of their house. The guard

Thatcher had requested from Moral America. The man behind the wheel had wisps of white hair and flabby cheeks. He didn't look much like a guard. She pulled next to him and lowered her window and introduced herself.

"I'm Sam Browning, Mrs. Thatcher. Bob Roberts at Moral America hired me to watch your backside. I'll be here during the day until the Senator gets home. I'll follow you when you drive your son to and from school. I'll try not to be intrusive. You don't need to worry about anything."

Carol thanked him and a few minutes later gunned her car into a parking space at the First Church of Christ. She jumped out and hurried toward the women's annex. Running up the stairs, she glanced at the Eye and wondered if she were recorded as late again to Women's Prayer Group. She opened the door.

In the front of the room, Reverend Mosser paced back and forth, preaching at forty-three women sitting at round tables. Most wore modest clothes and no makeup. Cinder-block walls matched gray-flecked plastic floor tiles. A neo-cross hung on the wall above a lectern centered between the ladies' rest room on the left and the door leading into the annex hallway on the right. Thatcher had told her that the men's annex was twice as large, carpeted and walnut paneled. She'd never seen it. Women weren't allowed inside.

She tiptoed in and looked for a seat. Heads swiveled. The only two empty chairs were close to the minister's lectern. She wove through the tables toward the front, wiping perspiring hands against her dress.

"Mrs. Thatcher! Once again you are late. Do you take pleasure in disrupting our Prayer Group?" Minister Mosser wore a conservative blue blazer, a freshly starched white shirt, a striped tie and dark gray flannel pants. Although he preached that cleanliness was next to godliness, his shoes were old and scuffed.

"No, I . . ."

"The Book tells us in Ezra, Chapter Six, Verse Seven: 'Do not interfere with the work of this temple of God'. Take this seat, so I can continue the work of the Lord." He pointed to an empty chair directly in front of him.

Mrs. Appleby snickered.

The minister strode back and forth in front of her. "As I explained before you interrupted, the male head of each family has been chosen to be the sole authority of God. Women and children are subordinate. Thus a witch is a woman who disobeys the God-ordained head of the house— her husband! The Bible says . . . ." The minister's words jumbled into a rushing torrent.

She felt the heat of the daily diatribe. That was the word for it, a bitter, abusive, prolonged discourse. She looked at the faces of the congregation. Mrs. Newell watched Mosser like an infatuated schoolgirl gazing at a handsome teacher. Mrs. Morel, sitting two tables behind Mrs. Newell, nodded and said "Amen" reverently. As usual, the loudest "Amener" was Gretchen Williams, whose head bowed over clicking knitting needles. Everywhere, heads nodded and bobbed in a hypnotic rhythm to the preacher's words.

The minister's unending stream of Bible verses proclaiming male dominance over women drove other thoughts from Carol's mind, forcing her to again listen to his tirade. An eternity later, he stood in front of her and held the Bible high over his head. His body odor rolled over her.

"Remember . . . your duty is to submit and obey your husbands." His accusing finger swung across the other women stopping at Carol.

"If you disobey, you are a witch in the eyes of God . . . a witch!" His eyes eagerly searched for a witch in the congregation to declare herself.

The rhythmic click of Gretchen William's knitting needles stopped. Carol looked at the folded hands in her lap. They trembled. There was a dry cough from the middle of the room. Minister Mosser waited for someone to come forward and witness that she was a witch. No one moved. Carol listened to her own breathing, wondering if someone might accuse her.

At last, defeated, the minister dropped his chin against his chest and said, with a voice tinged with disappointment, "Let us bow our heads in silent prayer."

She prayed God would give the minister laryngitis for a year.

He raised his head, gathered his notes from behind the lectern and, as a seeming afterthought, asked if there were questions or comments.

Mrs. Appleby rose. "I want to compliment our dear Minister Mosser for his wonderful work in gathering supplies and taking them, with the Word, to the poor across Africa. He leads a marvelous Christian effort to help those unfortunates in need, as our Savior Jesus Christ commanded. My husband and I support his efforts, as I'm certain many of you will also."

Mrs. Appleby scanned each face in the room, throwing silent guilt on those she knew had not contributed to the effort. "My heart goes out to those poor Africans caught up by events they can't control and, as good Christians, we must do everything in our power to help their plight. We can certainly do more than simply write a check to the cause. So I'd like everyone to think about what sort of fundraiser we can hold to really make a difference to ease their lives of misery. I propose we devote all of next Wednesday's meeting to developing a plan."

Everyone clapped. Mrs. Appleby's chest swelled. She nodded three times and sat down. The minister thanked her for her fine Christian thoughts. He walked out of the room.

Was Mrs. Appleby blind? Couldn't she see the homeless crowding the streets around her? Carol closed her eyes, listening to whispers grow into shrill gossip. Marsha, the hawk-faced woman sitting to Carol's left, said, "We should invite the Ridgeways into our Couples Prayer Circle."

Joyce, a young woman with a pleasant face and sweet smile, said, "They declared too late! We can't be certain they are sincere in their belief." She looked around the table for agreement.

A woman with blond hair pulled into a severe bun, sitting on the right of Carol, leaned forward and said in a conspiratorial tone, "Joyce is right. You have to question the motives of those declaring this late."

Carol looked at the faces of old friends. She remembered when the church was filled with loving people like Gretchen Williams and Mrs. Newell, who stepped into her life when she first joined the church. They became a caring family, the only family she had until she married Thatcher. Thank God for him.

There had been a joyous sense of community in the church when it respected individual differences and beliefs.

That fellowship represented a wonderful part of her life, but it changed. Slowly, a culture of intolerance, stridency and suspicion replaced Christ's teachings of love and compassion. She looked at the faces of past friends. Could she trust them now? Carol looked at her watch. Might as well give them something more to talk about. She stood up.

Betsy Simpson, the Daily Prayer Chairwoman, peered at her from the next table. "We still have ten minutes before the end of the meeting, Carol. You're not leaving alone?" Simpson had a hard face, but pretty even without makeup, with a thin body under a plain dress, a snake pretending to be a grandmother.

Conversations faltered. Everyone watched Carol.

She smiled. "I can take care of myself."

The chairwoman's hands opened in a Christ-like pleading movement. "But you know the rules of the Department of Virtue regarding Christian women traveling alone."

"Not edicts. Not yet. Only suggestions. When the Department of Virtue declares an edict that a woman not be outside her house alone, I'll be the first to ask you to accompany me."

Simpson sputtered, face contorting with rage.

Carol cut her off. "My husband ordered me to pick him up to take him to a meeting. And, as our dear Minister just preached, our duty is to submit and obey our husbands." The silence turned oppressive.

Mrs. Branch, an elderly woman with stringy white hair, rose from her table with difficulty and announced, "I have to leave as well."

Carol helped Mrs. Branch limp toward the door. The old woman leaned on Carol's arm and said in a loud whisper, "Just look at them. Just like a herd of cattle. No makeup. All of them wearing terrible plain dresses."

"You and I usually look just like them, Mrs. Branch."

"I know that! Don't you think I know that? What's happening to us?"

In the parking lot, she helped Mrs. Branch into her car and waited while she lowered her window. The old woman reached for her hand and stared through rheumy eyes. "Thank you, dear. You were brave to leave early. That was a matter of principle. The entire situation is disgusting! I'm an old woman with nothing to lose. I can get away with criticizing Virtue, but you're young and have more to lose. Be careful."

Carol watched as Mrs. Branch's old sedan lurched onto the street.

She checked her rearview mirror several times as she drove toward her neighborhood. She stopped at the brick guardhouse that blocked the cobblestone entrance to their McLean community. She ignored the Eye that recorded the car, license plate and driver. When she lowered her window, warm September air spilled inside. She breathed deeply, hoping to ease the tension in her shoulders. Waiting for the guard to inspect her car, she looked at the neighborhood's twelve-foot-high perimeter fence.

She felt safe inside this compound. Her neighborhood, like all upper class enclaves of Washington, was a fortified camp. The armed twenty-four-hour gate guards, face-cams, concrete walls and razor wire . . .

But something was wrong with a society where you only feel safe inside a prison of your own making. Without Thatcher, she would be living outside, unprotected. She felt bad for those less fortunate. Much of the city was dangerous.

The guard finally raised the steel gate. She drove down peaceful streets lined with trees, past well-manicured lawns and the expensive homes of her neighbors.

She lived in a red brick Georgian-styled home, nestled on a two-acre lot under a grove of ancient maples. A winding brick walk led from the sidewalk to the columned portico of their two-story house. She loved the thick lilac bushes that shielded their lot on three sides. Their springtime blooms and scent made her smile.

She parked in their two-car garage. She looked at the kitchen clock. Two hours before she had to pick up Billy. There would be plenty of time after that to get dressed for the reception at the French Embassy.

She leaned against the kitchen counter and remembered the day during grade school when her father had enrolled her in karate classes. Later, when she was older, he had taught her how to shoot a shotgun, rifle and pistol. She learned to outshoot him, which made him proud. He was determined his daughter would know how to protect herself in a violent world. In high school he taught her how to drive his motorcycle. Her friends had thought she was weird when she rumbled to school on a Harley Davidson Hog.

She had thought her father was a bit paranoid. Now she realized he had been prophetic. Locking the doors, she walked downstairs into the basement and tossed a few dirty clothes into the washing machine. She slipped out of her dress and smiled. The churchwomen would really gossip if they knew she wore nothing underneath.

She kicked off her shoes and stood naked and free. She dug the rest of the dirty clothes out of the hamper and stuffed them into a heavy cotton laundry bag. Standing on tiptoes, she tied the bag to a ceiling beam, hanging it waist-high. It swung like a man on the end of a noose. Reaching into the bottom of the hamper, she pulled out a white, loose-fitting coat and pants. After slipping on her karate *gi*, she wrapped a black belt around her waist.

She balanced on her left leg, and gave the bag a vicious kick.

CHAPTER 12

Hart Senate Office Building

Thatcher

THATCHER SAT AT HIS OFFICE desk, reading the minutes of the Senate Intelligence Committee meeting. His iCom vibrated. He looked at the text message.

French Embassy reception—tonight—Jamila

His hands trembled. He dropped the iCom on the desk. He hadn't heard from her in years. How many? Twenty? More? Didn't matter. A long time. He leaned back, stared at the ceiling and moaned.

His stomach was a vat of squirming eels. Elbows on the desk, he buried his head in his hands, struggling to drive out the desire, struggling to erase the images, struggling to forget the secret that could kill him. The secret only she knew.

He had been a twenty-two year old Second Lieutenant in Afghanistan standing next to his First Lieutenant at a forward base, thinking about the email he'd received from her. She was in the Mideast. He hadn't seen her since grade school. At eleven, she'd been tall and klutzy, yet they had formed a tight friendship—she'd shared her personal secret.

He heard a hollow thump. The First Lieutenant's head exploded: the beginning of his first firefight in Kunduz province. Covered in blood and brains, dragging his friend's body to cover, taking command, shouting orders, dodging bullets, crawling on his belly over moaning, dying comrades, gagging on the copper smell of their blood smeared over his hands, face and clothes, screaming on the radio for air support—denied—denied—denied—as his men died around him, praying to God for help. God took a long time to answer.

Later, he was recalled to headquarters to report to the Commander about the disaster. Lost in the sprawling office complex, he wandered into an off-limits area. He overheard a plan for a meeting that could end the war. He left without being noticed and gave his report about the battle.

He was qualified for a medal and earned a four-day pass to the Central Command's rest and rehabilitation program at Camp As Sayliyah, in Qatar. He contacted her.

Two days later, Thatcher met Jamila next to the reflecting pool at Doha's Museum of Islamic Art. He recognized her immediately. Tall, wearing a white blouse and dark ankle-length skirt, hair modestly covered by a scarf. A mix between a Moroccan mother and American father, she had grown to be an exotic beauty. Off balance in this Arabian culture, he smothered his first impulse to hug her, instead offering a battle-scarred hand. Her smooth fingers touched his, and a current of energy flowed through him.

They walked between rows of palm trees toward the museum, his eyes darting from trunk to trunk, scouting danger. After what he'd been though, he couldn't help being alert.

After touring the museum, marveling over the Islamic world's treasures, they had lunch at IDAM, the museum's elegant restaurant—French Mediterranean cuisine, with an Arabic twist. Coming off the battle, he was too wired to enjoy the food. He struggled to have a relaxed conversation.

Finally, she asked, "Has it been tough?"

"What?"

She looked into his eyes. "You don't know who your enemy is."

Was that a double entendre? Was she warning him about something? He'd let it play out.

"How's your Mom?" he asked.

Jamila looked out the window and studied the ocean for a moment. "She's gone."

"I'm sorry."

She turned back to him with moist eyes. "So am I."

"I shouldn't have gone there."

She sighed. "It's what we have in common. You want to know the rest."

"You don't have to. You told me about it when we were in grade school. Let's talk about something else," he put his napkin on the table.

She stared out the window at a sailboat far out on the ocean. "The only time my father ever gave me any attention was in bed. I was special to him. I felt loved."

"He was a sick bastard."

Her head snapped toward him. "He still is."

"But that's the past. You've moved on," he said.

Her laugh was like a moan. "That's the sick part."

"You still live with him?"

"In a compound in Marrakesh. He has armed guards. I can come and go as I wish. I work for him."

"Why the hell do you go back?" He hated the judgmental anger in his question.

"He has my daughter."

He shook his head, closed his eyes and kneaded the bridge of his nose. Sitting across the table, she was so beautifully vulnerable. She stared at her hands in her lap.

"Let me get this straight. You can't get your daughter out of the house past the armed guards and he's forcing you to work for him?"

Without looking up, she nodded.

He knew the answer before asking, but had to hear it from her. "How is he blackmailing you?"

"He groomed me. I can't let that happen to my daughter. She's still too young, but I have to break the cycle. He promised not to touch her if I bring him enough money."

"Sex?"

She looked directly at him, her eyes angry. "No! Not sex. I . . . I pick up and deliver forbidden things."

"Drugs?"

"No! But that's beside the point. You wanted to know. And now you know. Are you happy?"

The serrated edge to her voice brought heat to his face. He'd pushed too far.

Later, walking along the oceanfront, she took his hand and leaned into him. "I want you to come with me. We're going to chase the . . ."

The roar of a passing jet ski drowned out her last word. He thought she had said dragon, but that didn't make sense. He watched the jet ski skim waves. Just a few hours' away American boys were being blown up. What a screwed up world.

She opened the door of the suite. It was like stepping into an Arabian palace from *One Thousand and One Arabian Nights*. The sunken living room's walls and ceilings, covered in colorful mosaic tiles in ancient Islamic patterns, with low tables and hundreds of pillows scattered across Oriental rugs, made him dizzy. At the tall windows, an ocean and flower scented warm breeze caressed white silk drapes. There were faint calls to prayer from a minaret.

"I . . ."

She held up her hand to cut him off. "We'll talk later."

She held his hand and led him to the center of the room. They settled into a nest of pillows.

She opened a table drawer and took out a cigarette lighter, a piece of aluminum foil and a packet of white powder. After pouring the powder on the foil, she reached into the drawer and withdrew several one-hundred-dollar bills. She rolled two bills into tubes. He held the foil while she brought the flame underneath.

She smiled. "Now I'll show you how to chase the dragon."

When smoke rose from the heroin, she inserted a rolled bill into her right nostril, held the other closed and inhaled the fumes. Her eyes turned glassy. A look of ecstasy spread over her face. She moaned and leaned back against the pillows.

He watched in amazement, taking in the scene, so peaceful, so different than the heat, cold and blood of Afghanistan.

"It's your turn. Chase the dragon," she said in a softer, slower voice.

He shook his head.

"Join me."

He had lived through the firefight where most around him had been wounded or killed. He was going back to more, facing death everyday. He'd either be wounded or killed. What did he have to lose?

She held the lighter under the foil until smoke rose. He put the rolled bill in his right nostril, closed the other with his forefinger, moved the tube into the smoke and inhaled.

A transcendent wave of euphoria rolled through his body. He fell back onto the pillows and watched the mosaic tiles on the ceiling morph into wonderfully strange patterns, swirling like the Northern Lights.

The pupils of her eyes were enlarged. He looked deep into her soul. He loved what he found. He had a revelation: while there were purely evil people in this world, many of the best souls hid behind a façade.

She held his gaze, daring him to look directly at her fingers unbuttoning her blouse, revealing velvet smooth skin, a glorious contrast to the dirt and grit of the battlefield.

Six hours of rapture and then, during withdrawal, the drug causing her extra sensitivity, the ecstasy of incredible sex. And then they chased the dragon again, over and over during three days.

Years ago. Never smoked again. Never would. Still consumed by the memories. Still consumed by desire. A desire for heroin or for her? Would it never end? And why, after all this time, after his fruitless Internet searches, did she suddenly appear out of the mists of the past? He'd never told Carol about her. There would be hell to pay.

And worst of all, trying to impress Jamila, he'd told her about the planned meeting between the CIA station chief and an important Taliban leader, assuring her that the war would soon be over. That was the moment he committed treason and became a murderer.

And the question that had haunted him was: had Jamila betrayed him by telling the enemy about the peace meeting?

He rose from his desk, walked to the neo-cross, knelt and prayed that he'd have the wisdom to navigate between Carol and Jamila during the embassy party. He couldn't betray Carol.

And then he once again prayed for forgiveness for the maimed and dead children. God didn't answer. He rose to his feet.

Perhaps God didn't answer his prayers because God didn't think Thatcher was worthy of an answer. God wouldn't bother to speak to a bad man.

CHAPTER 13

Reverend John's Office

Reverend John

REVEREND JOHN AND DEVERENCE SAT at the round table discussing plans. They were interrupted by a knock on the office door. Mack Bradley walked in, carrying a tablet.

"Yes?" Deverence asked.

"Good news! I have proof of your theory about Steve Brooks of Network Two. They've finished shooting their investigative report on us. It's scheduled to run the day before the Senate vote on the *Voting Act*," Bradley said.

"Have you seen it?" Reverend John asked.

"An unedited cut."

"And?" Reverend John asked.

"It's not good. The program raises a lot of questions. No Senator in his right mind would vote for the bill."

"We'll destroy that program. Show us your proof," Deverence said.

"I've been tracking Brooks for two months. He works all the time on his investigative reports for the network. He's private about his personal life. He's cautious and circumspect. He has a younger assistant who I suspected was his lover."

"The proof?" Reverend John asked.

Bradley propped the tablet up on the coffee table in front of the couch. He turned on the screen. "I've edited it down to five short scenes. There is plenty more footage to back that up."

The first scene was an empty bedroom.

They watched as Brooks led his assistant inside. They struggled out of their clothes, fell on the bed. Moans. After-sex pillow talk. The other four scenes where shot in another bedroom, a living room, even on a kitchen table.

The screen went black.

"Well done! Well done indeed! Great program content. Brooks will star in our Public Punishments," Reverend John said.

"They have a rendezvous tonight," Bradley said.

"I understand Brooks is an expert in martial arts," Deverence said.

"That would make an exciting scene," Bradley said.

Reverend John held up his hand. "No. Brooks has a huge audience. I want him arrested during the middle of his prime-time news broadcast. Think of the value of that scene. And tell your source to delete the files and videos of the investigative report."

"I'll do it right after I pick up Brooks."

"Great job, Bradley." Reverend John noticed the man looked distracted. "Is there something else?"

"Perhaps it's not within my area of responsibility, but I understand Senator Thatcher is being difficult," Bradley said.

"So?" Deverence asked.

"I served under Thatcher in the army. I know him, how he thinks. We need to get rid of him."

Reverend John said nothing.

Bradley picked up the tablet and started to walk toward the door and then hesitated. He turned toward Reverend John. "Could I ask a favor?"

"What?" Deverence asked.

"If we take Thatcher, I want to be his executioner."

"Why?" Reverend John asked.

"In Afghanistan, the son-of-a-bitch killed my best friend."

"Don't use that kind of language." Reverend John said.

"I'm just saying . . ."

Deverence cut him off. "We understand. Now leave. We have work to do."

That night, Reverend John's driver took him home for the first time since Linda had hit him with the frying pan. He still had headaches. He dreaded going through the charade of an amicable dinner with Pearl serving. He would either have to confront the issue, or not, with his wife. He'd let her take the lead on that. He wasn't in a position to argue. In fact, he was thankful to her for saving him from sin.

He touched the foreign lump under his collarbone. He'd leveraged technology into power, yet this pacemaker, with its wires connected to his heart was an abomination—unnatural—a manmade intrusion into a holy-made body. Yet God had directed the inventors of pacemakers, so his implant had been blessed. Still, he worried it would malfunction before he could carry out God's command to trigger the Rapture. But that was silly—God controlled everything.

As they approached the house, he noticed the lights were off. Strange.

"Wait for me," he told the driver. He got out and walked toward the front door. Several yards from the house the motion-activated lights snapped on. There were dark plastic bundles scattered on the lawn under a window. He bent over and opened one. It was filled with shirts. His shirts. He stood up and looked at the bags; at least twenty garbage bags. His clothes. She had thrown out his clothes. Out of the window. His clothes. The woman had lost her mind!

He went to the front door. His key would not fit in the lock. He understood her anger. He deserved it, but she should understand he had not been in control. His actions had been controlled by the Devil.

He walked back to the car, concocting a story so the rumor would not spread. Something about the yard man leaving bags of grass clippings. Something about Linda traveling and he had forgotten he had the locksmith change the locks. Yes, that would do. It would have to.

He settled back into the backseat. As the driver turned the limo around, he looked at the dead house. He would not return. He would sleep at the office. Time was short. He had Heavenly work to do. God had sent him a message through Linda; he should concentrate on His task.

CHAPTER 14

French Embassy—Washington

Felix

WEARING HER OFF-THE-SHOULDER red evening dress, Felix presented her Moroccan diplomatic credentials at the French Embassy reception. She used her real name, Jamila Murr, for her diplomatic cover. She was eager to meet Thatcher again after all these years.

She accepted a flute of champagne from a waiter before cruising the crowd, chatting with other guests, and ignoring men's admiring looks. Her breath seized when she spotted him.

His Internet pictures presented a tall well built man, sandy hair, honest blue eyes set on either side of a sharp nose, teeth so bright they had to have been whitened, a cleft chin on a rugged face. All in all he'd grown even more handsome than when they had met in Qatar. He looked better than the Internet pictures. She smiled to herself and began stalking him like a tigress.

Thatcher talked with diplomats and their wives, shaking hands, smiling, nodding, listening and laughing. She noted he wasn't like an insecure politician who constantly looked over the shoulder of the person with whom he talked, scanning the room for someone more important. That hypocritical trait bugged her. Point for Thatcher. Was he as extreme as many in the government? He didn't look like a zealot. Knowing his past, she understood why he had been attracted to religion. Perhaps he had changed. Everything else had. She'd been gone five years. Upon returning, she had not recognized the country. How could a culture change so quickly? He could provide an answer to that . . . and other things.

A rotund bald man talking with Thatcher looked at her. Thatcher followed the man's gaze and spotted her. His eyes caressed her figure. Their eyes met. A fleeting shadow crossed his face—a mixture of joy and anger. She smiled. He glanced around the room, obviously looking for his wife, excused himself and approached her.

"So we meet again," he said.

She offered her hand. "I'm the cultural attaché with the Moroccan Embassy."

His laugh seemed uneasy.

"Aren't you happy to see me?" She smiled, sipped her champagne and looked into his eyes.

He signaled a waiter, grabbed a glass of champagne and drained half its contents. "I never thought I'd see you again. You've changed. You're more beautiful than . . . I didn't recognize you out of context."

"You mean with my clothes on?"

"Yes . . . No!"

She imagined his mind racing. Was she a threat? Had she planned this meeting? What did she want? Or was this one of those . . . unpredictable . . . dangerous and wonderful circumstances in life?

"Who did you tell?" His face looked angry.

"What?"

"Innocent little kids were killed after I told you about the meeting between the CIA and Taliban leader."

She put her hand on her chest. "You think I betrayed your trust?"

"You're denying that you were behind the suicide bombing?"

She flared. "Oh, for God's sake!"

He took her by the elbow to stop her from walking away. "So why are you here? Why now, after all these years?"

"I was just curious about my childhood friend—my Qatar lover. Haven't you ever wondered about me?"

"Looked for you, but you aren't on the Internet."

"I don't believe in technology."

"Yeah, sure," he said. "So what now?"

She smiled and slid closer, penetrating his personal space. "Do I make you nervous?"

"Of course not." He took half a step back, eyes scanning the room, laugh insincere. "Just curious."

"I've been stationed in China for the past five years. So much has changed since I was last here. I don't understand the cultural implications. We'll have lunch tomorrow. You can help me understand what happened."

"I'm busy," he said.

"Change your plans."

"You've certainly read about it in your diplomatic reports, read it on the Internet."

"Believe it or not, America is not as important as it was once. It's like the Roman Empire, decaying. Still, I'd like you to brief me."

"As the cultural attaché with the Moroccan Embassy?"

She touched his arm and smiled. "And to catch up with an old friend."

A tall woman wearing a dark blue evening gown moved toward them.

"Here comes my wife."

"I hope she's not the jealous type." She watched Thatcher's wife approach like an enemy destroyer. The smile was one of those looks wives paste on their lips when their antenna says a competitor is hitting on their husband. "I'll call you in the morning."

Thatcher turned to his wife, "Oh there you are. Carol, I want you to meet a cultural attaché with the Moroccan Embassy." He turned to Felix. "I'm sorry, I forgot your name."

So he'd kept their relationship secret. "I'm Jamila Murr, Mrs. Thatcher." She took Carol's hand. "It's so nice to meet you. I'd love to chat, but as I told your husband, I need to get back to the embassy for a meeting." She nodded goodnight, walked away from them, squaring her shoulders and standing tall, feeling their eyes on her, remembering her last time in Qatar with him, chasing the dragon.

CHAPTER 15

Washington

Carol

THEY WAITED IN FRONT OF the French Embassy for the valet to bring their car. Carol wore a light coat and hugged herself. He moved from foot to foot.

"Nice party," he said.

"Really? Did you meet anyone of particular interest?"

"I always meet interesting people at these affairs." He looked relieved when the valet brought their car. The young man accepted a tip and opened the passenger side door for Carol.

Thatcher pulled onto the street, merging with light traffic. She waited, looking out the passenger window.

"Have fun tonight?" he finally asked without looking at her.

"So what's going on?"

He shot her a look. "I had a rough time at the office today."

"I'm not interested in what happened at the office."

"Oh?" He swung around a van.

"I asked what's going on."

"What?"

"Cut it out, Thatcher. Stop avoiding the issue."

"The issue?"

"Miss Sexpot"

"Sexpot?" His laugh was forced.

"Your Moroccan 'cultural' attaché, as if you didn't know."

He lifted his hands from the wheel in frustration. "What did I do wrong?"

"You acted like an idiot, first ogling her and then acting like a virgin teenager propositioning a call girl."

"You're imagining things."

"So tell me. I'm interested."

"She looked familiar . . ."

She interrupted. "That's . . ."

He slapped the steering wheel. "Let me finish."

"You'd better."

Thatcher cleared his throat. "At first I didn't recognize her. It was out of context. You know how it is. You know someone in a certain setting and sometime, years later, you meet them in a totally different venue. You think you've met them before, but can't place them. It turns out I met her when my Dad was posted to the Air Force base in Saudi Arabia. We lived within the same compound. We were kids in school together. She was a friend. He was reassigned and I haven't seen her since."

Carol turned toward him, straining against the seat belt. She pulled it away from her breast. "So, suddenly, after all this time, your childhood 'friend' shows up at an embassy party and targets you."

"'Target' isn't a fair term."

"Really? Then how did she find you, Thatcher? And why now, after all these years?"

"She said she was curious. Did an Internet search."

"Haven't you Googled her?"

The light changed as they approached an intersection. He slowed to a stop. A group of homeless approached their car. He gunned it through the red light.

"Well?"

"You know how it is. You wonder about what happened to old friends, so you do a quick search. I couldn't find her."

"That's unusual in today's world. You can find anyone."

"I know it's strange, but I couldn't find her."

"When was the last time you looked for her?"

"Years ago. I couldn't find her, so I stopped trying."

"What makes her so special?"

"I forgot about her until tonight."

"I'll bet." She regretted her sarcastic tone.

He glanced at her. "What's with this jealously bit? She's no threat to you."

"She's a threat to you."

"Oh for God's sake Carol, you didn't say two words to each other."

"It's a woman's intuition. She wants something."

He pulled into their driveway, pushed the door opener, pulled into the garage, turned off the ignition and reached for her hand. She pulled away.

"So why did Jamila give you that 'call me' signal at the door?"

"Oh. That?"

The garage light went out, plunging them into darkness. "Wait. I'll get the light."

She waited in the dark.

"She hasn't been in the States for years. Assigned to China. She wants to understand what's happened here. So much has changed. She's confused."

"Aren't we all? She and I have that in common."

"She wants me to tell her about it at lunch tomorrow."

"I'll bet. A little romantic lunch to catch up with the times?"

He paused before opening the door into the mudroom, his voice cold. "She is a cultural attaché. It's her job."

"Don't be naïve."

"You have no idea how many women, attracted to power, have thrown themselves at me. I've always been true to you."

"I believe that. But that woman is different. She frightens me."

After paying the sitter and checking on Billy, they turned on their bedroom TV to catch the news. The anchor announced breaking news: Chief of Staff General Amos Slater had been inspecting the Air Force Academy in Colorado Springs. His plane had exploded shortly after takeoff, killing all aboard.

They watched a film clip of the General's jet exploding. A massive fireball hung suspended in the night sky. Fiery pieces jettisoned from the main explosion, rocketing outward, up and down like ball lightning. And then the fireball arced toward earth like a meteor. It was beautiful, as if the finger of God traced light against darkness.

CHAPTER 16

Huntington Residence

Karen

AFTER A LEISURELY SHOWER, KAREN toweled off. She turned to the full-length mirror. Not bad for her age. Not bad at all. Working out three days a week, a combination of cardio and weights, plus 150 stomach crunches first thing every morning, helped. She was toned, with firm biceps without underarm flab, shapely legs and flat stomach. Her fingers traced from her navel to her breasts, cupping and raising them. She caressed and gently tugged her nipples, relishing the tingling feeling. Her breasts looked better than most boob jobs she'd seen at the gym. God blessed her with a figure men admired, a figure only Ralph knew, and figure only Ralph touched.

She brushed her hair and slipped on a silk robe. She would put on her make-up just before leaving for the luncheon banquet where she'd be the honored guest—Washington's Volunteer of the Year. News about the tribute last month had been a surprise. There were so many other people doing worthy things, so many more working in the trenches, making a bigger difference in needy people's lives. Giving to others created happiness and satisfaction in her life.

She found Ralph at the kitchen table, drinking coffee and reading a financial report. She kissed him on the cheek and received a loving pat on the behind. She poured a cup of coffee.

"We had a message from Susan last night," she said.

"Something new about her love life?"

"Joe invited her to dinner tonight to celebrate a special occasion."

"Knowing her romantic track record, he'll announce he's received a promotion for a job in London."

"That's not kind." She sat at the table with him.

"True. She's doing great in her job, but she seems desperate to settle down."

"Kids her age are getting married later in life, if at all."

"Don't blame them. World's gone to hell. I wouldn't want to bring kids into this mess."

"But you would have married me. Right?"

"Of course . . . dear," he said teasingly. He slipped the report in his briefcase and then smiled at her. "On another subject, I want to know how my famous wife feels this morning?"

"Did I tell you that a man called and said both the *New York Times* and *60 Minutes* want to do a joint interview after the luncheon?"

He grinned. "Not more than ten times."

"I'm happy you'll be there to share it with me."

"Bad news on that front. Reverend John called when you were in the shower. He's demanding to meet with me at one."

She sat back and took a deep breath. Leaning forward, she lifted her coffee cup with both hands and took a long sip. She finally looked at him. Her eyes felt moist.

"Say no!"

"I told him I was tied up. He told me to break whatever I was doing. I told him I was going to support you and I could meet with him at any other time . . ." he paused.

"And?"

"He reminded me he had the contractual power to break our single-supplier contract."

"So?"

"That means others could manufacture and sell neo-crosses. We just mortgaged ourselves to the hilt to build three new manufacturing plants to meet demand. Our profits would disappear. Our business would fail."

"He's bluffing. You have a patent on the design."

"He said the patent doesn't matter. He'll open up the contract and then fight us in court and we won't have a business by the time the case is settled. We'd go bankrupt."

"I can't believe it."

"He wants to be majority owner of our business."

"We talked about that. He's being a hypocrite. Immoral. He pretends to be a Christian. He signed a legal agreement. He has to live up to it."

"I agree. In any event, I have to talk to him."

During the pre-luncheon reception at the Washington Hilton on Connecticut Ave, an intriguing looking man cuddling a Shih Tzu introduced himself to Karen as the interviews coordinator.

"We'll conduct the interviews in a suite upstairs to eliminate background sound problems. So you won't be interrupted by well-wishers. I'll meet you in front of the elevators immediately after lunch. Everyone will want to congratulate you, but we're on a tight schedule. Don't linger."

He walked away as though she didn't exist. She wondered how he could have gotten his pet into the hotel or reception.

She thought only service dogs were allowed in public places. Still, it was a cute little dog. He had called it 'Bebe. He hadn't given his name. It didn't matter. After today, she would never see him again. She mingled with the others, graciously accepting their congratulations.

A few minutes later, the host led her and the rest of the guests from the reception room down a wide corridor toward the banquet hall. She became aware of a buzzing sound that grew louder until the sounds separated into different categories; murmurs, voices, laughter, scraping of chairs, clinking of silverware. They walked through a side door into the banquet room on a runway carpet leading to the long dignitary table, raised on a dais above the crowd.

What a crowd! There must have been a thousand people seated at round tables. They were there to honor her. She was astonished. Ralph should have told Reverend John to go to hell. He would have been amazed at the number of people gathered for her. He would be proud of her.

She followed the host up four steps onto the platform, walked between chair backs and a blue curtain that contrasted nicely with her red suit. She spotted the man with the Shih Tzu standing in the back of the room. He nodded and waved at someone and then pointed to her. She looked for the person he waved to, but saw only a waiter, carrying a pitcher of water toward the dais. She spotted her fellow Meals On Wheels board members sitting at a round table near the podium. She waved and they waved back. There were other faces she recognized, but most in the audience were strangers.

"What would you like to drink?"

She turned to the waiter who poured water into her glass, "Iced tea would be wonderful."

"I'll be right back." He hurried off and returned moments later with a glass of iced tea with a wedge of lemon stuck on the rim.

She looked down at the empty seat where Ralph should have been. The experience of receiving a prestigious award meant little in the scheme of life. Having your loved one share that experience was more satisfying than the award itself. If it weren't for Reverend John, Ralph would be there. That man irritated the heck out of her.

She took off the lemon wedge and dropped it on the plate. She preferred lime or nothing but sweetener in her tea. She asked the host, a tall slender and rather unattractive man of her age, to pass the sweetener. She tore the packet, poured it into her tea and stirred it. The tea tasted peculiar. She tried her glass of water. It tasted the same. She wrote both off to her nervousness, but she didn't particularly feel nervous. The more she drank the thirstier she became.

A few minutes later, she chatted with the master of ceremonies. He seemed more attractive than before. A bit later, after she refused to eat because she didn't want to give her acceptance speech on a full stomach, she noticed she was leaning closer to her host, even though she had no trouble hearing the man.

She felt strange, a little disoriented, a part of her mind gained clarity she had never experienced. It was as though that part, the objective side of her brain, was a video camera woman floating somewhere outside her body. Filming her. Watching her, listening to her conversation with the host. It shook its head with disapproval.

At the same time, she became aware of the scent of the man, a cloying bouquet underlying the fragrance of his aftershave, a primitive aroma teasing some dark level not previously recognized. Their knees brushed. Delicious tingling rushed from her knee, sliding up the inside of her thigh, tracing a feather-like stroke between her legs. She spread her knees, savoring the sensation, relishing the longing.

At the same time, she watched the eyes of her objective self widen and its mouth form a slow motion "No-o-o-o". She laughed at her self-righteous self. It needed a name. Under her breath, she giggled and named it Little Miss Good Girl. Bor . . . ing!

And if that part had a name, surely she should name that other part which was rising from some shadowy, damp, delicious place. She had a name! Miss Slut. Miss Slut was a lot more fun. Besides, Miss Slut could not control her any more than Little Miss Good Girl. She was her own woman. Wasn't she the one getting the award for being a good woman? Bor . . .ing!

She took another drink of tea. What was it? Her third glass? She should pee before her talk. She couldn't remember drinking so much tea. Every sip created a desire for more. And that's not all she desired.

The audience was still working on the main course.

She leaned close to her host, pressing her breast against his arm. He did not yield, but gave her a questioning smile. She felt the sensation of his bicep tighten against her, wanted to feel his naked skin against her bare nipple. "Do I have time to pee?"

Little Miss Good Girl told her, with schoolmarm precision, "You should have said 'bathroom' rather than 'pee'. What do you want that man to think?"

In the Ladies Room, she smiled at herself the mirror. Miss Slut told her to unbutton the top buttons of her white silk blouse and take off the prim choker of pearls. Her red suit jacket looked prim enough. She bent forward and could see the swell of her breasts. When she returned, she'd give her host (what was his name?) a tantalizing peek.

Little Miss Good Girl was proud of the way she walked back to her seat with a confident self-assured gait, shoulders back, steady, back straight and proper. That pride evaporated in a look of horror when Miss Slut slid her finger across the back of What's-His-Name's neck as she passed behind him and sat down.

As her host (it bothered the heck out of her that she couldn't remember his name) introduced those sitting at the head table, she scanned the crowd, finally concentrating on the Meals On Wheels table. They clapped as the host introduced someone at the head table. He rose, walked to the podium, adjusted the microphone to his height, looked down at her and then began recounting her accomplishments. Little Miss Good Girl, hovering somewhere in front of the speaker and reminded her it was too bad Ralph wasn't here to hear this.

She looked at the faces of the men that served on her board. Those faces were now so interesting. She realized the men hid behind masks, sincere innocent expressions hid concealed desires . . . for her body. She'd worked with them for years and only this instant understood they secretly lusted for her, imagining it was her body when they thrust between their wives' legs, pretending to shoot their passion into her. How could she have been so naïve? How could she not have known they wanted her?

She picked one board member out each time a new speaker began, looking at his upturned face, so attentive, nodding in agreement, and so innocent looking. She concentrated hard, imagining his face changing as she sat next to him, her hand reaching under the long tablecloth, touching him, unzipping his trousers, coaxing out his phallus. Stroking.

She would watch his face contort, the mask of innocence melting away, revealing his animal instincts. And then, pretending to pick up her dropped napkin, leaning low, head hidden by the tablecloth, a quick ice-cream-cone lick. Surfacing in time to watch him struggle to maintain the mask as he came. And then watching his face grimace with cold realization that he'd shot all over the front of his pants. She giggled.

She drank more iced tea. All of her senses seemed to be concentrating in her breasts and between her legs. She fought the urge to touch herself. Wondered if she could play with herself to orgasm without anyone of the thousand sitting in front of her knowing.

As though looking through a haze, she saw her good self. Little Miss Good Girl hovered high over a man's head, the orgasmic man, waving and shouting at her. She struggled to hear the words through all the clapping.

"Stand up! Give your acceptance speech. Now! Don't screw up. For God's sake, don't stray from your notes. Now! Now!"

She stood, nodded to the crowd and then walked to the podium. She scanned the crowd while reaching into her jacket pocket for the notes she'd prepared yesterday. Eyes on the orgasmic man, she smiled and winked at him. He pretended to be surprised. Surprised after what they'd just been through?

"Concentrate! Your notes! Don't screw this up!" Little Miss Good Girl rushed toward her, merging with her, clapping her hand over Miss Slut's mouth. "Now!"

She thanked the audience for the honor bestowed upon her and then gave a stunning acceptance speech that caused a standing ovation. It even pleased Little Miss Good Girl. She shook hands with the host.

He grinned and held her hand a beat too long. "I'd like to take you to lunch to hear more about volunteering."

She laughed, turning as if to pass behind him and then brushed her body against his. "Since I haven't eaten, I'd like to lunch with you right now. I'm so hungry, I could eat you."

His eyes widened. "Now?"

"I'm sorry. Not now. I have to give interviews to the press." She slipped her hand from his. "But why don't I meet you in the bar after my interview? We could spend the afternoon together." Miss Slut's laugh was low and throaty.

Little Miss Good Girl, hovering behind the host's shoulder, turned red with anger and began screaming at her. "Don't you understand what you're doing? Stop it right now! Get to your interview."

The entire scene freaked her out. "You're no fun," she said to Little Miss Good Girl.

"Huh?" the host asked, a perplexed look on his face.

"Just kidding. I meant let's have fun later. Got to run. See you at the bar in an hour or so." Her hand brushed the front of his pants. He was hard. She smiled at him and then walked off the platform and through the side entrance, avoiding well-wishers. She hurried to the elevator where she spotted the man with the cute little Shih Tzu.

"Are you ready for your interview, Mrs. Huntington?"

She petted the top of the dog's head and ran a finger across the man's chest before looking at his eyes. His blue eyes stared at her like a surgeon examining a patient.

He motioned a handsome blond man over and introduced them. "Tom will escort you to the interview. He'll give you anything you want. Are you nervous?"

"No, I'm not nervous, just eager"

"Relax and have fun, Mrs. Huntington."

She watched him walk away, disappointed he wouldn't be joining them.

"Mrs. Huntington?" The man held the elevator door open for her.

She stepped past him and smelled the scent she'd picked up earlier. Her nipples felt like they were going to rip out of her lace bra. Her panties were warm and wet. She turned and pressed her hip against the chrome bar in the back of the elevator. The man entered behind her and stood facing her. The door closed. They were alone. He stepped close, smiling, looking into her eyes.

"How far to our floor?" she asked.

"We'll be there soon."

"I hope not." She pulled him to her, lips on his, feeling his hands pulling her close against his body.

They stepped apart when the doors opened on the sixth floor.

She had never done this before, never felt this way before, as if all the sensation in the universe flowed to her sensitive parts. He held her hand and led her down a long corridor to a double door at the end. He took a key from his pocket and inserted it into the lock and then, before opening the door, kissed her again with passion.

"We're throwing a special party in your honor, Mrs. Huntington." He kissed her again. "Are you ready for the time of your life?"

She looked down the corridor. Little Miss Good Girl was nowhere in sight. She must have gotten lost in the lobby by the elevators. Good!

He opened the door and let her walk inside the gigantic suite. "You wanted to party, Mrs. Huntington. Here we are."

She stopped and held her breath. There were two handsome men standing next to a sofa, one Hispanic, one Black. A cameraman stood to one side with a handicam. He panned from the men to her, filming her reaction.

Somewhere, somehow, her objective self watched. She didn't give a damn.

The door shut behind her. The bolt latched.

She sensed her physical self disappear piece by piece until all that remained were her breasts, nipples and clitoris.

The man who brought her reached around her shoulders and slipped off her jacket.

Her fingers rose slowly across her breasts and felt for the buttons on her blouse, unbuttoning as the men walked toward her.

CHAPTER 17

Hay-Adams Hotel

Thatcher

THE NEXT DAY THATCHER WALKED into the Hay-Adams Lafayette dining room. Jamila, dressed in a stylish professional outfit, waved him over to a table next to a window that overlooked Lafayette Square and the White House.

"Thanks for joining me, Thatcher. I can only imagine how busy you must be." She offered her hand.

Surprised again at her strength, he admired her arm's muscle tone. She held his hand a bit too long. He pulled away.

She gestured toward a bottle of red wine on the table. "I hope you enjoy red."

The waiter poured him a glass.

They talked about the embassy party, comparing notes. She was stunning. Unflinching almond eyes, soft and warm, searched his face. Her eyes were what he had most remembered throughout the years. Her full lips were quick to smile, smooth sensual skin reminded him . . . He thought he could smell her from across the table, a sweet primal scene full of promise.

She sipped her wine. "Just think, a US Senator chased the dragon with me," she said.

His sphincter muscles tightened. There it was again. "Do that often?"

She smiled. "Not since our time together. I knew I couldn't top that, so I've never tried."

"Ever think about it?"

She blinked. "Us? Often."

He looked away and then said, "Well, tell me about your life."

She swirled her wine close to the lip of the glass, studying the red skim sliding back down the sides. "It never changes."

"I don't understand."

"Yes you do." Her voice was flat, emotionless.

"As in, with your father?"

Her furrowed brow knit her eyebrows together. She avoided his eyes.

"You're still living with him?" He persisted.

Her head swiveled back to him, eyes hard, with a look that made him want to shudder—it was as if he was staring into death.

"No, not living with him. I live on the road, but he has my daughter, so I'm forced back."

"She must be in her late twenties. You haven't gotten her out?" he asked.

"My first daughter . . ." her voice broke . . . "died."

"Died? How the . . ."

She held up a hand to cut him off. She picked up her glass of wine and stared into it a long moment with moist eyes.

"You don't understand the power of evil, Thatcher. But the point is, I had another daughter. She's the same age as your Billy. He's grooming her, just like he did with me and with my first child."

"Jesus Christ!" He shook his head. "He impregnated you again?"

"My daughter is still a virgin. He uses her to force me to make a fortune for him."

He leaned over the table. "Why the hell don't you get her out?"

"He has armed guards. They watch me constantly. I've tried to . . . kill him . . ." She shook her head. "You couldn't understand. He says he'll release her if I bring him enough money."

"You believe him?"

There was a long pause. "I can't give up hope."

"The authorities?"

"Women's rights in the Mideast?" Cynicism burdened her laugh. She didn't blink, but held his gaze, her lips taut.

He shook his head. "So why now? Why did you want to meet, after all this time?"

She shrugged her shoulders as if shaking off something cold.

"Your country is changing in a way that much of the rest of the world considers to be dangerous. You've become an important political player. It's my job to understand what might happen . . . and . . ." she tailed off.

"And?"

"Have you shared our relationship with your wife?"

He felt heat in his cheeks. "You're the only one who knows. What will you do with that?"

Her hand touched her breast. "Absolutely nothing. My telling your wife would ruin your marriage. I'd never do that to you. You're the only one who knows my secret. We're each other's secret keepers."

He hid his discomfort with a laugh. Which secret? Chasing the dragon with her? Or telling her about the meeting between the CIA and Taliban leader, the leak that caused the murder of innocent kids? Was she putting him on notice that she held information that could destroy him?

She glanced at the entrance. Her eyes widened. She whispered. "Here comes your wife!"

Carol strode across the room toward them. A tight smile curved her lips. She stood tall, determined and beautiful. It seemed as though everyone in the restaurant had stopped talking to watch her. He stood to greet her. Jamila's lips formed a curious smile as she stood to greet Carol.

Carol shook Jamila's hand, her voice professional. "Thatcher told me you were talking about cultural changes. I thought you'd benefit from a woman's point of view, so I decided to join you."

"Men get so involved with their work . . ." Jamila said.

"You're absolutely right." Carol glanced at him. "Some men don't have a clue."

The waiter brought a place setting and wine glass for Carol.

"Carol, I have a confession to make . . ." Jamila said.

Shaking his head, Thatcher held up his hand and interrupted, "Wait a minute . . ."

Jamila poured Carol a glass of wine. "I only made a reservation for two. I would have been delighted to have known you could join us."

"It seems the three of us are destined to be together." Carol raised her glass and looked at him. "What should we drink to, Thatcher? Old friendships, new beginnings, or scheming intrigues?"

"Let's toast to peace," Thatcher said.

The women laughed.

Jamila put her glass on the table. "Thatcher told me how proud you both are of your son, Billy. That he's quite an athlete."

Carol glanced at him and arched an eyebrow. "Do you have children, Jamila?"

"My daughter Sara is Billy's age."

"Really? Is she in Washington?" Carol asked.

"Sara stays with her grandfather."

"Sara is a beautiful name." Carol said. "That's the name we'd picked had Billy been a girl."

"Sara means 'Princess' in Islam," Jamila said.

"Do they live in Morocco?" Carol asked.

"Marrakech."

"That sounds romantic," Carol said.

"The city can be romantic for some, and terrifying for others."

Carol looked at him. "I forgot, Thatcher, did you visit Marrakech when you were in the service?"

"No." He suggested they look at the menu.

After the waiter took their orders, Jamila said, "I haven't been in the States for years. I've been busy in China. Your country has changed since I last visited. I've read our embassy dispatches, but I'd like to understand how it happened."

"What do you want to know?" Thatcher asked.

"I know about the terrorist attacks, the food and economic problems and your jobless problem, President Lopez-Chin's election, and the Department of Virtue."

"Seems as though you're well informed," Carol said.

"I've also heard Thatcher and Senator Alan Long are behind a legal attempt to have the Supreme Court block the

Security Act as unconstitutional, but Virtue will tie you up, claiming their new Supreme Moral Court has jurisdiction. That will take years to decide. In the meantime, there's no one to stop Virtue."

Jamila continued. "The Act also established new Moral Courts that have jurisdiction over Biblical Law cases with death sentences for homosexuality, adultery, kidnap and rape."

"And many other offenses," he agreed.

"It's terrible. Biblical Law is like your Sharia Law," Carol said.

"I'm not a Muslim."

"Just what are you, then?"

Jamila smiled. "Historians outside the US are calling you hypocrites for fighting Islamic theocracies while building your own Christian theocracy."

The waiter brought their lunches.

"It sounds like you know just about everything," he said.

"I know what happened, but I don't understand how it happened," Jamila said.

Carol's voice rose. "It happened because of fear: people were afraid of terrorism, disgusted with ineffective government, and didn't want to be involved in the process. They let the Christian fundamentalists worm themselves into power, first at local county levels, then state and finally the national level. Everyone laughed at them, thinking that if, by some fluke, they did win the elections, they wouldn't carry through, and even if they did gain control, our lives wouldn't be affected. And we woke up to this nightmare!

Jamila asked "So what do you think will happen now?"

Carol leaned forward. "You're an impartial observer. You tell us."

"I've seen similar things happen in other countries. I can sense patterns. Your country is plunging into a fascist theocracy. Things will get worse. If you continue fighting them, you and your family will be in danger." Jamila opened her purse and pulled out a diplomatic card and pen. She wrote on the back and handed it to Carol. "I'm giving a phone number to you, Carol, because I don't want you to think I'm after your husband. Keep it. If you get into serious trouble, call that number and leave a message for Felix."

CHAPTER 18

Hay-Adams Hotel

Thatcher

JUST AS JAMILA WALKED OUT of the Hays-Adams dinning room, Thatcher's iCom rang. He looked at the screen— Senator Alan Long. He apologized to Carol and answered.

"Thatcher, where the hell are you? What are you doing?"

"Having lunch with Carol. What's so important?"

"Well, you tell that beautiful lady she's too damned good for the likes of you. Kiss her, pat her on the ass and send her home. We need to meet with your buddy, Caleb Gates, over at Moral America. He might have some ideas about additional senators we might influence to defeat the *Voting Act.*"

"Have you made an appointment?" Thatcher asked.

"Hell no! You're the one with the relationship. You told me the guy's like a father to you. You set it up."

"Are you flexible?"

"Hell yes! I'm my own boss," Long said.

"Have you told Martha?" Thatcher asked about Long's wife.

"Stop being a smart-ass and call Caleb. He probably won't have time for you until next year."

After talking with Long, Thatcher called Caleb. They agreed to meet that afternoon. He told Carol he'd see her later at home and kissed her goodbye.

Later, when Thatcher arrived at his office, his chief aide,

Richard Bowman needed to talk. They walked into Thatcher's office and shut the door.

Bowman said, "Bob Roberts told me he'd run into Mack Bradley at the Eighteenth Street Lounge last night. Bradley was drunk and said something about getting even with you for killing Jessie."

"Bradley is shooting off his mouth. He's a coward. He'll never do anything."

"Just saying." Bowman walked out.

Thatcher sat at his desk and remembered making the rounds one night in Afghanistan when he caught Bradley sodomizing a private named Jessie. Jessie assured Thatcher it had been consensual, so Thatcher didn't press charges.

Jessie ended up being Bradley's partner. Claimed they loved each other. Their personal life was none of Thatcher's business, so long as they did their jobs, were discrete, and didn't cause trouble. Everyone knew about their relationship, but compared to the possibility of getting killed at any moment by an unseen enemy, their affair wasn't all that important.

The platoon was ordered to set up a small forward base at the edge of a village. The land, purchased from the village elders, sat at the bottom of a giant bowl, sloping up to the village. It was a terribly exposed position, with dead zones where you couldn't see the enemy. The base was exposed to fire from the buildings and the mosque. The land on the other side was a terraced mountain.

As platoon leader, Thatcher objected to his superiors about the position, but he was overruled. The base needed protection from high ground, so Thatcher set up an observation post several hundred yards above the base on the mountainside to give them cover from shooters in the town. Thatcher ordered a fire team, with an M240 machine gun, grenade launcher and three riflemen to set up in the post. Jessie was the machine gunner.

Before they could secure their post, all hell broke loose. The base was caught in the middle of a firefight, with bad guys shooting down from the heights of the mountainside above their machine gun post, and from the second stories of the buildings. It was a trap. Thatcher called for air support. It was denied on the grounds that another unit in trouble had priority.

Thatcher's men were being wounded and killed. The men in the machine gun nest put down suppressing fire and saved them, but ran low on ammunition. The Taliban poured everything they had at the post, machine gun fire, RPG's, everything. Thatcher kept screaming for air support. Delayed. The situation went from bad to worse. Before the Blackhawks arrived at dusk, Jessie and the other gunners were mortally wounded. Mack Bradley fought his way up there. He held Jessie in his arms, screaming over the radio for a medic. The medic had been wounded. Jessie died. Bradley vowed to kill Thatcher. Later, someone tried to frag him. Bowman pushed him over a metal footlocker and dove after him, but lost his leg. They could never prove Bradley had thrown the grenade.

Now Bradley worked for Virtue. Maybe Thatcher should be a bit more alert. He shook his head and turned to business.

Later, walking with Senator Long toward their meeting at Moral America, they passed FREEDOM, SECURITY, FOOD banners lining the sidewalks. The flags fluttered gently in a light breeze that carried the scent of the Tidal Basin, a humid smell tinged with the stink of brackish water and dead fish. The warm afternoon sun added to the humidity. All in all, it was one of Washington's better days, but it didn't help their mood.

They walked through Virtue's banners toward the Moral America offices on K Street. They stopped at an intersection for a traffic light. An Eye, mounted on a pole at the corner, tilted down to examine them.

Senator Long looked at the lens and gave it the finger. "Ever worry about those?"

"Frankly, I never thought about them before the *Security Act* created Virtue. Now they make me uneasy," Thatcher said.

"Yep. I feel the same way. Never noticed before. Now I watch them watch me. Like right now, someone is watching us."

"Someone or a computer."

"They know we normally don't walk here. We've broken a pattern. That'll raise a question. Betcha five bucks every Eye we pass from now until we walk into Moral America will turn to watch us."

"Is betting approved by Virtue?" Thatcher asked with a grin.

"Okay, smart-ass. Tell ya what. Let's moon the next Eye. Put a little excitement in their day."

"Or *its* day. I wonder if they've programmed mooning into their artificial intelligence? Think it'd send a red alert . . . 'watching Senator Alan Long's skinny Montana ass?'" Thatcher asked.

"They're so fucked up, they'd probably spend a week trying to classify my ass as a derrière."

They walked at a brisk pace toward the Moral America building.

Thatcher said, "You're in good shape for your age."

"Careful, sonny, don't go pulling age discrimination on me. Seriously, I take a long walk around my neighborhood every night before going to bed. It keeps me in decent shape and it helps me decompress from the pressures of the day."

"Martha walks with you?"

"No. She gets ready for the return of her lover." He laughed.

"How long have you and Martha been married?"

"Fifty years of heavenly bliss . . . seriously. I can't imagine loving anyone else."

"I can't imagine any woman putting up with you that long," Thatcher laughed.

Bob Roberts, another member of Thatcher's old Afghanistan unit, greeted them at the Moral America building. They were ushered through security and rode an elevator to Caleb Bates' office on the top floor.

Thatcher thanked Roberts for providing a security guard to protect Carol and Billy.

Roberts said, "Tell Carol to come back down to shoot with me in our pistol range."

"You want her to humiliate you like last time?"

"Gotta admit she's a hell-of-a shot," Roberts said.

Caleb, a short balding man with a kind face, greeted Thatcher with a bear hug.

After greeting Senator Long, Caleb suggested they use a small room to the right of his immense office with its view of the Capitol Building. He closed the door, opened a wall panel and flicked several switches. He held up a finger, until they heard a low humming noise and then he nodded and motioned them to sit down at a small conference table. "I assumed you want our conversation to be confidential," Caleb said. "I can't guarantee it, but this is supposed to be a state-of-the-art secure room."

The room also contained a kitchen, bathroom, bedroom and an informal area with couches and chairs.

Thatcher looked around. "This room is new since I was here. You could live in it. Sort of like a safe house."

Senator Long leaned back in his chair and looked at the ceiling, "If you have done nothing wrong, you have nothing to fear."

"Exactly." Caleb said. "However, under Virtue the definition of 'wrong' keeps changing."

Roberts said, "The old saying 'Better safe than sorry' seems to be today's watchword."

"The minute we deviated from our predicted route every Eye traced us here. Whoever or whatever is watching knows we're here," Thatcher said.

"I'm afraid we backed the wrong presidential candidate in Lopez-Chin," Caleb said.

"And everyone misjudged Reverend John. Everyone thought he was a joke," Senator Long said.

"That's what German voters thought about Hitler," Caleb said.

"I believe everyone thought the party would jettison him after the election. He must have a hold on the President and many others in power. But that's obvious. The horse is out of the barn and the damned barn is on fire. The *Security Act* was just the beginning. And now we're faced with this so-called *Voting Act*. What a sick fucking joke," Senator Long said.

Caleb winched. "I suppose you wanted to meet for some reason other than to swear."

Thatcher said, "Exactly. We have a list of Senators we've targeted to help us defeat the voting bill. We'd like you to review that with us. Perhaps you might know something, some connection or have an idea about one or more of them that might help us."

They went over the list, name by name. Caleb offered several ideas, but no solutions. He offered to talk to three Senators he felt he might influence. They sat back, silent for a moment before Caleb broke the silence. "Like I said before, I'm afraid we backed a movement that's spun out of control and been taken over by a fanatic. Reverend John called in his campaign debts and consolidated unprecedented power under Virtue. The entire nation should thank the two of you for fighting him, but I suspect you'll get little support.

"Virtue's created a chill through the halls of Congress. I worry that if you aren't careful you and your families could be in danger," Caleb said.

Senator Long's laughed. "They wouldn't have the guts to hurt a U.S. Senator."

Thatcher would have thought that himself a month ago, but Frank's warning, Billy's incident with the man with the dog, and Bradley's renewed threat, were telling him that it was no longer true. They would hurt you, especially if they thought you could hurt them.

CHAPTER 19

Three days later—
Golden Triangle, Thailand

Felix

FELIX STOOD MOTIONLESS IN THE jungle. Her backpack contained neat stacks of one-thousand-yuan bills, a total of ten million. Another ten million in gold awaited in a Swiss bank. The backpack was heavy, yet she dared not put it down. Easing the shoulder straps, she hid in shadows at the edge of a moon-lit clearing where she waited, watched, and listened.

The smell of rotting vegetation and fragrances of strange flowers reminded her of the smells of the funeral of a hill tribe elder in the village she had visited. Scents of death.

Tourists loved this part of the world. The Golden Triangle, the mountainous intersection of Myanmar, Vietnam, Laos and Thailand, was one of the world's largest producers of heroin, a hotbed of violence, wars and corruption.

Everyone had guns for sale. Everyone was on the take. That's why she had picked the Golden Triangle for the handoff. She could bribe any policeman or customs inspector.

She leaned against the tree, listening to the hum of insects. The earth grew heavy, intent on suffocating her. She preferred the arid open lands of the Mideast. If her plan worked she'd save Sara and would never have to do this again. She slapped a blood-filled mosquito against her neck.

She had checked into a suite at the Chiang Mai 4 Seasons and then driven a rental four-by-four up Highway 107 deep into the Golden Triangle. She then rented an ATV from the headman of a nearby hill tribe to drive through a muddy, water-filled rutted track deep in the jungle to the drop zone. After this was over, she would return to the hotel, spend the day sleeping, and then meet her chartered jet to fly to Morocco, where she would kill the man who threatened her daughter.

Animal sounds filled the jungle night; screeching night birds, a cough of a tiger from somewhere across the clearing. She knew pythons slithered through the jungle, seeking warm-blooded victims to squeeze to death before swallowing. A drop of sweat tickled from her shoulder blades to waist.

The tiger coughed again. Did it smell her?

The derringer tucked into her back pocket, so effective in close encounters with human enemies, seemed like a toy against a tiger. She should have a AK-47. She could have easily bought one in the village.

A full moon painted the meadow silver. A humid breeze swayed the knee-high grass. A moonbeam climbed the branches of tall pines, and struck the chrome handlebars of her ATV parked thirty yards away.

The tiger coughed once more. Closer now. Much closer. She spotted a movement of the grass, a line swaying against the breeze. Big. She slipped the derringer out, selected the lower barrel for multiple pellets and thumbed back the hammer. She pressed her back hard against the tree trunk. The breeze caressed her face. She prayed the tiger would not smell her. She was so close to her goal.

She felt the tree's rough bark and smelled its vanilla scent. A movement. A fleeting ghost sliced the black sky three feet above her head. She ducked and raised her gun. Too late. It had been an owl on the hunt, silent and deadly. She shivered and whispered to herself, "Time to quit." Losing her discipline could be fatal. Covert meetings like this used to spark adrenaline rushes, but tonight the rush gnawed her gut.

Her father had promised this job would be her last. Twenty million should be enough. But he would want more. He always wanted more of everything. It would go on forever, until she was dead—or he was.

The grass stopped moving. The tiger had either walked away or crouched, waiting to attack. The breeze carried a rotten scent. High above her, male cicadas sang mating songs, punctuated by the call of a night bird and the distant bark of a fox. But it was the sound of an owl hooting that filled her with brittle loneliness. She felt that way every time she heard an owl. While she had no childhood memories of listening to an owl, the hooting triggered a hollowness that pushed her to the edge of a dark abyss. She pulled the collar of her jacket close to her neck and waited.

Another sound—the high pitch of a four-by-four. The machine wound its way up the rutted track through the pines. It would pull up behind her ATV, then they'd get out and look for her. The engine coughed and then died. Still far off.

Several minutes later, a new sound puzzled her. Not a vehicle. A noise she couldn't place. She spotted a small light weaving through the trees and then recognized a man bicycling up the lane. He stopped twenty yards behind her ATV and eased the mountain bike to the ground. He crept to the ATV and put his hand on the motor to determine if it was warm. Was this the Colonel?

Not wanting him to see her armed, she lowered the hammer, slid the derringer into her back pocket, flattened against the massive pine and watched. He leaned against her ATV as if he were waiting for someone. For her.

He looked at his watch and then sauntered into the center of the meadow. She expected to see a movement of grass as the tiger either fled or charged. Nothing happened. The man placed something on the ground. Hand above his brow, he shielded his eyes from bright moonlight. He searched the shadows.

He returned to her ATV with a bear-like stride. He was much larger than most Chinese men. Even from this distance he appeared menacing. He leaned against the front fender and lit a cigarette. The flare from his match revealed a hatchet-like face and cruel black eyes. She knew him by his picture. He waited again.

She didn't like surprises. The Colonel should have had the devices with him. Perhaps he'd left them back at his vehicle. But why park far down the road and then bicycle here? She watched him for ten minutes before moving.

The weight of the backpack forced her to be even more cautious than usual. She circled behind him. She balanced on her left heel and then felt for the next silent step with her right toe. Speed wouldn't matter if she died.

Eight minutes later, she stood on the far side of her ATV. She pointed the derringer at the back of the man's head before she spoke softly in Mandarin Chinese.

"Why are you leaning against my vehicle?" She smelled the bitter tobacco preferred by the Chinese military.

The man flicked the cigarette down and then ground it into the dirt with his boot. He knew better than to turn around. His accent was coarse. It was the same voice she had heard over the phone.

"I wait for a man."

"What man?" The muzzle of her derringer held steady. She couldn't miss at this range.

"Felix." The man still didn't move.

Relieved, she lowered the derringer's hammer and then slid it into her pocket.

"Felix sent me."

"So it's true. The reason no one has ever seen Felix is that he's a coward. He sends a woman in his place." The Colonel spat.

"Where are the devices?"

"A helicopter will bring them when I signal."

"Signal now, Colonel."

"After I see the money." He slowly turned to look at her. He took in her tall body and then looked into her eyes. "Felix has a beautiful woman."

Her saliva soured. They were all the same. "Call for the helicopter."

"The money," he growled.

"In my backpack."

"Show me."

"When I see the devices."

"You act tough. You good fuck?" His laugh was crude.

"Call the helicopter or the deal's off."

He shrugged and reached into his jacket for a portable radio, spoke into it, then smiled at her. In the moonlight, she saw his teeth, yellowed by cigarettes, uneven and cracked.

"How long?" She touched her leather jacket.

"Three minutes. Show me the money." He started around the ATV toward her.

"Stay. You'll see the money when I see the merchandise."

"You are beautiful and bright."

She cocked her head when she heard the distinctive thump of rotor blades.

"What did you put in the clearing?" she asked.

"A homing device."

The blast of the chopper's blades spiraled the meadow grass into violent waves as a Chinese Z14 bounced onto the ground. She recognized it as the newest model, designed to evade radar. Three uniformed men, two with machine guns slung over their shoulders, jumped out. The third man lugged a carry-on suitcase to her ATV.

The Colonel pointed to the front rack. "Here."

"Yes, sir!"

"Bring the other!" The Colonel lit a cigarette.

She smelled the sulfur of the match. She felt her lips tighten while the three soldiers trampled yet another trail through the meadow grass.

The soldiers cut an even larger swath as they returned with something nestled in a sling of military webbing.

"Put it there." The Colonel pointed to the back rack of her ATV.

"Stop!" She recognized the bomb from stolen intelligence pictures—a two-by-three foot, stainless-steel nuclear device with the destructive power to destroy a city of one hundred thousand.

She ran her fingers over the gear-shaped opening in the top of the rectangular casing. There were no other openings, doors or panels. She nodded to the Colonel and then watched the soldiers put it on her ATV. They returned and stood at attention.

"Return to the helicopter to await my instructions!"

"Yes, Colonel!" The three men saluted, ran toward the chopper and ducked under its rotating blades before jumping inside. She looked at the trampled meadow grass and heard the helicopter door clang shut.

The Colonel held out a ballpoint pen. The top part of the shaft that protruded from the pen's body was gear-shaped, matching the opening on top of the bomb.

"This is the trigger for the bomb. The ballpoint is a popular American brand that we've modified, but it will still function as a normal pen. You can see it has a digital time and date display. It also has an alarm function, which is preset and locked to 6pm—September 14, as Felix instructed. When the alarm goes off, the ballpoint shoots its shaft into the bomb and detonates it.

"Boom!" He flung his arms wide.

She flinched.

He laughed.

"Why the gear on the top of the ballpoint shaft?" she asked.

"Insert the pen into the bomb and turn the gear to lock it into place to open the bomb's safety switch." He made a circle with the fingers of his left hand sliding the ballpoint in and out in short strokes, a universal gesture. Grinning, he offered the pen to her, but held tight to it.

She spit a bad taste from her mouth, just missing his hand, surprising him. She ripped it out of his hand and zipped it into the pocket of her jacket.

"All right, so much for the bomb. Show me what's in that." She pointed to the carry-on suitcase.

"A shame . . . all business." He flipped a cigarette away in a fiery arc. He unzipped the carry-on so she could see it contained a metal case. A dial, a recessed switch and power inlet were the only things that marred its smooth surface.

"It, too, is beautiful. So simple. Harmless to humans. It is a HERF gun. HERF, for high-energy-radio-frequency. Push this switch and it will destroy any computer circuits within a one block area, no matter how well shielded."

"What do you mean?"

"Everything today runs by chips; not only your computer, but your watch, microwave, washing machine, maybe even this expensive ATV of yours." His thick fingers caressed the ATV's handlebar.

"So that's why you rode a bicycle?"

His coarse laugh made her want to hurt him.

"I thought HERF guns didn't work well."

"We have made great advances with the technology. You are getting a great bargain. Maybe we should negotiate for something more."

"How do I know it works?"

"What's the expression? Show me yours and I'll show you mine."

She walked to his side of the ATV and shrugged off her backpack. She smelled his fetid breath and felt the heat of his body.

He opened the backpack, his thick fingers fondling the tightly stacked rows of cash.

"Money is the best thing . . . other than sex. Yes?"

It was always this way. She felt sick with disgust for the man. She jerked the backpack away from his fingers and pointed to the HERF gun.

"How do I know it works?"

"Killing is the best aphrodisiac of all, don't you think?" His eyes assaulted her body while he spoke into his radio and ordered the helicopter to leave.

The speed of the rotor blades increased to a whine. The Z14 shuddered and then slowly rose from the clearing. It was tree height when he shouted at her.

"Do it!"

"What?"

He pointed at the HERF gun. "Push the switch."

"Go to hell!"

Laughing, he forced her fingers onto the switch.

Overwhelmed by his strength, she felt the toggle flip over.

"Now, my beauty, watch the helicopter."

The Z14 rose and then dipped its nose for forward flight over the jungle.

She jerked her hand away from his rough grasp. "It doesn't work."

The helicopter, a black silhouette against the full moon, began an erratic, uncontrolled spin. It flipped upside down, plunging into the jungle at the far edge of the meadow. It erupted into a fireball.

His eyes were bright in the glow of the flames.

"That helicopter had the most advanced electronic shielding ever developed. You've just killed all the witnesses to our transaction."

Her mind raced; if her ATV did not start she'd have to burn it to destroy the evidence, use his bike to pick up his car, drive it back here, load the weapons and escape. The tiger would do away with other evidence.

"You killed your own men."

"Not me." He grabbed her in a bear hug and kissed her.

He was too strong. Pretending to resist, she finally gave in. She slipped her tongue between his lips and fought from gagging on the bitter tobacco taste of his mouth. Rubbing her pelvis against his thigh, she caressed his growing hardness with her left hand. His breathing quickened. She slipped the derringer from her pocket and put its muzzle against his temple. The hammer cocked with an audible click.

His eyes snapped opened with shock. He stiffened. "You bitch!"

"You should know something, Colonel."

"What?" He hissed.

"*I* am Felix." She squeezed the trigger.

And the animals of the jungle fell silent.

CHAPTER 20

Virtue's Chamber

Karen Huntington

HER WORLD WAS BLACK. SHE didn't know if her eyes were open or shut. How long had she been held captive? Two or three days? She couldn't tell. They'd taken her watch. There was no cell window. The door was lightproof. Day or night?

The lights snapped on, flooding her cell with harsh light, forcing her to shield her eyes with her arm. Thank God they had not used the strobe lights. Not this time. The flashing of the strobes, the discordant rhythm, battered her mind. Made her feel disjointed, body disassembled. Drove her crazy.

Shivering, she crossed her arms over her chest for warmth. She studied her cell once again, trying to discover what they had changed during the darkness.

The cubical was just long enough for a stainless steel bed and a lidless steel toilet-sink combination. There was no blanket, no towel, no toilet paper. The walls were smooth concrete. A camera lens, speaker and a vent embedded flush into the ceiling. They watched her. Probably could hear her. But that speaker screen was new. It had a different shape the last time the lights were on. Or not. Maybe. Yes. She was certain they had changed out the speaker during the darkness. How could they have changed it without her hearing them? Maybe it was not new. She wasn't sure. Not certain of anything.

She waited for the vent to spew out its surprise. When hot air gushed out, she lay on the floor to escape the heat. She feared she would die of heat stroke. When freezing air poured out, she curled into a fetal position to preserve body warmth. Right now she felt no air. Maybe they had stopped the airflow. After she used all the oxygen in the cell she would suffocate. She breathed deeply. Her lungs burned. They were going to kill her.

The floor sloped to a large drain covered by a metal grate. Several times she watched her body dissolve, melting into small fluid pieces—a tiny part of a finger, flakes of skin, bits of muscle—flowing over the side of the bed, across the floor, eddying, then whirl-pooling through the holes of the drain into oblivion. Her life sliding into nothingness.

The steel door, set flush into the wall, had two openings; a small one at eye level and a larger opening at waist level, both covered by sliding doors. The larger opening, the one they pushed a bowl of rice through, was too small for her to escape. She wondered if they had welded the door shut. She would be captive here until she died.

She remembered the horror when, after capturing her after the incident at the hotel, they had slipped a hood over her head. She heard a click as they locked it around her neck. The hood's fabric sucked tight against her nose and mouth, blocking the air. She was going to suffocate.

"I can't breath! Please take it off. Please!"

"Stop breathing so hard. You'll be fine."

"Oh God!" Heat seared her lungs. She knew she'd die.

Later, in the corridor outside her cell, blinded by the hood, rough hands emptied her pockets, stripped off her watch and pearl necklace, the one her mother had given her as a wedding present, feeling the string break, hearing the pearls bounce on the floor. Hands pulling down her pants, fingers exploring her. Probing. Everywhere. Hands jerking off the hood, hands on her back, pushing her into the cell, the door slamming shut, the cold metallic sound that froze her heart. Hearing the upper slide open, looking at the eyes of the man with the dog —those clear, innocent eyes.

"Get comfortable Mrs. Huntington. I'm Deverence, your confessor. Think about your sins. Let me know when you're ready to confess. We'll have a nice little chat."

"You can't do this to me!" she screamed. "Let me out of here."

The sliding spy door clanged shut, cutting off the sound of his laughter.

Now, days later, as she thought about her capture, the lights switched off, plunging the cell into pitch-black. She sensed she was falling. Her hands sought the reality of the wall and bed.

She heard an indistinct voice that seemed familiar, yet she couldn't make out the words. The words grew louder. She recognized her voice, growing louder until even the bed vibrated from the sound. She covered her ears, yet could not block out her words recorded at the orgy.

"Fuck me! Oh my God, fuck me now!"

Her words. Repeated over and over. Assaulting her, her very skin attacked by the vibrations of her pleas.

"Stop it! Stop it. For God's sake stop," she screamed, palms slapping the wall. As if that would help.

The sound stopped. She knew the words, her voice, would come again. They would play with her. Drive her insane. She waited. Waited in black silence broken only by her breathing. Her body emanated a sour smell.

Later, she didn't know if it had been hours or days, the waist-high door clanked open, throwing a blinding shaft of light into the cell. She squinted and made out the silhouette of a bowl. She staggered off the metal slab and reached for it. Just as her fingertips touched the bowl, it was withdrawn. The door slammed shut.

Sometimes they gave her the food, sometimes not. Playing with her. She slid to the floor and sat, leaning against the door, staring into the black void. Her stomach growled. And then the words came again, softly at first, rising in volume until every syllable beat against her chest. She covered her ears and then pulled her hair and screamed, "Stop! For God's sake have mercy!"

The sound faded and then disappeared.

"Please turn on the lights," she begged.

Nothing happened.

She crawled across the floor on knees and one hand, the other exploring the black void until she found the toilet. She dropped her underwear and sat on the lidless rim. Urine splashed against the metal until it dribbled to a stop. It smelled bitter. Its scent mingled with the odor of her body. She was certain they were watching her, even in the dark. She stood, fought dizziness.

She felt her way to the slab and curled up, resting her head on her hand, waiting for the silence to once again be broken by her words, filthy words that proved she was a whore, an adulteress. No! That was wrong. She wasn't an adulteress. They had drugged her. They had forced her into that orgy. She wasn't an adulteress. She wasn't. Wasn't!

She heard the words, even when she covered her ears with her hands.

Time cycled between deadening silence and her screaming voice begging to be fucked. Pleading for them to stop. And as time shifted, during the silence, she wanted to hear the voice, wanted the sound of her words to break the dread of being alone in the cold and darkness. Wanted any human assurance, even though they were her words, filthy words, untrue words, words forced by drugs. Even those words were better than being alone. No control. She needed the words to help stop her from imagining what would happen when they came for her.

After a long while it dawned on her that each time she pleaded, "For the love of God . . ." they turned off the sound. Those words, or perhaps it was the entire phrase were a code for them to turn off the recording.

Perhaps she was wrong.

Her mind played with the possibility that she could control the sound by saying the code. She waited for the next sound with anticipation. Eager to hear her voice again. Eager to try word combinations. Eager to cling to her sanity.

The next time she begged them to turn it off, but it went on and on and on until she pounded the back of her head against the wall. Her voice finally died. And then she waited. Waited for what seemed hours. As soon as she heard her voice begin, she begged them to turn it off, "for the love of God!" The sound stopped. It worked! She tried the code again the next time. It worked again! She was victorious. She had gained a little control. Maybe she had more control she had imagined.

"I'm ready to talk with Deverence," she shouted.

As she waited, she decided they wanted more from her than using her for leverage to force Ralph to give up his neo-cross company. How were they going to use her? Why? She was innocent. Why pick her? What were they going to do?

CHAPTER 21

Washington

Thatcher

THATCHER CANCELLED AN APPOINTMENT IN order to pick up Billy after school. Leaning against his front fender, he waited for the bell announcing the end of classes. Sam Browning, parked nearby, nodded. Good to have Sam for extra safety.

The bell rang. Seconds later kids burst through the door like they were fleeing the devil himself. Boys and girls flowed out, walking, running, backpacks weighing them down, shouting, forming pools of friends. He spotted Billy talking with two girls and a boy. Billy looked up, waved, said goodbye, trotted to the car, threw his backpack into the back seat and jumped into the front.

Several minutes later, they merged with traffic, driving toward home. Sam followed two car lengths behind.

"Have a good day?"

Billy looked out the passenger window. "Un-huh."

"What was the best part?"

"I'm hungry."

He drove to a shopping center and parked in front of an organic food store. "Bet there's something inside for us."

Billy homed in on the snack section, looking at chocolate chip cookies, muffins, cakes, chips and other goodies. He rushed up and down the aisles, scanning the food cases, picking up one item, carrying it until he saw something better, and running back to replace the first and then picking up the second.

Watching Billy made him think of his own childhood. He'd been forbidden to eat between meals. Finally Billy selected a plastic box containing half of a key lime pie.

"Whoa! Think you can eat all that?"

"Dad! I got this for the two of us."

"Well, in that case, let's get forks, pay for it and get out of here."

A few minutes later he parked next to a small park. They sat next to each other at a picnic table, opened the box and attacked the pie. Sam parked on the opposite side of the park.

"This is going to ruin our dinner," Thatcher said.

"Let's not tell Mom. Okay?"

"It'll be our secret. Why did you get three forks?"

"One for Sam." Billy ran a piece of pie across the park to Sam and sprinted back.

They ate in silence for several minutes, savoring their treat.

"Dad?"

"Huh?"

"Can I ask you something?"

"Something troubling you?"

"Girls."

"Girls?" He knew Billy had friends who were girls. Was this something new?

"I don't understand them."

He laughed. "Join the club. Women are confusing."

"What club?"

"That's just an expression. Means you're not alone in not understanding girls."

"Oh."

"Well?"

"Sometimes they're mean."

"Yeah?"

"Like this girl, Emma. She sits two seats in front of me."

"Is she mean to the other boys?"

"I don't think so."

"What did she do to you today?"

"The teacher had me write on the board and on the way back to my desk Emma stuck out her foot and tripped me."

"Do you like her?"

"Not really. I don't talk to her. She always laughs and has fun with other kids. But she hangs around. You know. Not with my friends and me, but she's always around, if you know what I mean. She bugs me."

"I'd say she likes you and she's trying to get your attention."

"Huh."

The clock showed 1:42 a.m. Thatcher moaned, muscles twitching, moonlight on his skin reflected perspiration. Carol rose on her pillow. It was about to happen. Again.

She reached across the bed for him. She touched his arm. He tensed. It would get worse. Soon. She rolled on top, naked skin against his, her breasts, stomach and legs pressed against his damp body. His legs jerked. Entwining her legs around his, she locked down, preventing his movement. She leaned on her elbows, held his head between her hands and kissed him hard, muffling a scream that rose from deep in his chest. She didn't want Billy to wake up and hear him.

His eyes snapped open. Unfocused eyes stared.

She kissed his ear and whispered, "You're here with me. You're safe. Come back."

And then, thank God, he shuddered. His eyes blinked. He shook his head, slowly returning to her, eyes filled with fear and confusion.

"Again?" he asked in a hoarse whisper.

"Yes."

She kissed him gently and rolled onto her back, head against the pillow, staring at moonlit shadows on the ceiling. She hated the men who declared war. Hated them for sending kids to strange lands, into horrific firefights, watching their friends get slaughtered, getting emotionally scarred forever. Politicians who declared war should first be made to send their children and grandchildren.

He reached for her hand. "Was it bad this time?"

"No worse than the others." As many times as she had tried, he refused to talk about the nightmares. Refused to talk about what happened in Afghanistan. Something terrible had happened. If he could only let it out, confront his terrors, his torment would lessen. How many times had she asked him to talk with her, or go to a support group, or talk with a shrink. Just talk. He maintained his silence, like a stubborn mule, a trait that she hated at times, admired at others. Depended on the issue.

"But it's getting better? Not as often?"

"No. Not as often," she lied.

She watched the moonlight and listened to him toss and turn with agitation. Finally, about a half hour later, she reached for him.

"What?"

"I know how to get you to sleep." She caressed him with her fingertips.

"There's no way, I could . . ."

She kissed him to shut him up.

Later, straddling him, feeling his hands on her breasts, her hands pulling his hair, arching his head back, moving together, moans swelling, she heard the door open.

Billy stood in the doorway. She slid off Thatcher in one smooth motion, pulling the sheet over them, hoping Billy's eyes had not adjusted to the dark. "Is that you, Billy?"

"I heard noises."

Thatcher rose on his elbows, looked across her and said, "Mom and I were just talking."

"Why was Mom sitting on your tummy?"

"Uh, I wasn't feeling well."

"Oh. When I feel sick, I feel like a monkey with a hippopotamus sitting on my tummy."

"That's what it felt like when Mom sat on my tummy."

She elbowed him in the ribs. "Everything's okay, honey. You run back to bed. I'll be right there to tuck you in."

"Sure you feel all right, Dad?"

"I feel better now that I've seen you. Get to bed and I'll come with Mom to tuck you in so you'll be safe and sound."

They listened to his footsteps patter down the hall. They giggled, and got into their robes before walking down the hall to kiss Billy goodnight.

The next morning, driving Billy, she checked the mirror when she pulled up in front of school. Sam, in his brown Toyota, was close behind.

"Hey Mom. Let me ask you a question."

"Okay," she said, hoping it wasn't about catching them making love.

"Why did the computer go to the doctor?"

"Why?"

"Because it had a virus!" Convulsing with laughter, Billy got out of the car and ran up the sidewalk toward friends standing near the door.

Where did that sense of humor come from? Neither she nor Thatcher was humorous. She wished she remembered jokes and could see things in a funny light.

Life didn't seem much fun now, living under Virtue.

CHAPTER 22

Senator Alan Long's Home

Deverence

DEVERENCE SAT IN THE PASSENGER seat of the van outside Senator Alan Long's house. He looked at his watch: 9:45. Long's front door opened, casting light onto the steps. He watched the lanky Senator kiss his wife. She watched for a moment as he walked down the steps toward the sidewalk. She closed the door.

How sweet of her to make certain he didn't trip on the stairs on his way to his nightly walk. That's what loving couples do—look out for each other. Deverence marveled at how people fell into unconscious routines, adopting habits that made life easy, and all so predictable, unaware of their vulnerability.

Senator Long strode away at a brisk pace and turned the corner. Deverence ordered the men out of the van and led them to the door. They stood out of sight. He tried the door. It was locked. He knocked softly. Heard footsteps approaching from inside. The lock turned. He pushed the thumb latch down. Someone stood on the other side of the door. He rammed his shoulder into the door. The door slammed into Martha's forehead. She collapsed. He stepped into the hallway, dropped a knee on her chest and covered her scream with a rubber-gloved hand. Her widening eyes watched his companions slip in and close the door. He slammed his fist into her jaw, knocking her unconscious. He stood up, pointed to two of the three men. They picked her up and carried her into the kitchen and dropped her on the floor. The remaining man stood next to the front door, waiting to surprise Senator Long when he returned from his nightly walk.

Deverence opened kitchen drawers until he found a long carving knife. He felt the weight of the knife in his hand, walked to Martha's inert body, bent over, picked up her hand and sliced 'defensive' wounds on her palms and fingers. He cut her other hand, before driving the knife deep into her chest. Once. Twice. Three times. He stood over her and watched blood pump out. He backed out of the way, so one of his men could video Martha's death throes. After the cameraman said he had enough footage, Deverence nodded to the other men. They shook her arms to splatter blood over the kitchen. Deverence swept dishes onto the floor, simulating a fight had taken place.

They waited next to the door for Senator Long. Deverence heard a key rasp the door lock, waited until Long walked in and hit him on the temple with a blackjack. Long collapsed. They carried him into the kitchen, held him upright while one of the men lifted his ankle and dropped the Senator's foot on top of a pool of Martha's blood. They dropped him on the floor. Deverence wrapped the Senator's fingers around the bloody knife handle. He backed up, careful not to track blood, and surveyed the scene. One of the men videoed the scene before Deverence picked up the house phone, took a recorder from his pocket, and called 911. When the operator answered, he pushed the play button on the recorder and played Tim

Oliver's computer generated magic—Martha Long's panicked voice screaming for help . . . her husband was trying to kill her.

Deverence and his men secured the house, returned to their van and drove around the block. Soon they heard police sirens approaching. They waited a few minutes after the police arrived before screeching to a halt before the Senator's home. He led his men into the house past several protesting policemen, brushed aside another trying to block his way into the kitchen. Deverence showed the police detective his Virtue credentials. They surveyed the crime scene while a photographer took pictures.

Deverence said, "It's obvious Senator Long murdered his wife. We'll take him into custody." He motioned for his men to pick up the unconscious Senator.

"You don't have jurisdiction," the detective protested.

"Virtue has total authority over moral crimes. The Supreme Moral Court has jurisdiction.

"Don't give a damn. Gotta follow protocal," the detective said.

"Take it up with your boss. We will incarcerate the Senator." Deverence pushed the detective out of the way.

Deverence's men carried the Senator out of the house toward their van. He called over his shoulder to the objecting detective, "You and your guys can clean up this mess. We'll be in touch."

They bound Senator Long's hands with plastic tie-straps and tossed him in the back of the van before driving back to Virtue headquarters.

The Senator had regained consciousness by the time he was led down a long corridor of cells. "What is this?" Senator Long asked.

"Holding cells for Biblical Law breakers like you, Senator," Deverence said. He pointed to a steel door to the left. "That cell holds a 15 year-old kid Virtue caught accessing Internet porn. The next is reserved for someone we'll catch for cheating, and the one across from it holds a 29 year-old who lied about her virginity. This one is for you."

They threw the Senator in a cell next to Karen Huntington.

CHAPTER 23

Virtue Headquarters

Thatcher

THATCHER WALKED INTO VIRTUE HEADQUARTERS, wondering why Reverend John demanded a meeting now, after refusing to meet earlier about the return of his wooden cross. The unadorned lobby, unfinished concrete walls, floors, tall ceilings with cold florescent lights, was a soulless place. A Virtue man, wearing a scarlet shirt and black pants, met him at the guard desk and led him through security. The man told him to sit in what looked like a leather massage chair, legs and feet fitting into recessed slots. His stomach tightened as a cover hissed over his legs, embracing them.

"What the . . ." Thatcher felt something clamp around his right ankle. He tried to calm his breathing, not wanting to show his fear.

"Don't be alarmed, Senator Thatcher. You've just been fitted with a security device, an ankle bracelet. Like the old ones, it contains a GPS, so our computers will know where you are at all times. But it is important for you to understand that bracelet also contains two needles. Either can be fired on command. One needle will knock you unconscious. The other is a kill needle."

"Take it off. Now!"

"Standard procedure, Senator. Terrorists, you know. Every visitor has to wear them. We'll remove it when you leave."

The leg cover hissed again, sliding back into its recess. Thatcher looked at the innocent looking black rubber bracelet encircling his ankle. He stood and his trouser cuff dropped, hiding the bracelet.

"Please follow me."

Fleeting shadows preceded them. He should have followed his first instinct and refused to meet Reverend John. The man inserted a key and a steel door slid open to a small elevator separate from those used by Virtue employees.

"This will take you to Reverend John's floor."

He walked into the claustrophobic elevator, turned around and punched the only button. The man's unblinking black eyes stared at him as the door closed. The elevator did not move. He hit the button again. Video cameras, embedded into the ceiling, watched him.

He spotted a tube he assumed could flood the elevator with poison. Trapped. Would he ever be permitted to leave? Alive? He felt beads of sweat on his forehead. He would not wipe them off. Damned if he'd show fear. Adrenaline pumped through his body like when he dodged bullets in Afghanistan. He pushed the button again, several times. Finally, the elevator rose swiftly, gravity pressing his stomach down.

Another agent met him as the elevator door opened and led him to a cavernous dark office. Reverend John was on his knees, bowing to a gleaming neo-cross hung against the wall at the far end of the room. Thatcher held his breath. It looked like the cross's vertical arm had plunged into the man's back like a dagger. He exhaled.

The Reverend stood and nodded at him. "What a pleasure. Why don't you sit down? We'll chat before I show you around."

"I'll stand. This won't take long."

"Ah yes. You live up to your reputation of being a man in a hurry."

"I want this damned ankle bracelet off."

"Of course you do, Senator. I certainly understand. However, we have to be consistent with our security measures. There are so many terrorist threats. I do apologize for the inconvenience. I can assure you that it will be removed when you leave the building."

"Your men trespassed into my office, stole my personal property and hung a neo-cross. I want my possession back."

"How very interesting. You raise several issues here. First of all, if you were a good Christian, you would obey the Commandment that God's law is above man-made law and therefore you would have welcomed the installation of the neo-cross. And . . ."

Thatcher interrupted him, "*Security Act* gave you the power to install neo-crosses in official places. That was a man-made act, not a Commandment . . . ."

"Blasphemy! God breathed the words of that act into my mind. You should fall to your knees!"

"I'll bow before you right after God answers my prayers. In the meantime, I want the wooden cross your men took from my office."

Reverend John stared at him with unfocused eyes for several uncomfortable moments. He shook his head slowly. He asked in a calm voice, "You want your wooden cross?"

"I made it when I was a kid. I've prayed before it ever since. I want it back."

Reverend John leaned back and formed a steeple with his fingers. "I wonder what you prayed for? Did God answer your prayers? Have you heard His voice?"

"That's between God and me."

Reverend John arched his left eyebrow. "We burned your little wooden cross." He shook his head, looking sorrowful, "Ashes to ashes, dust to dust."

Speechless, Thatcher turned toward the door.

"Please wait, Senator. Spare me several more minutes of your precious time. I want to show you what we're doing here at Virtue."

He felt the bracelet around his ankle. How could he refuse?

Reverend John led Thatcher to Tim Oliver's office.

Oliver looked up from a desktop computer screen.

Reverend John chuckled. "Tim sits here, in his own personal Heaven, surrounded by every toy a nerd could wish for. He even has a secret lab for advanced research—developing human-like robots.

"Everything in this room is state of the art. In fact, most is beyond state of the art. Any equipment or software that's not commercially available, Tim either builds himself or has his staff build for him. There's no one in the world better at manipulation of data and images."

"So why do you work for Virtue?" Thatcher asked.

Tim turned back to his screen.

Reverend John said, "What's important, Senator, is for you to know we can not only change the future, but change the past. Data records define everyone's past. Your past is history, but history can be revised. For example, if I wanted to give you an immoral past, all I'd have to do is change the figures in your bank account to make you a thief, or establish an email trail that proves you are a homosexual. Tim could alter your past in minutes."

"That sounds like a threat," Thatcher said.

"Not a threat, just the reality of today's world." The Reverend turned to Oliver. "Pull up the senator's bank account."

Oliver's fingers flew over the keys. "Here it is."

Thatcher looked at the screen. It was their household account.

"Now put three million into his account," Reverend John said.

Several more keystrokes and Thatcher gasped as he watched his account increase by three million.

"Remove the money and then show the senator what we know about his recent activities."

Oliver nodded and Thatcher's throat constricted as he watched a video of him walking with Senator Long toward their meeting at Moral America. He heard their conversations about the *Voting Act*.

"Such a shame that Senator Long is behind the misbegotten lawsuit against our *Security Act*," Reverend John said. "He will regret that.

"However, the point is that you have allowed Senator Long to influence you before you've had the opportunity to understand the consequences of opposing the *Voting Act*. I'm certain that you will now change your mind and support the bill. I need your leadership and I'm counting on your support."

Behind the Reverend's back, Oliver shook his head.

Feeling the weight of the ankle bracelet, Thatcher said, "You've made a convincing case for my support, Reverend."

"You can prove your support by making a public announcement before the end of the week, senator."

"I'll need a bit of time to talk with others about the bill. I appreciate your advice, Reverend."

Thatcher glanced at Oliver's computer screen and watched the video continue, showing them walking to the Moral America office. Thatcher noted with relief there were no inside pictures, or scenes from Caleb's office or safe room. But that didn't mean Virtue could not spy inside the Moral America headquarters.

"Tim does impressive work," Thatcher said.

"I pulled him out of prison. He had hacked into sensitive government computers. If he disobeys, I'll send him back. He'll spend the rest of his life staring at the walls in his cell. What would his life be without his computers?"

Tim took a deep breath.

"I'll show you out." Reverend John turned and walked toward the door.

Thatcher squeezed Tim's shoulder. The man touched Thatcher's hand, and then looked at him, eyes moist. Thatcher gave him another reassuring squeeze. The computer genius glanced at Reverend John walking away, hit a key and nodded at the screen. An image of Reverend John's office appeared, showing Thatcher talking with Reverend John. The picture disappeared as fast has it had appeared. Then Oliver typed, "I'm Brutus!"

Thatcher followed Reverend John as he disappeared into the corridor.

Thatcher stopped at the door, turned and gave Oliver a thumbs-up. Oliver returned the salute. Thatcher nodded and followed Reverend John back to his office.

Reverend John opened his office door. "I'll let you out the same way you entered. My assistant will be waiting for you in the lobby to accompany you to the street."

Thatcher started to leave. Reverend John touched his elbow.

"Thank you for joining me to make America a Christian nation. I know you and Senator Long called for a meeting of the dissidents to the *Voting Act*. You'll tell them you changed your mind. You now support the bill. You'll convince them to do likewise."

Thatcher nodded, rode the elevator down to the lobby, where the ankle bracelet was removed. He pushed through the front door and walked out of Virtue. He stopped on the sidewalk and took a deep breath of clean fresh air tainted by the sour smell of his armpits. He called Senator Long. There was no answer. His office did not know where the Senator could be reached. And what did the computer guy mean by 'I'm Brutus?' Exasperated, Thatcher looked up.

An Eye watched him.

CHAPTER 24

Virtue Dungeon

Karen

THE DOOR OPENED, FLOODING THE cell with bright light. She covered her eyes.

"Step into the hall."

She stumbled to the door, lost her balance and caught herself on the doorframe.

"Four steps forward."

She stepped toward two guards.

"Stop! Bend over until your chest is parallel with the floor. Clasp your hands behind your back."

They bound her hands, raised her elbows and slid a rod between her arms and back. They lifted the rod so she stood, arms behind her back, bent double and face down. They walked her down the corridor into a bare concrete room.

Somewhere nearby, a man screamed in agony.

They forced her to her knees. She glanced up. At the end of the room a man in a red robe knelt in prayer below a floor-to-ceiling neo-cross. The man rose slowly, and then spun to face her. "God is Sovereign!"

She recognized Reverend John's voice. She heard his footsteps approaching until she saw the tips of his highly polished black shoes and the hem of his robe.

The man being tortured next door screamed again, a long screech ending in a wet, blubbering sound.

Reverend John said, "God is Sovereign over all things!"

"Amen!" she murmured.

"Lift her to her feet. Remove the rod, untie her hands and then leave us."

They jerked her off the floor by lifting the rod. Excruciating pain shot through her shoulders. She bit her lip to keep from screaming. The men removed the rod, untied her wrists and then pushed her into a metal folding chair. They placed another chair close in front of her.

Reverend John swirled his cloak around his body. He sat facing her. Their knees touched. She shifted her legs to the side of her chair.

Deverence, holding the little dog close to his chest, walked into the room and stood behind Reverend John, impartially observing, watching with honest blue eyes.

"Do you know who I am?" Reverend John's voice was gentle, the pupils of his eyes dilated.

"Yes."

Your husband made a fine contribution to our cause with his stunning neo-cross design. Just look at it," he turned toward the shining metal. "It captures mythos of spirituality with the logos of reality—a dagger poised to strike down our enemies."

The dog squirmed in the man's arms. He put it on the floor. It trotted to her and smelled her foot. She felt the dog's tongue on her ankle. She felt like kicking it.

Reverend John turned back to her. "Do you have questions?"

She stared at him in disbelief. The little dog's tail wagged as it leaned against her leg. She picked it up and held it on her lap. She stoked the dog's soft fur while fighting tears. She would be damned if she would let these bastards watch her cry.

The victim next door shrieked. Perhaps the screams were faked. No one was being tortured. She was caught in a sick psychological game.

"What do you want?" she asked.

"I want your help, Mrs. Huntington. God needs clarity."

"I don't understand. Why me?"

"Why you?" Reverend John smiled. "Of course you need to know why you were chosen. You're mistaken if you think you're here so I can blackmail your husband for the rest of his company.

"No. You were chosen because hypocrisy and sin is rife in our nation. God wants me to lead the country back to its moral foundations. God commanded me to reinstate the divine!"

She held the little dog close to her chest. "What does that have to do with me?"

"You will be the perfect example of God's punishment for adultery. You are a powerful woman, respected by your peers and by the nation. But, like so many, you are a woman with a secret, a woman with a sinful soul, a woman who willfully breaks Biblical Law."

"I didn't . . ."

Reverend John shook his head, looked at Deverence. He turned back toward her. "I'm so sorry you don't understand the greater need and your role in God's plan."

"You still haven't explained why you are doing this," she said.

"You ask why? You know why!" The pupils of his eyes constricted to angry pinpoints. He leaned forward, face animated, a vein in his forehead throbbing.

She recoiled against the back of her chair and gripped the little dog closer to her chest. Deverence took a step closer to Reverend John, resting his hand on the Reverend's shoulder.

The door to her left opened. Two guards dragged a naked semi-conscious older man across the room. His hands were tied behind his back, elbows bent over the rod the men held. He moaned incoherently. A thin line of red blood trailed on the concrete behind him.

"Bring him here," Reverend John said.

The guards dragged the man to them, dropping him to his knees and holding him upright. His head hung, snot hung from his nose. Terrible smells flooded her nostrils.

"Perhaps you recognize Senator Alan Long. He murdered his wife. We offered him the opportunity to confess, but the poor deranged man claimed he was innocent. He refused to sign the confession. You heard God punish him for lying. Now he's begging to confess, but it's too late.

"How can we possibly tell if he has truly repented, or he wants to admit his guilt to avoid more pain? We certainly don't want him to sign a false confession. So he's made it terribly difficult for us to determine whether or not he's telling the truth.

"The only way to be certain is to subject him to more pain. God will tell us when Senator Long is telling the truth. Then we'll allow him to confess.

"Tell Mrs. Huntington what it's like in the next room, Senator."

The man uttered something incoherent that ended in a moan.

"Take him back to his cell."

The guards dragged him out of the room.

Reverend John turned toward her. "Allow me to get back to your question. Secular humanism tried to destroy us with logic and reason and scientific discourse, tried to destroy that which cannot be explained in rational terms, tried to destroy the spiritual.

"Haven't you felt the hole in your soul? Haven't you felt empty? Haven't you gone to a party, been surrounded by so-called friends yet felt alone? Have you wondered about the meaning of life? Why you don't feel whole? Something important is missing? Material things don't bring the lasting joy you thought they would?"

"Yes." She was all but hypnotized by fear.

"Of course. Of course you have. All your toys, your big house, fancy cars, beautiful clothes, high-tech toys, all your shrinks and therapists can't assuage that emptiness, that aloneness, that feeling of lost wholeness.

"No amount of humanistic rational discourse can fill that void. Secular humanism tried to destroy God. But we fought back. Years ago Jerry Falwell founded the Moral Majority. He also founded Liberty University. Bob Jones had already started his university. Those schools trained a spiritual army to infiltrate all walks of life, the professions as well as politics.

"It took forever, but we are now in the position to save the people of America, to teach God has dominion over all. There never has been separation of Church and State, despite what man-made law says. We are reorganizing society on Biblical terms, so that every single law of the Bible will literally be put into place.

"We are so close. Time is short. The Rapture is near." He began to breath faster. "There are so many to be converted.

We must help God save America! Great sacrifices will have to be made."

"Sacrifices?" she asked.

He leaned forward, suddenly calm, smiled and patted her knee. "That's where you will help, Mrs. Huntington."

"What?"

"You want to help God, don't you?"

She was panting again. "I don't know."

"You will help God by confessing you are an adulteress. You will become a martyr."

"Fuck you!" She gripped the seat of her chair. The dog jumped off her lap and ran to Deverence.

"Deverence, show her the confession. Sign it, Mrs. Huntington and save yourself terrible pain."

This was all an elaborate trick; the screams, an actor made up to look like Senator Long, all an act to frighten her into signing a confession. She was innocent.

Deverence handed her the paper. She tore it in half and threw it at Reverend John.

He shook his head. "I'm so sorry, Mrs. Huntington." He stood and then walked to the neo-cross, knelt and prayed out loud for mercy for her soul. He stood up, walked to the door, paused and then turned back toward her. "One last chance, Mrs. Huntington. I beg you to sign now, before I turn you over to Deverence."

"Go to hell."

"No, my dear. Not I. She's all yours, Deverence." He walked out of the room.

She stared at the neo-cross, avoiding Deverence's eyes. There was a long silence that grew even more uncomfortable.

"Her name is Bebe," Deverence said.

She looked at him. "What?"

He was holding the little dog close to his chest. "She is a Shih Tzu."

"I'll go back to my cell."

"It's too late for that."

"I'll sign the confession."

"Yes you will, Mrs. Huntington, but if you sign now you'll be acting out of fear. As Reverend John said, a confession under those circumstances would be disingenuous. After you are purified you'll beg to confess."

"No! I'll do it now."

Deverence said, "Allow me to show you the confession room." The door opened. The two guards walked in, grabbed her arms and walked her toward the other door.

The confession room, bare smooth concrete, held a sour smell. A video screen covered the entire left wall. A floor-to-ceiling neo-cross stood against the right wall. A water hose coiled beneath a faucet. The wet floor sloped toward a drain in the center. There was a metal desk to the left of the video screen.

A harness dangled from the ceiling at the center of the room. Two chains bolted it to the floor, two chains to the ceiling. Padded leather wrist and ankle constraints, small belts, attached to the end of each chain.

Her knees buckled. She collapsed in bowel-loosening terror. She struggled to escape. The men held her upright while Deverence approached, Bebe at his heels.

He stood close. "This is a tool of God." He held up something for her to see. The round head and first twelve inches of the shaft were stainless steel. Thick rubber coated the handle. He touched its smooth head to her cheek. She recoiled.

"This creates unbelievable pain. I can control the intensity of the electric shock with this knob at the end of the handle. He turned the knob. Let me show you." He touched the shaft on Bebe's back. The little dog howled, fell to the floor in spasms, and moaned.

"You bastard!" she said.

He smiled and whispered. "I am your confessor, Mrs. Huntington. I will be your teacher. I will teach you Biblical commandments, Leviticus 20:10. 'The adulteress must be put to death'. "

He picked up the unconscious dog, held her gently, and told the guards. "Take Mrs. Huntington back to her cell. So she can think about what will happen if she refuses to confess."

CHAPTER 25

Morocco

Felix

HER PRIVATE JET LANDED IN Tangier. She'd had the nuclear warhead boxed to look like she had acquired a small piece of furniture. The HERF gun was concealed in its roll-along suitcase. Thanks to her Moroccan diplomatic passport and another wad of cash, she cleared Customs without inspection. She was happy that in Morocco, unlike so much of the rest of the world, women were still permitted to travel without male companions.

She made a phone call, spoke several words of code and hailed a taxi which drove her to a crowded bazaar. She got out with her luggage and watched the taxi disappear. A car swung to the curb, the driver helped her put her baggage in the trunk and passenger front seat. She got in back and they sped off.

Forty-five minutes later, after backtracking several times to throw off anyone following them, the car pulled into a garage in a nondescript building owned by a black market electronics genius. The driver loaded her luggage onto a dolly and wheeled it through a door, which led to several other doors, guarded by security cameras. They finally arrived in a room that looked like a mixture between a high tech machine shop and a laboratory.

A swarthy, bearded man wearing a white djellaba, a long, loose, hooded garment with full sleeves, and a pair of yellow soft leather balghas on his feet, ordered his driver to leave.

He gave her a slight bow and touched his heart. "You have returned. Praise be to Allah. No harm on you?"

"All is fine."

"And your boss, Felix?"

"Felix sends his regards and great appreciation for past services."

"Serving Felix has been my great honor. I hope I might be of service now and in the future."

"You heard what happened to the man in France who was indiscreet and talked about Felix?"

"I fear the knowledge, but I'm certain you will enlighten me," he said.

"His tongue was cut out, then he was skinned alive . . . a video sent to his wife and family."

The man winched. "May Allah protect us."

"Allah did not betray him; his mouth betrayed him."

"Great lessons come in the form of stories."

She unpacked the HERF gun and nuclear device. "Felix wants you to hide tiny homing devices inside the circuitry of both of these."

The man's eyes widened and then he bent to inspect them, running the tips of his fingers across their surfaces. "Beautiful in design and simplicity. May I ask if they might be booby trapped?"

"Only Allah knows."

"Allah might know, but I will be the one to find out."

"Your fee shall be doubled."

"If this detonates, my family will not find enough pieces of my body to bury, nor will they find my head to face south toward Mecca. My name and my family will be dishonored. Therefore my fee will be triple."

"Felix will agree, under the condition that you do one more thing." She pulled out the bomb's trigger disguised as an American ballpoint pen and explained what she wanted.

He agreed. She could pick up her items in two days. She ran the tips of her fingers over the nuclear warhead and then walked out, saying, "Peace be with you."

"And may peace be with you," he replied.

As the driver returned her to the train station, she thought again about the dilemma debated by philosophers, politicians and the press: were the lives of tens of thousands of strangers worth more than the life of a loved one? But she was not the one to make the decision to detonate the warhead. She would not be responsible for pulling the trigger. Perhaps the weapon would simply be used as blackmail. Besides, there were thousands of nuclear bombs scattered across the world. As a delivery person, she would be as innocent as a truck driver delivering a bomb from the factory to the U.S. military.

Two hours later, disguised by a burka, Felix rode the high-speed train from Tangier to Marrakesh, carrying an aluminum suitcase containing ten million Chinese yuan. At the Marrakesh station she stepped off and wheeled her suitcase through the station, declining aggressive offers of help from young men and boys. She stood on the curb, looking through the slit of her burka for a taxi.

A taxi stopped for her. Before the driver could get out to help, she heaved her suitcase onto the floor of the back seat. "Les Jardins de la Koutoubia."

The driver nodded and flipped the meter. He drove toward the five-star hotel at the heart of the Medina, with its thousand and one perfumes and colors of Marrakesh. She had chosen

Les Jardins de la Koutoubia because it was next to the Djemaa el-Fnaa, the UNESCO Masterpiece of the Oral and Intangible Heritage of Humanity, commonly known throughout the world as the huge square known for its storytellers, dancers, water-sellers, musicians and other performers.

Sounds from the Djemaa el-Fnaa filtered through the open taxi window, familiar sounds that filled her with hope. The Koutoubia Mosque, its tower adorned with four copper globes, rose on the left. The legend said the globes were originally made of pure gold, and there were once only three globes. The fourth globe was donated by the wife of a ruler as compensation for her failure to keep the fast for one day during the month of Ramadan. She had her golden jewelry melted down to form the globe. The Koutoubia's minaret became the model for thousands of church towers in Spain and Eastern Europe. Most people were ignorant of Morocco's contributions to the world.

The bellman showed her to her rooms. She double locked the door, slipped her derringer under a bed pillow, threw off the oppressive disguise and undressed. After a hot shower, she wrapped on a robe and then walked onto the balcony. The snow-capped Atlas Mountains shimmered in the distance.

She looked at the familiar square and the Medina, the old quarter with its narrow streets, some less than a meter wide, the constricted and winding passages designed to confuse and slow down invaders.

She had grown up here, in a compound hidden within one of these streets. When she had been an innocent child he had called her his Princess. Once, he took her to Italy. Standing high on a mountainside overlooking the ocean, he promised to build her a glass castle. Later, at bedtime, he put her to bed and cuddled her. And stroked her. She thought she had been loved.

He had kept her hidden like a prized jewel, having Hajar home-school her, keeping her away from others. It wasn't until he allowed her to go to a private high school and she talked with other girls that she understood he had violated her.

After the death of her first daughter, he raped her again, impregnating her once more. Now, she did his bidding in return for his promise not to violate Sara. But he'd replace her with Sara when she was worn out or dead. After all, he said, he had to maintain the cash flow to maintain his lifestyle.

But the sickest part of it, the part that tore her apart, the part that suffocated her in guilt and self-hatred, was that she had loved his touches. Loved his caressing fingers. His fondling made her feel special. Those same feelings now tore her apart.

She had to kill him to protect her daughter. She knew his guards would find her gun, but this time she had hidden a hard plastic shiv disguised as a part of her bra. Touched by inexperienced hands, the shiv would feel like the wire uplifting her breasts. The plastic would not set off the metal detector. It was long enough to penetrate his heart.

She imagined her father entering the room, his charm concealing an evil soul. He would spread his arms in greeting. She would step into his arms, twist a bit to the left, raise her hand, push and feel the shiv penetrate his chest on its journey to his heart. His face would contort with surprise and confusion. She would step back and watch as he looked down at blood spurting out, staining his white garment. He would swear at her. Stagger toward her, she taking short steps to just be inches from his grasping fingers. He would fall on the tile floor, convulse and then die. And then she would laugh and dance on his corpse.

CHAPTER 26

Virtue Dungeon

Karen

SHE WAITED IN THE CHAMBER for an eternity, naked, strapped spread-eagle, wrists and ankles bound by the constraints, her mind torn by fear.

The door opened. Deverence walked into the room, wearing nothing but black briefs. A gold neck chain held a small silk sack and a silver neo-cross, its foot pointing to washboard stomach muscles. She wondered what was in the silk sack. He studied her body as he walked toward her. He stood close. His breath smelled like mint-favored mouthwash. His eyes were curious and friendly. At the same time they looked as hard as obsidian.

"Jehovah wants you to learn the Fourth Commandment."

"Who?"

"Jehovah. God is 'dog' spelled backwards. I learned that when terrorists cut off my fingers." He held his deformed hands close to her face, and then held up the sack. "I keep the bones here, so I'm a complete man." He turned and walked to the desk. He opened a drawer, took out the torture instrument and walked back.

"Repeat after me, 'I committed adultery.'"

"Oh God. Please. I'll confess," she whispered in a voice that seemed distant and hoarse.

"No, Mrs. Huntington. It's not that easy. I'm only your confessor. God will judge when you truly repent. He will tell me when you're ready." He slowly walked around her, gently touching her with the prod.

"Deuteronomy. 'You shall not commit adultery' . . . Leviticus. 'The adulteress must be put to death.'"

He began chanting:

"The adulteress must be put to death."

"You shall not commit adultery."

"The adulteress must be put to death."

    "You shall not commit adultery."

    "The adulteress must be put to death!"

He touched her with the prod and pressed the trigger.

She screamed.

Many times.

After that first lesson, they dragged her back to the cell. Time lost meaning. She knew he would come for her to teach new lessons. Soon the anticipation of torture became worse than the session itself. Now, when she heard the footsteps approaching, she wanted them to open her door and take her to the chamber. Get it over!

Sometime after the third lesson, she heard footsteps pause on the other side of her cell door. Deverence opened the door. He wore his Virtue uniform. "Stand up!"

She stood, clutching the blanket over her naked body.

"Drop the blanket."

She complied.

"Are you ready to confess?"

"Yes! Oh, please, yes." The panicked sound of her voice frightened her.

He handed her some printed papers. "This is your confession. Read it. I will be back in a few minutes to ask if you will sign it." He turned and slammed the door shut.

She pulled the blanket over her shoulders, sat on the bed and stared at the words on the pages. When he returned, she signed.

A short time later, she stood naked in a small Courtroom someplace near her cell. Deverence stood close behind her. Three Supreme Moral Court judges, wearing Virtue's scarlet robes, sat behind a raised dais. A clerk read the charges. She began to cover herself. Deverence touched her thigh with his probe and whispered, "Stand at attention."

The judge in the middle looked like her beloved grandfather. The man on the right wore wire-rim glasses, had a huge fringe-lined bald head, with thin lips pressed together as though he had tasted something sour. The judge sitting on the left seemed like a disinterested public clerk.

"Do you agree with these charges?" the head judge asked.

"I confess to being an adulteress."

"Have you signed your confession?"

Deverence stepped forward and handed the document to the head judge.

All three judges signed as witnesses.

The head judge cleared his throat. "You have confessed to violating the Seventh Commandment, in Exodus 20:14. 'Thou shalt not commit adultery'. This court hereby condemns you to the punishment prescribed by Biblical Law. That concludes these proceedings."

Deverence walked her back to her cell. He waited at the door. She sat on the edge of the bed, too numb to cover her nakedness with the blanket. She stared at the floor.

"I'm worried about you, Mrs. Huntington. You need to lift your spirits. After all, you will be a lesson in morality for the nation and the world. You need loving companionship."

"No. Please, no." She shrank against the wall.

Deverence whistled. Bebe trotted into the cell. It jumped upon her bed, wagging its tail. It crawled in her lap.

"She's broken, too. I'll let her keep you company until the Punishments."

CHAPTER 27

Thatcher's neighborhood

Carol

SHE AND BILLY DROVE TOWARD the house with a load of groceries. Sam, driving his brown Toyota, followed. At first she had been uncomfortable with the bodyguard hovering nearby, following her. But now she was thankful Thatcher had arranged for the security. Approaching the house, Sam pulled around her and parked next to the curb in front. She pulled next to his car, lowered the passenger side window and asked Billy to hand Sam a plastic carton of double chocolate muffins. Billy unbuckled his seat belt, leaned out the window and handed the muffins to Sam.

"Boy, you're lucky. Mom won't let me have one."

Sam smiled. "Why not?"

"She says it's too close to dinner."

"You tell your Mom a man should eat every chance he gets. Could be his last meal." Sam winked at Carol.

She shook her head. "You men are impossible. I have to put away the groceries before the ice cream melts." She drove into the garage.

Billy helped carry a sack of groceries into the kitchen. "I'm going out to practice lacrosse, Mom."

Several minutes later, she walked back to the car for a box of laundry detergent. On the way back, she looked through the family room window. Billy threw the lacrosse ball into a net.

She walked into the kitchen and heard the faint iCom ring—Thatcher's unique sound.

Thatcher's voice was tight and controlled. "I'll meet you for dinner at the Red Wings."

She had never heard that commanding tone of voice. Her stomach tightened, remembering their code word. "Okay."

"Do you remember where Red Wings is located?"

"Yes."

"Bring Billy. I'll meet you there."

She hung up and reached high to the top of the doorframe and found the key to the locked top drawer of their bedside table. She tried to insert the key into the lock. It slipped out of her fingers, bouncing off the hardwood floor and under the bed. She fell to her knees, felt under the bed frame, found it and unlocked the drawer. She fingered through the contents until she found her passport and emergency cash. She picked up her 9mm Glock, slammed the magazine closed and chambered a shell. She put the pistol in her back pocket. No one was going to take her son.

She ran downstairs and through the door to the backyard for Billy. The yard was empty. She stopped, paralyzed. She listened. Started to call his name. Thought better. One of the thick bushes between the houses moved. She pulled out the pistol. Fighting through the bushes, sharp branches scratched her face and hands. She sensed a movement to her left, something on the ground under the branches. A foot. Billy burrowed deep in the tangle.

"Hi Mom! Look at my neat fort!"

"Oh, my God!" She pocketed her gun, fell to her knees and squeezed him.

Billy tried to pull away. "What's wrong, Mom?"

She clamped her hand over his mouth. A man in a Virtue uniform walked around the garage into the backyard. He stopped and scanned the area. She hunkered deeper into the thicket, shielding Billy with her body.

"Sh-h-h-h. Don't say a word." She pushed him to the ground. She smelled fresh dirt, the odor of an eleven-year-old boy, and the copper smell of her own blood from the scratches.

The man, gun in his right hand, opened the back door, crept into the family room and disappeared.

She pulled Billy up, held his hand and then slipped through the bushes into the neighbor's yard. Using the bushes as a shield, they skirted through their backyard. A white van blocked her car in the garage.

The Toyota was still parked in front of the house. Sam sat behind the steering wheel, head against the headrest.

Using trees in the yard for cover, they ran to the driver's side of the stakeout's car. Crouching, she opened the driver's door. Sam toppled onto the pavement. Suppressing a scream, she covered Billy's eyes so he wouldn't see the round bullet hole in the man's left temple. She dragged him out of the car.

She pushed Billy inside and climbed into the driver's seat. The key was in the ignition. The engine purred to life. She eased down the street, slowly so the men inside didn't hear squealing tires.

At the end of the block, she accelerated, shot down two blocks, and swerved around the corner toward the guardhouse. She eased on the brakes as they approached the gatehouse.

"Get down. Down on the floor. Hide."

Billy slid to the floor. She realized he had not fastened his seat belt. The gate was up. She could see the guard through the bulletproof glass of his hut. She looked away, hoping he didn't recognize her. She drove through and merged with traffic.

"Get back up now. Put on your seat belt."

"Look at this gun, Mom." He held a revolver by the barrel, the muzzle pointing toward his belly. The hammer was cocked.

"Be careful! Give it to me."

He gave her the gun. She released the hammer and then put the gun in her lap.

"We're going to a secret place where Dad will meet us." She checked her review mirror. It didn't look like anyone was following them.

A few minutes later she merged with traffic on the Beltway toward Columbia, where Captain Charles Maxwell lived. Thatcher had asked her to marry him on the porch of the Captain's house. Maxwell had been her dad's best friend and classmate. They'd served together at the end of the Vietnam War. Captain Maxwell became a surrogate father to her after her father's death and a grandfather figure to Billy.

Her iCom rang Thatcher's tone. She answered.

"Are you all right?"

"Yes. Sam's gone."

"The car and your phone will be tracked. Get rid of them."

"Understood."

"Meet you there." He hung up.

She powered off the iCom. He had kept the conversation short, hoping it couldn't be tracked. She had to get rid of her phone. She lowered her window to toss it out, and then she had a better idea. Pulling off at the next exit, she pulled into a busy gas station where she spotted a pickup with out of state license plates. She waited for the driver to walk inside before dropping her iCom in the pickup's bed.

Thirty-five minutes later, she pulled the Toyota into an overflowing Walmart parking lot. She left the keys in the ignition, hoping someone would steal the car. She tucked the pistol in the waist of her pants and then pulled out her shirt to hide it. Her Glock was hidden in her pocket. They began to walk the several miles to Captain Charlie's neighborhood.

One of America's first planned communities, Columbia had been middle-class in the seventies, but the area was deteriorating fast. The houses looked even more rundown than the last time she had visited. Almost every other house was vacant or had a 'For Sale' sign in its unkempt lawn.

Captain Charlie's two-story house badly needed paint and was indistinguishable from other sad houses on the block. A white-haired slender man in a wheelchair opened the door. His eyes widened and he smiled. "What a nice surprise! Boy, you've gotten bigger." He held out his arms.

The boy drew back. "Do you know why sea-gulls fly over the sea?"

"Gosh, you've got me. Why?"

"Because if they flew over the bay they would be bagels!" Billy erupted with uncontrolled squeals of laughter that drowned the Captain's soft chuckles.

She wondered how he could joke at a time like this. "We need to get inside."

The Captain frowned and then wheeled back out of the doorway. "Why don't you go into the kitchen and grab some chocolate chip cookies?"

Billy rushed inside.

"Say 'Thanks," she said as he disappeared around the corner toward the kitchen.

Captain Charlie stopped her. "What's wrong?"

"We . . . nothing . . . thought we'd drop in and say 'hi.'" She pushed a strand of hair away from her eyes.

"Where's your car?"

"We walked."

He grabbed her hand and looked at it. "That's dried blood."

"It's nothing . . . oh, Captain Charlie!" She sobbed.

He held her hand. "It's okay, honey. You can tell me."

She told him the story. "Thatcher should be here soon."

"You need a cup of coffee." He turned and wheeled toward the kitchen.

She followed, smelling a musty scent unique to old people's houses. They sat at the littered kitchen table, waiting for the coffee to heat up. Billy told him about scoring a goal at his lacrosse game. It started to rain. It had been over an hour. Thatcher should be here by now, she thought.

CHAPTER 28

Marrakesh

Felix

SHE WORE THE BURKA OVER slacks and blouse, and walked labyrinthine alleys toward his house. The smells and sounds were familiar; perfumes, spices and donkey shit, grilled chicken. Berber, French, Spanish, Arabic and English voices created an international melody. She heard strains of Chaabi music. The sights and sounds should have been familiar. Marrakesh had been her 'home' since she was eleven. The place created mixed emotions: familiarity and mystery, peace and violence. She wondered what it would be like to be a carefree tourist, rather than on a life or death mission?

She carried a gift for Sara. She prayed the girl would live to age gracefully. In spite of his claims of innocence, she knew he had killed her first daughter. She could not let that happen to Sara. She would end this charade today.

She sidestepped a braying donkey pulling a cart of bleating sacrificial sheep. Berbers, dressed in traditional blue djellabas with long hoods, leaned against a wall, watching her. Vendors shouted from their souks, displaying their wares on rugs thrown over the dirt.

She paused near a metal works to listen to a melodic rhythm created by three bare-chested men hammering a large sheet of copper. She stopped and bought a sprig of lavender to hold under her nose before walking past the nauseating stink of the leather tannery that used urine and pigeon shit during the processing.

She turned right into a narrow passageway that wove through high mud brick walls. There were fewer people there. No breeze to carry away the stench.

She stopped in front of a worn wooden door inset into a whitewashed wall, took a deep breath and then banged the iron doorknocker. A small window opened. Brown eyes peered at her.

"Jamila," she whispered.

Male voices, Arabic words, a command. An iron lock screeched. Hinges complained as the door opened. She saw the familiar fountain in the shaded courtyard. Sunlight reflected off the spray, turning the droplets into millions of diamonds. She stepped into cooler air.

Two men, dressed in white shirts and loose fitting black slacks, stood ten feet apart. They pointed Uzi's at her. Abdul smiled. "Allah sent you back."

Now for the security routine. If he touches me . . . She put her shopping bag on the ground, and dropped her burka on the floor. She locked her fingers together behind her neck and spread her feet wide. The guard on the left walked behind her while the other pointed the muzzle of his machine gun at her stomach. His hands felt her ankles, the outside of her slacks, up the inseam, too high. He explored her hips and back.

He found the derringer and laughed. "You always try, don't you?" He unloaded it and then placed the gun on top of a table. He returned to continue the pat down. His fingers slid inside her white silk blouse and then into her bra. He grinned as his fingers cupped her breast.

"Dirty bastard." She slapped him.

"Bitch!" He cocked his fist to hit her.

The other guard hissed, "Don't be a fool!"

The man in front lowered the muzzle of his machine gun. The pat down was finished.

The guard on her left motioned to the shopping bag. She reached into the sack. She had thought of buying Sara a Thai silk dress, but that would be provocative. She pulled out a small package. The guard opened it and looked at a plain pair of gold earrings. He nodded.

He motioned toward a hallway that penetrated the Moorish house through a mosaic arch. She left the burka, picked up the shopping bag before walking through a metal detector and followed him down the hallway. They passed a doorway to a large room where four young women were chained to a post. The man slowed and leered at them. They sat on the floor, cowering against the wooden pole. Two were natural blondes with strong jaws. Eastern European, she guessed. They would bring three times as much as the two Mediterranean-looking brunettes. The women's eyes begged her to help. She turned away, powerless. The blondes would live a little longer than the brunettes.

Sex slavery was not as lucrative as dealing in illicit weapons, but the product had fringe benefits. However, his greed for money was a bottomless pit. His specialty was the knowledge of who was developing state-of-the-art weapons and how to find a corrupt person to steal them. Her job was to make the connection, the pay off, collect and deliver the merchandise, collect and return the money to him.

There would never be enough money to satisfy his needs. He would set a dollar goal to buy Sara's freedom. Once achieved, he would set a higher goal. She wondered what motivated his greed. The missing mother of his childhood? The poverty of his youth? The sense of being deprived as a child? Fear of being poor in his old age? The feeling he could not be a whole person until he filled some emotional hole? His greed was caused by a lack of something, a lack she could neither determine nor fill.

The guard opened a door and she stepped through the scent of incense into a huge room. Ornate columns supported high ceilings. Colorful mosaic tile images of dancing naked women wound around the pillars. Carpets covered blue tile floors. Folds of indigo, yellow and red silk draped the walls. Low upholstered couches and overstuffed pillows scattered across the floor. Silver carafes and cups on trays lay on low tables in front of couches.

A polished mahogany platform, three feet high and twelve feet square, occupied the center of the room. A ten-foot high pole, thick as a man's chest, rose from the middle of the platform. Its highly polished wood was carved with the figures of naked women. Thick leather straps with wristlocks dangled from its top. The room where his customers selected their slaves. The room where he had violated her. The room where he would rape Sara.

The guard closed the door behind her. She heard the tumble of a lock.

Several minutes later, were the hiss of movement of the drapes on the left side of the room. The silk separated and an old woman wearing a burka stepped into the room.

"You have returned. Praise be to Allah!" The woman's eyes smiled as she approached and kissed her lightly on each cheek and then touched her right hand to her heart.

Jamila touched her heart and looked at the woman who had cared for her since childhood. She loved the old woman. She also hated her for not protecting her; hatred wrapped in guilt. What could Hajar have done? Tried to stop him physically and be killed or thrown out to starve to death? Tried to warn her? Warning her would have made it worse, because she would have known his caresses to be wrong, but would be powerless to stop him. Hajar had had to struggle to survive as well. "How are you, Hajar?"

"No harm on me, Praise be to Allah."

"And Sara?"

The old woman's cloudy eyes lowered. "I try to keep her safe, but I am old and helpless. I am sorry. Sara does not complain."

"I didn't either. I didn't know any better."

"I tried."

"How? You did nothing."

"He was all-powerful."

"And you still do nothing. How far, Hajar? How far has he gone with Sara?"

"I don't know. He takes her to her room at night to put her to bed. He shuts the door."

"But you listen, don't you?"

"No! No."

"I know you, Harjar. I know when you lie. You listen at the door."

"Sometimes."

"And what do you hear?"

"He hasn't taken her yet . . ." the old woman paused.

"But everything else?"

"Maybe. I don't know. Soon. Sara is the same age you . . ."

"Has Sara changed?"

"She is becoming a woman."

"That's not what I meant. I mean have you noticed Sara acting differently? Sad? Depressed? Different?"

"No, by the grace of Allah."

"I think Allah has little to do with this."

The woman's eyes widened and then she looked at her feet. "As you say. I must go to Sara. I shall bring her to you at his command." Hajar turned and disappeared through the silk drapes.

She stood alone, waiting in silence. Praying that when she met him, she would have the courage to act, to finish this macabre dance once and for all. She unbuttoned the top buttons of her blouse and slipped the shiv part way out from her bra, so she could reach it with ease.

A soft rustle of silk. The drapes parted and her father, wearing a white chiffon robe, walked into the room. His head was shaved, his eyes sparkled, his step was energetic, his voice deep and charming, "Welcome home, Jamila. Welcome home, my darling daughter!"

He held his arms wide to embrace her, as he had when she had been little.

She rushed into his arms, slipping out the shiv, raising her arm to thrust the needle-sharp plastic into his heart. Sensing the movement, he blocked her hand. The shiv plunged into his shoulder. He screamed. She pulled it out for another thrust. He twisted her wrist until the shiv fell to the floor. He kneed her stomach. She doubled over. His fist crashed into her jaw. Gasping for breath, she lay on the floor, partially conscious. Her fingers found the shiv. He stepped on her wrist and twisted until she screamed with pain. He stood over her, face contorted with anger. His wound barely bled.

He picked up the shiv, walked away, and then turned back toward her, his face calm. "Ingenious. What will you think of next? I'm proud you were able to get this past my guards."

Woozy, she staggered to her feet and felt her jaw. She lurched to the wall, leaned against it, hands on knees, sucking air into her lungs.

"I'm so sorry you forced me to hurt you. What else could I have done? That was no way to greet your father. How can I possibly make you understand how much I love you?"

"I want to see my daughter."

His face contorted with a look of annoyance. "Can't say *our* daughter, can you? You live in denial, my dear."

She staggered over to a bench, sat on a cushion, put her head in her hands. A minute later, she said, "I have a plan to get an additional twenty million for this job."

"An additional twenty? His eyes fill with greed.

"I can't do it myself. I'll need help. I'll have to hire someone when I get to America."

"But that will cost money."

"Several million."

"Are you out of your mind? You can't give away my millions!"

"Business expenses."

"It's too dangerous to bring someone else in. Save the money. Do it yourself. What's your plan?"

"I'm having a fake trigger made for the bomb. When Virtue realizes it won't work, they'll want the real trigger. I'll demand an additional twenty million for the real one."

"That's my daughter!"

"The problem is that I'll have to expose myself to hand it off and collect the money. They'll never let me escape. I need someone to help collect the money."

"You plan to use someone you don't trust handle my money?"

"Perhaps you can come up with a better idea," she said.

"Have Virtue wire transfer the money to the Swiss account, like they did before," he said.

"Virtue knew Felix's reputation of honest dealing. They deposited that money on the basis of trust. When they discover the trigger is a fake, they will feel betrayed. Now would they trust Felix? Of course not. The handoff will have to be the real trigger for cash, or we can forget the extra 20 million and simply give them the real trigger."

"No!"

"Now I'd like to visit with my daughter."

"*Our* daughter. *Ours.* Say it, Jamila. *Our* daughter." His smile faded into a tight line splitting his face.

"If you violate her there will be no more money for you."

"Delay several weeks for an additional twenty million? Of course."

"How do I know you won't break your promise?"

"I'm a business man. I've never reneged on a business proposition. Never will. That would be bad for my reputation."

"I want to talk with my daughter. Alone."

"You'll see our daughter as soon as I'm ready for you to see her."

She hung her head. "I'm sorry."

"I'll let you see our daughter now." He walked out of the room.

She took the earrings out of the shopping bag, and paced back and forth, waiting.

"Mom!" The drapes exploded and an eleven-year-old girl raced across the room toward her. Jamila sank to her knees to embrace her daughter. Not his. Hers. Only hers. Tears ran down her cheeks.

"I brought you a present." She handed the present to Sara.

Sara opened the box and smiled.

"You'll look lovely with those."

"Thanks, Mom."

"Are you all right, darling?"

"I miss you, but Grandfather's teaching me how to kick the soccer ball. I can kick it through the goal."

She remembered when she'd been at the center of his attention, when he taught her how to kick a ball, how to play cards. How she had loved him. Trusted him.

"And he's taught me Crazy Eights. That's a card game. I beat him most of the time," Sara said.

"He taught me the same game, honey."

"He's going to teach me how to shoot a gun when I get a little older, just like he taught you when you were my age."

She looked at Sara and asked, "Has anything happened with Grandfather that you'd like to tell me?"

"Grandfather gave me a white kitty," Sara said.

He walked back into the room. He stroked Sara's hair. His fingers traced her arms and brushed across her tummy when he gave her a squeeze, cupping her body from behind.

He bent down and his lips brushed Sara's ear when he whispered, "Why don't you show your present to Hajar?"

Sara ran out of the room.

"I might need your help, as well, to get that additional twenty million," she said.

"What sort of help?"

"I won't know until I get back to Washington."

CHAPTER 29

Columbia, Maryland

Carol

STANDING IN CAPTAIN CHARLIE'S KITCHEN, she pulled the collar of her white shirt up against her neck as if to ward off a cold draft. She leaned against the kitchen sink, smelled old coffee grounds and mold, and watched raindrops splatter against the window. Droplets ran in rivulets down the glass, distorting tree limbs into nightmarish shapes. She had used Captain Charlie's phone to call Thatcher. He had not answered. She assumed he had been captured. Maybe he had destroyed his phone. Tree branches swayed in the wind as if pleading to some higher power for salvation. She felt so alone.

Captain Charlie sat in his wheelchair in the living room, wrinkled face alert, listening to Billy and laughing, acting as if there were no problem.

Virtue would eventually track them to Captain Charlie's. Where the hell was Thatcher?

She had an idea—the only place Virtue might not discover would be Mary Lee's. Their casual working relationship had been years ago when Mary Lee joined Planned Parenthood. Virtue would never think of looking in the ghetto.

"Charlie, I need to talk to you in the kitchen."

He wheeled his chair toward her, calling over his shoulder, "I'll be right back, Billy."

She turned and leaned against the counter. "I need to borrow your car."

"It's yours, but it's old. I never use it. Might not start."

The TV snapped on, startling them. The evening news anchor, Steve Brooks, began the program with a news flash. "The Department of Virtue announces the capture of U.S. Senator William Thatcher, who was attempting to flee from an arrest warrant for grand theft."

"Virtue issued a public announcement of the warrant for his arrest five hours ago. Thatcher has just been seized by Virtue agents after a public minded Christian reported his location." Brooks went on to other news.

Billy shouted from the living room. "Hey, Mom. The man on TV said Dad has been arrested."

Captain Charlie looked at her. "Shit—the living room TV."

She cleared her throat. "It's all right Billy. Someone thinks your Dad did something wrong, but it's a mistake. Dad will be all right."

Billy stood in the doorway, looking at them. She turned her head to hide her tears. "Will Dad be okay, Captain Charlie?"

"You bet! You'll be okay too, Billy. It might take some time, but you'll be just fine. You wait and see."

"Then why's Mom crying?"

She wiped her tears and turned to him. "I'm sad because someone made a mistake. It'll be all right. Just like Captain Charlie promised."

They heard shouts from the TV. Virtue men walked into the picture. Steve Brooks looked up from the teleprompter. "Get out of here! I'm in the middle of a broadcast."

The weatherman, looking on with horror, fled.

The Virtue agents surrounded Brooks. He ripped off his earpiece and jumped to his feet. Two men grabbed his arms.

Brooks spun, knocked one man down with a martial arts move, but he was quickly subdued. He looked off-camera and shouted, "Get security!"

The Virtue leader turned so viewers could see his face. He held a sheet of blue paper. "This is a Virtue warrant for your arrest. The charge is homosexuality. You've violated Biblical Law." He motioned to the others. "Take this pervert away."

Speechless, Carol and Captain Charlie watched as the Virtue agents bound the anchor's wrists with a plastic strap and marched him out of the studio.

Captain Charlie put his hand on her shoulder. "You wanted to borrow my car. The keys are in the far left drawer."

She got the keys, ran outside through the rain, opened the garage door and smelled a faint odor of gas and oil. After a few cranks, the old sedan's engine kicked over and, after a few minutes, began to run smoothly. The gas tank was full. She killed the engine, slipped the pistol into the driver's side pocket and then stepped out of the car. There was something large in the corner of the garage covered by a plastic tarp. Curious, she lifted the tarp. An old Harley Davidson Hog. Two helmets hung from the handle bar. The motorcycle had huge old-fashioned leather saddlebags. She ran her fingers over the seat. She had not touched a Hog since high school.

She walked back into the house. Captain Charlie and Billy were in the living room, looking at metals he had been awarded during the war.

"My Dad gave me a medal he won in college. It's a discus thrower. Look." Billy pulled the medal from underneath his shirt by its chain.

"Okay, boys, time to break it up. We have to go now."

"You can stay here," Captain Charlie said.

"They could trace us here. We have to go someplace they can't find."

"Need anything?"

"I can't use my credit chip. Do you have any cash? Or an extra iCom?"

"A little. I'll get it." He returned with a handful of cash. "And here's Doris's credit chip, her ID and her iCom. I haven't closed the accounts."

Carol walked into the kitchen, stood next to the door and watched raindrops splatter the porch stairs.

Charlie wheeled to her and put his arm around her waist and pulled her close. "Be careful, honey."

"I'll call to check in, Charlie."

"The phone might be tapped."

"I'm sure it will."

Captain Charlie said, "If I say Doris died, you'll know not to come back. If I say Doris is fine, that means no one has been here." He tousled Billy's hair. Billy shook his head.

She wrapped her arms around Captain Charlie's neck and held him tight before leading Billy through the rain to the car.

She was close to Interstate 95 when she looked in her rearview mirror at the car behind her. Whoever was driving had kept one car between them. No one knew she and Billy were visiting Captain Charlie. How would Virtue have known she was driving his car? It was old enough that it hadn't been equipped with a locator beacon. Perhaps the men in the Ford were simply going her direction.

The rain slowed and then stopped. She turned off the wipers. The Ford turned onto an off ramp. She watched it disappear, exhaled and rubbed the back of her neck.

Could she remember where Mary Lee's place was in Anacostia? It had been at least three years since the last visit—maybe more. She swung onto the Beltway, catching the beginnings of the rush hour traffic.

Billy asked, "Where are we going, Mom?"

"To a friend's place. Do you remember Mary Lee?"

"No."

"You were a baby. Mary Lee worked with me. She has a son a little older than you. I remember the last time we visited her she held you. You were fussing, and . . ."

"What was I fussing about?" Strapped into the seat belt, Billy stared out the passenger side window.

"I can't remember. You were young. Mary Lee will be surprised how big you are." She turned on Route 50, followed it to Kenilworth Avenue, which led to the ghettos of Anacostia. Turning onto the street where Mary Lee lived was like driving into a war zone. They passed deteriorated buildings and burned-out cars.

People slept on the sidewalks and in alleys, covered with ragged blankets, or newspapers. Men huddled in cardboard box shelters. Others lay propped against walls, grasping bottles of cheap booze. Gangs of men skulked on street corners. They stared at them, white strangers.

Teenagers stood on the curb on the left side of the street. Someone lobbed a bottle at her car. It fell short, shattering on the pavement. She sped up.

Mary Lee had told her that night was the most dangerous time. "No time for a woman, or man, for that matter. Fact is, best stay out of here altogether."

She was glad it wasn't dark. This was bad enough.

In the next block three kids squatted next to a car, stealing its tires. They barely glanced as she drove past. She looked in her rearview mirror. The street was full of burned-out cars, garbage and stragglers.

She spotted the four-story brick building where she thought Mary Lee lived. Did she still live there? Was she home?

She pulled next to the curb in front of the building. Two young toughs walked toward her car. One leaned on the hood. The taller one shucked-n-jived to her window. An outline of a switchblade bulged in his jeans pocket. Jaguar-built, black cornrows adorned with pieces of silver. He pressed his hands on the roof and looked through the window at her, staring with curiosity, as if he had seen her before, but could not place her.

The fingers of her left hand wrapped around the pistol grip. "I'm looking for Mary Lee Brown."

His eyes widened. "Wha' fo?"

"I'm a friend. I need to talk with her."

"How you know this Mary Lee Brown?" He leaned close to the crack in her window. She could smell his breath. A lime scent, like he had been sucking breath mints. She had expected marijuana.

"We used to work together." She looked at the kid in front and decided that she would have to jam the car in reverse to get him off her hood.

"Who you?" A man-boy's voice. Not threatening. Just curious.

"Carol Thatcher." She'd had enough of this bull. She slipped the gear into reverse.

A grin broke his face. "No shit! Mrs. Thatcher! I thought you look familiar. I'm Leon, Mary Lee's son."

"Leon?" Carol studied him closely. The last time she saw him, he had been a shy, scrawny little kid.

"Yeah."

"Leon! You've grown up!" She smiled and relaxed.

"Take you up to see Mom, but she be asleep. She works nights. Still, she'll be pleased to see you." He tried to open her car door. It was locked.

Carol took the pistol with her. She got out and then turned for Billy, who crawled over the seat. He stared at Leon. "Billy, this is Leon."

Leon's grin was genuine. He held up his palm to let Billy slap a high-five.

Billy grinned. "Hey, Leon, do you know why the picture went to jail?"

"No." Leon's face wrinkled into a grin.

"It was framed!" Billy laughed hysterically.

"That's good." Leon turned to the boy who slid off the hood and approached. "Jesse, you watch Mrs. Thatcher's car, hear? Don' let nobody fool with it."

"Yo." The boy opened the car door, reached in and then tossed the keys to Leon. He handed them to Carol.

"Shouldn't never leave keys in your car in this hood."

She pushed the button on her keypad and heard the doors lock.

Leon led them up a crumbling staircase though the smell of garbage, and other things she could not identify. Billy wrinkled his nose and was about to say something. She gave him a warning look. The walls were covered with graffiti. She hadn't remembered the place being this bad.

They stopped on a third-floor landing littered with broken whiskey bottles, fast-food wrappers and a broken chair. Cockroaches scooted under a piece of paper, making it move. Leon paused at the door and turned to them.

"Things ain't so good no more."

What did he mean? Was Mary Lee on drugs, or booze? Depression hit Carol. She could not leave Billy here. They would have to leave. Before she could react, Leon opened the door and ushered them into the apartment. He motioned for them to sit on a worn couch in the combination living room-kitchen, and then he disappeared through a door she assumed to be to Mary Lee's bedroom.

A broken couch spring pinched her left thigh. The vinyl top of the kitchen table curled at the edges, the metal legs brown with rust. A dripping faucet had stripped the enamel off the sink. A piece of cardboard was taped over a broken window. The TV looked old, not like the opto-mirrors now mandated by Virtue. Two armchairs flanking the TV were losing their stuffing. Despite all that, the apartment was as clean as possible.

Leon walked back into the room, looking serious. "She out in a minute. Hey Billy, come talk to me."

They sat at the kitchen table. Leon began drawing graffiti designs on a pad of paper. Billy watched.

The bedroom door opened. Mary Lee shuffled out in a tattered but clean robe. Ringlets swayed as she walked into the room. The ghost of her smile at seeing Carol vanished.

Carol stood up. "Hi."

Mary Lee ignored her. She walked over to Billy at the kitchen table. "I remember you when you were a little boy." She smiled and mussed up his hair.

He stood straight and ran his fingers through his hair.

Mary Lee eyed her. "Where's your Virtue smock?"

"I don't wear a smock."

"Come to convert me?" She sat next to Carol.

"Thatcher's in trouble. I need help."

The bitterness of Mary Lee's laugh surprised her. "You need help?"

"Yes. I need . . ."

"You need! You got nerve to come here and ask for help! Who you think you are? Your kind tossed me back into this shit-hole. Blacklisted me. Your Almighty White God says Planned Parenthood is a sin. Outlaws it. Tosses us on the street. No money. Do you have any idea what I have to do every night?" Mary Lee's eyes moistened.

Carol sat back, stunned by Mary Lee's outburst.

"Well, do you?" Mary Lee hissed.

"No." She wiped her sweating palms against the couch.

"Well, let me tell you. There isn't any work since those people took over. No welfare neither. I'm too old to turn tricks. I stand on a street corner and . . ." Mary Lee looked at Billy and Leon.

Carol put her arms around the woman's shoulders to console her. Mary Lee's body relaxed into her. They both cried.

"I'm sorry, Carol. Lord knows you tried to help. One year you sent me all that money."

"But the next year you sent back my checks. Why?"

"Pride. Stupid pride. I had hope then. I felt terrible every time I cashed one of your checks. I didn't want your gifts after that first year, even though we needed it."

"Why didn't you call me? I would have helped."

"Hell, woman, what could you have done? Your husband is one of the higher-ups. You're one of them. And all I've got left is my stupid pride. But you can't eat pride," Mary Lee said with a bitter laugh. Her voice lowered to a whisper. "My biggest worry is Leon."

"I'm sorry." Carol didn't know what else to say.

"You aren't here to hear about my troubles. You've got your own."

"Did you see the TV announcement about Thatcher?

"No, I didn't hear anything."

"Doesn't your TV set come on automatically for Virtue announcements?"

"Not unless we turn it on. Rumor is we only get certain channels, different programs than you folks."

"Virtue arrested Thatcher for theft. It's a lie. They're holding him. He's a prisoner. I have to figure out how get him out, but I can't do that without putting Billy in danger." She decided not to tell her about the kidnap attempt.

Mary Lee looked at the boy sitting with Leon. "So you want to hide him with me?"

"This is the only place they can't find him."

Mary Lee looked at Billy. "He was a sweet one when he was a baby."

"He still is. I'd die if anything happened to him."

"I feel the same way about Leon. He's a sweet boy, too. Sometimes he acts like a man, but mostly he's my sweet Leon. I know how you feel."

"Will you keep Billy while I try to get Thatcher out?"

Mary Lee stiffened and looked at Carol for a long moment, "I have to work after dark. He'd be alone with Leon. I think Leon goes out after I leave."

She reached into her pocket and handed Mary Lee the wad of cash.

Shaking her head, Mary Lee looked at the bills in her hand and counted them. "Good Lord! There's over five thousand here."

"You won't have to work while Billy's here."

Mary Lee stuffed the cash in her robe pocket. "What if something happens to you?"

She gave Mary Lee Captain Charlie's phone number and then she walked over to Billy. "You have to stay here while I try to help your father."

"I want to go with you."

"The best way you can help get Dad back is by staying with Mary Lee and Leon. I'll be back as soon as I can."

"I . . . I want to go with you."

"I can't get your father if you come with me. You want to see him again, don't you?"

Tears ran down his cheeks. "I guess . . . yes."

"Mind Mary Lee while I'm gone. I love you." She hugged him and walked out, trying not to cry.

On the street, she gave Jessie fifty dollars for watching the car. She got in, locked the doors and started the engine. She was eager to get someplace safe. She would drive back to Captain Charlie's after she called to make certain it was safe and then spend the night. She needed help. She could trust Bob Roberts at Moral America. Who else? That Moroccan diplomat, Jamila, who had given her a phone number in case she needed help. She would exchange Charlie's car for his motorcycle. A motorcycle was more maneuverable than a car. A leather jacket would hide the pistol and a helmet would hide her face.

CHAPTER 30

Virtue Dungeon

Thatcher

HE HUNG STRAPPED TO THE chains in Virtue's interrogation chamber, spread-eagled and naked. Fear exploded into hatred when Deverence, wearing nothing but black briefs, walked into the room. A neo-cross and a small leather sack hung from gold chains around his neck. He knelt beneath the large neo-cross and mumbled a short prayer. He approached Thatcher and stood so close that he could smell the man's sweet aftershave. Deverence looked up at him with honest and kind blue eyes. Lying eyes.

Deverence walked a slow circle around Thatcher, examining his body, touching him lightly. "You and I have something in common. We both served our country, fighting terrorists. I respect you for that, but I don't see any marks of wounds."

"I wasn't wounded."

"You were lucky, because someone tried to kill you. And that someone works for Virtue. Mack Bradley still wants to kill you. Doesn't he?"

"Let's get on with this."

"Don't be impatient. We are embarking on a delicate process," Deverence said.

"I'm not going anywhere."

Smiling, Deverence moved closer, standing inches away, examining his face in a sensual way that made him feel uncomfortable. The man's body heat felt obscene. "I will be your confessor. You will tell me your secrets, but you need to know about me as well, because the role of confessor is intimate and requires mutual trust."

Deverence held his hands close to Thatcher's face, turning them, staring at his finger stumps. "First, I will confess to you and then you will confess to me. I'll tell you how I was wounded. My missing fingers are the only outward evidence that I was captured during a botched raid of a terrorist head-quarters in the mountains of rural Pakistan.

"I was tortured nearly to death. My confessor sawed both my index fingers off, so I could never pull another trigger. I was delusional and starving in a filthy dungeon. The bastard gave me my bloody fingers to eat. I refused to eat my own flesh.

"Instead, I used my severed fingers as bait to catch rats. To keep from starving to death, I ate them raw, guts and all.

"I was lucky. A drone missile strike destroyed the compound and killed my captors. I escaped and was discovered by a missionary. I was spirited through an underground Christian network back to America.

"After I retired from the Navy, I moved to Colorado Springs because of its large retired military and evangelical communities. I sought out Reverend John, who was known as an aggressive Christian advocate. I became born-again and vowed to devote my life to Jehovah, and to help Reverend John create a Christian World.

"I saved my finger bones. They are in this little sack." He shook the leather sack close to Thatcher's face, rattling the bones. "These bones are a reminder of heathen brutality . . . and I still have them. They make me whole."

Deverence walked across the room to a metal desk. He opened a drawer and took out the probe. Walking back, he said, "There are more efficient methods of extracting confessions, like chemicals and high frequency sounds, but I find this old fashioned way is much more personal. He gently played the probe's head across Thatcher's skin, touching places that made Thatcher shrink with fear. The anticipation of a shock was unbearable. Anticipating where he might be shocked was agonizing.

"We'll start with the smallest charge."

He swore he would not give the bastard the pleasure to hear him scream.

Deverence gently placed the probe between his legs.

He watched in horror as the man's thumb pressed the trigger.

He screamed.

It was a day, or two days, or three days later—he couldn't tell—maybe the third session, when Deverence used the maximum charge. Thatcher's bodily spasms rattled the chains.

"I confess! Oh God. Please. I confess." He wept.

"Good, Thatcher. Good! Tell me your confession."

"I committed treason when I revealed the plans for a meeting between a tribal leader and the CIA. As a result, hundreds of children were maimed and killed." He would not have had to confess if God had ever listened.

Deverence blinked and stepped back.

Thatcher told him everything.

Deverence walked out of the room, leaving him hanging. It seemed to be an eternity later before the man returned.

"Your so-called confession was interesting, Thatcher. I talked with Reverend John. We decided your treason is not covered by the Biblical Laws, so we cannot accept your confession. You must confess to theft. You do remember stealing the money don't you? You saw it when you were visiting Reverend John. When Tim Oliver pulled up your bank account on his computer? Confess to stealing the money."

"Go to hell!" Thatcher said.

Deverence touched the head of his penis with the electric probe.

Thatcher's agonizing screams echoed from the room's concrete walls.

Several hours after he had confessed, Thatcher stood naked and humiliated in a small courtroom. He looked at the floor with unfocused eyes to avoid looking at the three Supreme Moral Court judges staring down at him from behind their bench. He covered his privates. Deverence touched him with the probe and ordered him to stand at attention. His body refused to straighten without pain. He barely heard the words of the judges. He agreed to the charge of theft, a violation of Biblical Law. A judge ordered him to look at him when he said, "You have confessed to theft, violating the Commandment as recorded in Exodus 20:15: 'You shall not steal.' This court condemns you to the punishment prescribed in the Bible. That concludes these proceedings."

The judges stood. The one on the right, the one whose huge bald head rose from his scarlet robe, seemed familiar. Wire rimmed glasses, thin lips pressed together, dark judging eyes appraising him.

Thatcher gasped, "Frank!"

The other two judges stopped and turned to look at their colleague. The man stood silent.

Thatcher ripped out of Deverence's grip and stumbled forward, "Frank, for the love of god, you're my brother-in-law!"

Frank straightened to his full height and said, "I warned you, Thatcher. Deuteronomy 22:7, 'If a man be found stealing . . . then that thief shall die.' "

CHAPTER 31

Nassau, Bahamas

Felix

FELIX LOUNGED IN A RECLINER on the sea-view terrace of her suite at Sandals Royal Bahamian. She wore a bikini bottom, a wonderful change from oppressive niqubs and burkas. A gentle breeze carried a stronger bouquet than the Moroccan Mediterranean. This sea breeze, mixed with the fragrance of gardenias from the garden below, triggered sensations long buried. Her fingertips brushed suntan oil over her skin. She surrendered to its sensual pressure, arching her back, offering her body to the sun. The rays caressed her like soft fingers of a lover. An imagined lover, she corrected herself. Other than those days in Qatar with Thatcher, she had never known a lover. She would never let another man touch her, but she enjoyed imagining a faceless man caressing her with long gentle strokes. That blank face morphed into Thatcher's face, the touch his. He was the only man who knew her secret, her relationship with her father and Sara's situation. Thatcher was the most appealing man she knew. She trusted him. He claimed he had not told his wife about their affair in Qatar. She wondered. In any event, no matter how much she was attracted to him, she would never allow anything to happen between them. Besides, she rather liked his wife.

She watched the hotel's ferry transport guests a half-mile across the shimmering blue water to an offshore island, with its beaches, pools and restaurant. The lagoon between the hotel and island was deceptively clear. Even though the multi-colored bottom varied between twenty and forty feet deep, the guest boat looked like it would run aground at any moment.

It had been too risky to smuggle the weapons into the U.S., so she landed in Nassau, just ninety miles from the East Coast, perfect for a handoff. She bribed the Customs inspector to look the other way when she unloaded her 'luggage'. Now the bomb and HERF gun lay under a tarp on a twenty-foot-long fishing boat she had rented. The boat was anchored three hundred yards offshore the island's jetty, its engine disabled. It could not be moved without towing.

A pair of Leica ten-power binoculars lay on a table next to her derringer and the bomb's trigger. She picked the glasses up and focused on the boat floating so still it looked like the subject of a still life painting. She glanced at the clock on her iCom. Virtue's men should arrive soon. The plan was for them to rent a boat, motor to her boat, board, and inspect the weapons, to which she had locked an explosive device. Satisfied with their inspection, they were to authorize a wire transfer of twenty million to a Swiss bank. After she had been notified the money had arrived in her account, she would send an electronic signal from her iCom, disarming the explosive device on the weapons so they could be safely transferred or towed. If they attempted to move her boat or transfer the weapons before the money had cleared, the men and boat would be destroyed.

A man and woman walked hand-in-hand along the beach. They laughed, touching with an intimacy that made her sad.

The couple chased each other into the water. They wrapped their arms around each other and kissed. She moaned. She closed her eyes and shook her head trying to shake off thoughts that seized her mind like the claws of a predator.

Her hand hovered over the derringer. Her fingers touched its cold steel. Picking it up, putting the muzzle to her temple and pulling the trigger would be so simple. Her end would be quick, painless. She could end it now. But there was Sara.

A speedboat, powered by two outboard engines, sped around the island and approached her boat. She focused the binoculars on the four men in the speedboat. Two men boarded her boat. The man who pulled up the tarp stepped back as if he had uncovered a cobra. He must have seen the digital readout and explosive she had locked to the weapons. The other man stepped forward and inspected the HERF gun, opening the lid and powering it up. Apparently satisfied, he turned his attention to the nuclear device. He ran his hand across the bomb's smooth surface, and found the false trigger she had made in Morocco.

He picked up the bogus trigger and turned the gear-shaped top. He put on a pair of reading glasses and looked at the digital readout showing the date—September 14. He nodded and said something to his companions.

She exhaled.

Their boat driver pulled a phone from his pocket. She could see his lips moving. It shouldn't take long now.

Ten minutes later, her iCom rang.

"Yes?"

"Twenty-million U.S. dollars have been transferred into your account," the Swiss banker said.

"Thank you."

"Is there anything else I can do for you?"

"I want to transfer all the money from that account into another account."

"By phone authorization?"

"Yes."

"I'll need a code word to be used during our phone authorization."

"The word is Thatcher. Spelled out: T-H-A-T-C-H-E-R." She hung up. The money now lay in a personal account, one her father could not touch.

She made another call and watched through her binoculars. The men on her boat jumped when the phone rang. She punched in a series of numbers to disable the explosive device on the weapons. The men looked at the digital readout, gone dead. They detached the anchor and tied lines from their boat to hers and then began to tow it, and the weapons, back to wherever they had come from.

She picked up the real trigger, rolled it in her fingers and looked at the digital readout, "6p.m. Sept 14". The trigger had been locked. The date and time could not be changed. She was pleased with her deception. She would not have the deaths of tens of thousands of innocent Americans on her conscience. It might be splitting hairs, but running high-tech weapons and software was one thing; killing innocents another. Still, there was the issue of trading the real trigger for more money, if she couldn't figure out another way to save Sara. A lose-lose situation.

She rose and walked into her suite to soak under a hot shower. She had to work up courage to call her father and set up the money trade-off for Sara. He would try to double cross her. He wanted everything.

Later, she made the call.

"Did you get the money?" Greed tinged his voice.

"Yes."

"Twenty?"

"Safe in my bank account."

"Transfer it to me now. Get another twenty from Virtue for the real trigger."

"I made a mistake today," she lied. "Virtue agents almost caught me during the handoff. They would have killed me. I'm lucky to be alive. I've never made a mistake before. I'm scared. Losing my nerve. I can't go on."

"You must! You'll be fine. I have faith in you, Princess."

On the lagoon, a jet ski carved the crystalline water. A puff of breeze brought the sticky sweet smell of gardenias. Her stomach heaved. She fought to control her voice.

"I contacted a man to help with the trigger handoff. Five million."

"Are you out of your mind?"

"It's high risk."

"Find someone else," he said.

"No, it's impossible. Let's forget about it. We have enough."

"No! We have to get the last twenty. You'll figure something out." "First transfer me the money from the Swiss account. Then go to Washington, sell Virtue the real trigger and bring me the additional twenty."

She sobbed. "I can't do it without your help."

"Enough of your self pity!"

"Yes, it is enough. I've had enough. Enough!" she screamed. "I can't stand it. I'm going to end it now."

"What?"

"I . . ." She moaned and sobbed and then blew her nose. "I can't save Sara from you. You'll never get the money. I'm going to kill myself!"

"No! Wait!"

"What?"

"Give me the Swiss bank account number!"

She screamed, hung up and dropped the iCom on the floor as if it were poisonous. She used the wall to steady herself as she stumbled onto the balcony. She looked at the derringer on the table. Picking it up, she walked to the railing, stared six floors down at the gardenia bushes and then looked at the ocean. Tears streamed down her cheeks. She cocked the pistol's hammer. As she raised the gun, her iCom rang. It rang and rang. She listened to its ascending trill and she smiled. She'd set the hook. Now let him dangle.

CHAPTER 32

Public Punishments Day
Eleven a.m., New York City

Virtue Agent

A VIRTUE MAN, IN PLAIN clothes, wheeled the suitcase-disguised HERF gun down a busy sidewalk, oblivious to the rumble of traffic. He stopped at a nondescript building housing the Internet Network Providers and Metropolitan Area Exchange serving the northeast United States. He unzipped the suitcase cover and slipped in his hand, pretending to look for something. He pushed the power button switch.

Other than hearing a faint hissing, nothing happened. Then he noticed the quiet. There was no traffic noise. People pointed at the street where cars had stopped like crazy pick-up-sticks. The computer chips controlling their engines had been fried by the HERF gun's electromagnetic blast. Several minutes later, he took out his iCom and tried to open the browser. It would not work. The gun worked! The blast destroyed all the servers inside the building. He'd already destroyed the backup servers in New Jersey. Virtue could now control the functions of the Internet, sending only Virtue-approved content. Reverend John would not have to worry about negative social media reaction to this afternoon's Public Punishments.

His car was parked blocks away, out of the HERF gun's range. He would drop off and recharge the weapon at the

Save-a-Child orphanage. He smiled. He'd just killed the Internet. New technology was amazing, but not as satisfying as using a gun or knife.

Twelve Noon, Virtue Headquarters
Reverend John

Wrapped in a red silk robe, Reverend John sat behind his desk reviewing the Public Punishments schedule. Everything was ready. The HERF gun had killed the Internet and Virtue engineers applied their 'work-around' so every channel would show The Punishments broadcast. Constant TV announcements about The Punishments had worked the public's curiosity into a feverish pitch. Newscasters, preachers and TV evangelists had followed Virtue's script. The public was guessing who would be punished, what the punishments would be, how they would be carried out. Censored newspaper editorials added to the hype. Many wondered if the golden stanchions on Constitution and Independence Avenues were to play a part in The Punishments.

The International Video Game Championships, which now had higher viewership than the Super Bowl, had been sold out for months. Halftime had been extended to accommodate The Punishments. During the past three days TV crews had set up for the most elaborate coverage of any event in history. Virtue had denied media requests for the layouts, timetable or schedules for The Punishments. Reverend John's program director, working as the Department of Virtue's censor, would select what would be shown to the worldwide TV audience.

Posing as fans, Virtue employees had been seeded throughout the stadium. One group dominated a large block of seats. TV cameras would focus on them for audience shots, so the viewing public would see only their reactions. Other Virtue plants were scattered throughout to lead cheering and put down negative reactions from other spectators, by force if necessary. Others were assigned the duty to whip up audience participation in The Punishments.

Reverend John turned to the wall of opto-screens showing different camera shots of the stadium, locker rooms, interviews with video game champions, and TV broadcasters speculating about the halftime show. He walked to his neo-cross, knelt and then prayed for God to fill the hearts of those who watch today's punishments with His spirit and make them agree that His Laws must be obeyed.

Reverend John felt relaxed. He had listened to the Voice and followed His instructions. He had made certain all was ready, including the pre-recorded videos of him leading The Punishments. There was nothing more to do. Now all he could do was watch The Punishments unfold. He ordered popcorn and Diet Coke to be brought to his office. He hung up his robe, kicked off his shoes and settled back on the couch to watch the performance.

Thirteen o'clock—Stadium
Thatcher

Clean-shaven and in a dark blue suit, hands bound behind his back, Thatcher sat with four other convicts on a bench deep in the stadium. They were forbidden to talk. He knew news anchor Steve Brooks, Secretary of the Interior Michael Zeller and Senator Alan Long. He recognized the woman wearing bright red lipstick, high heels and a fashionable dress—Karen Huntington.

He heard the screams of the fans, a sound that rose to a bellow that shook the walls. He heard drumming. Last year's International Video Game Championships had begun with an elaborate drumming ceremony.

Virtue agents guarded them. Mack Bradley, leaning against the wall, glared at him, made his fist into a pistol, and "shot" him. Bradley grinned.

Deverence stood before the prisoners. He slapped the electric prod against the palm of his left hand for attention.

"Today you have the unique privilege of being the stars of the first of the Department of Virtue's public punishments.

"Your performance will be viewed by the largest TV audience in history. The Punishments will be broadcast to every country in the world, reminding everyone, Christians and non-Christians alike, of the swift and just retribution meted out by the Department of Virtue for breaking Biblical Laws.

"Each of you has been convicted of crimes against God.

"The Department of Virtue is not responsible for your punishment. It was your own refusal to obey the Word of our Lord. You broke Biblical Law. You have done this to yourselves. We are not responsible. You alone are responsible."

The woman prisoner's head slumped. She moaned. Deverence placed his prod under her chin and raised it until she looked him in the eyes. "Not so enjoyable now, is it, adulteress?"

Her body trembled. Deverence turned his attention back to the rest of the prisoners. "I will now lead you in prayer." He had to shock Steve Brooks before the man would bow his head. The sound of the spectators grew from a constant hum to a growl. The room vibrated with the roar of the fans.

Fourteen-thirty—Virtue Headquarters
Reverend John

Listening to Wagner's *Meistersinger* overture playing from the stadium's loudspeakers, Reverend John scanned the eight screens on his office wall. He concentrated on the screen showing the relatives of the condemned. Ralph Huntington sat between two Virtue men. He tried to lift his hand to wipe wet eyes, but it was handcuffed to an agent's wrist.

The camera focused on Carol Thatcher. Like Huntington and the other relatives, she sat on the front row. Next to her was old Caleb from Moral America. On the other side, an exotic looking woman had her arm around Mrs. Thatcher's shoulder, probably some neighborhood friend. The other six or seven men surrounding them were obviously Moral America security men. Mrs. Thatcher's face looked tired and haggard.

He watched the other opto-screens. The crowd fell silent. Two robot crawler-installers crept across the field, aligning themselves in a straight line in the center of the field. The robot's arms positioned two giant domes in place. The domes looked like transparent igloos, a glass circle with an entrance tunnel pointing to the home team's side of the field.

Another crawler deposited a steel cage bolted to a waist-high metal platform to the right of the two domes. A self-propelled aerial lift positioned itself to the left of the domes. The two robots returned to the far end of the field where they lowered themselves like compliant dogs to wait for the next command.

A hollow feeling of loneliness swept over Reverend John. He had to share this moment of triumph with the one person who had helped make it possible. He called Tim Oliver and ordered him to his office. A moment later, the door opened and the man walked in. Tim's hair was combed, face shaven. He wore a clean white shirt, sport coat, slacks and polished shoes.

"Sit in that chair."

Ignoring him, Oliver sat next to him on the couch.

"I told you to sit in that chair. You disobeyed my direct order."

"It won't be the last." He put his feet on the coffee table.

"Get your feet off my table!"

"I want to watch my work."

"You know where you're going if it's not successful." Reverend John studied the alignment of the domes. He had been right to eliminate the third dome for the sake of perfection. Long and Zeller would be exclamation marks on either side of the punishment domes. The Punishments' finale, the execution of Thatcher, would take place at the fifty-yard line. Kneeling, Thatcher would straddle the out-of-bounds line, just a yard or two from his wife sitting in the front row.

The audience pointed to two scarlet-shirted Virtue men pushing wheelbarrows of fist-sized rocks toward each dome. The men guided their load inside each tunnel to where it met the circumference of the dome. They dumped the stones on the field immediately to the right of the junction.

Five golf carts, backs modified into stretchers, drove single file into the stadium. Each contained a driver, convict and guard. The first dropped off Senator Long. His guard marched him to the aerial lift stand, hands bound, to stand under its raised skeletal arm. They dropped Karen Huntington and Steve Brooks at the two domes, and then Interior Secretary Michael Zeller at the cage.

Karen's guard led her through the tunnel to the center of the first dome and removed her handcuffs. He walked back to block the tunnel entrance. She stood alone, beautifully dressed, hair and makeup perfect. She turned slowly, uncertain, tripping once when a high heel caught on the Astro-turf. She looked at small robotic cameras watching from the ceiling before staring at the stadium's attentive audience. She spotted Ralph in the front row. She screamed and ran down the tunnel toward him. The Virtue guard blocking the entrance walked slowly toward her, menacing her back into the dome. She ran to the closest spot to Ralph, shouting, pounding the Plexiglas with her fists, gesturing to him. He raised his shackled hands.

Reverend John watched the third cart drop Steve Brooks at the second dome, while the fourth cart deposited Secretary Zeller at the cage. Locked inside, Zeller grasped the steel bars and stared at the crowd.

The last cart drove stopped at the fifty-yard line in front of Carol. Mack Bradley pushed Thatcher, hands bound behind his back, to the player's bench. She screamed something at him and rose to get to him. Caleb and the woman restrained her. Thatcher turned toward her and shouted something. Bradley twisted Thatcher's arms and shoved him forward off the bench onto his knees.

Reverend John noted Mack Bradley's enjoyment. He decided Virtue would make an example of Bradley at the next Punishments as a hypocritical homosexual.

The music faded and a deep male voice-over announced:

"The half-time public punishments are brought to you by the Department of Virtue!"

"And my genius!" Oliver pumped his fist.

"Shut up!"

Oliver grabbed a handful of popcorn and burrowed deep into the couch pillows.

The camera zoomed to the gigantic screen built above the end zone.

"Here is the Director of the Department of Virtue, Reverend John!"

When his red-robed image appeared on the oversized screen, exotic shivers flowed through his body. The monitors pictured a silent, expectant crowd. The propaganda screen that his censors broadcast to the world pictured an applauding Virtue section. Sound engineers cranked up pre-recorded sounds of wild cheering.

"The Department of Virtue, upon the direction of God, will lead our nation, the United States—New Jerusalem—into the arms of our Lord. These Public Punishments are the first step to prepare for the Rapture and Second Coming. We hereby declare open the first Public Punishments!"

The sound of his voice, computer-altered into a rich tone, made him tremble with delight.

"Like that, Reverend John? That's not your voice. I created a computerized voice just like yours. Can't tell the difference, can you?"

"What?"

The sound engineer at the stadium dialed up sounds of cheering, while the main camera crew shot the Virtue block of seats, that audience now giving a standing ovation.

"You're not watching an image of you. It's an image of an avatar of you that I created."

"Shut up and let me enjoy this!"

His character on the screen said, "The Bible tells us, in First Corinthians, Chapter Six, Verse Nine, 'Do you not know that the wicked will not inherit the kingdom of God? Do not be deceived; neither the sexually immoral nor idolaters, nor adulterers nor male prostitutes, nor homosexual offenders will inherit the kingdom of God.'

"We must purge our nation of these wicked evildoers before the Lord, in His infinite wisdom, will return to take Christians into His arms. It is prophesied in the Book of Revelations that those who do not embrace Jesus Christ as their Savior will be thrown into the lake of fire and brimstone when he returns.

"He is coming soon!

"God tells us in Exodus, Chapter Twenty, Verses Three and Four, 'Thou shalt not make for yourself an idol, and Thou shalt have no other god before me.' Many in our nation have worshipped the false idol of technology in place of the one true God!

"Just this morning, we witnessed the hand of God as He began the destruction of the temples of technology! He shut down the Internet to show us His power over the temporal.

"Tomorrow, God will demonstrate His ultimate power, with a force of fire and brimstone in New York.

"God will continue to wreak havoc on those of you who continue to resist declaring for Christ. You will feel God's wrath!

"God is telling us that we are in the final battle against Satan. We are at the beginning of the Battle of Armageddon. It is not too late to convert! Convert today, after The Punishments. Run, don't walk, run to your churches and give your life to the Lord! You have but a day or two to be saved. And then it will be too late.

"Let me warn those of you who ignore these words. God has personally spoken to me. He said, 'It is time! The Rapture is upon us. Christ will win his battle against Satan.' Christ will win! CHRIST Will Win! CHRIST WILL WIN!"

Virtue employees in the crowd picked up the chant. "CHRIST WILL WIN!" The sound swelled, joined by the rest of the audience, now on their feet. The chorus grew hypnotic.

He hadn't planned on an emotional outburst from the mob this early in the performance. The TV censor froze Reverend John's picture until the crowd exhausted the chant. When the voices quieted, the censor again began playing his image.

"Today, in this stadium, those who have sinned against Biblical Laws shall be punished. The Commandments warn us against adultery, against false idols, against theft, against murder, against homosexuality, and other acts.

Each of you will have the opportunity to participate, either by using the box at each seat to vote on each punishment, or to contribute by your physical involvement. You shall be the hand of God Himself!

"Today, you can punish those who broke Biblical Laws!

"Today, by your actions, we will declare the glory of God!

"Today you can smite a blow against Satan!"

Reverend John heard the swelling of voices. He scanned the monitors picturing the crowd. A majority of the spectators were stomping their feet, shouting and cheering, overwhelming the computer-generated crowd-voices his production manager broadcast to the world. The main camera cut to a picture of applauding fans and then shifted back to Reverend John's image on the end-zone screen. He looked resplendent in his red robe that flowed outward as he raised his arms. The crowd hushed.

"Today's first punishment is of a sinner who defiled the Commandment 'You shall not murder.'"

CHAPTER 33

Virtue Headquarters

Reverend John

IGNORING TIM OLIVER, REVEREND JOHN scooted to the edge of the couch, concentrating on The Punishments. His image filled the opto-screen and his computer-enhanced voice filled the stadium.

"The Bible commands us, 'You shall not murder!' Senator Alan Long killed his loving wife Martha. Watch the evidence. Watch his confession before the Supreme Moral Court."

The screen filled with graphic images of Senator Long plunging a knife again and again into his wife. Her screams filled the stadium. Spurting blood images filled the screen. Her eyes rolled back. The Senator, in front of the Supreme Moral Court, the justices' faces hidden, confessing he murdered his wife.

Tim Oliver slapped Reverend John on the shoulder. "It's a masterpiece of deception. Tell me I created a masterpiece."

"Shut up and let me watch in peace," Reverend John said.

The video-Reverend John said, "Now use the box on the seatback in front of you. Push 'Yes' or 'No' to punish the senator."

A split screen in Reverend John's office displayed the votes, tallied in real time, real votes on the left, and computer algorithm fake votes on the right. The split between men and women voters were displayed below.

"Look! Women are outvoting the men to punish the Senator," Reverend John said.

"And we don't need to use the computer generated votes. It's a real majority," Oliver added.

Reverend John's image appeared in the stadium. "Punish Senator Long for murder!"

A Virtue agent grabbed a rope hanging from the Ariel lift's arm and knotted the end around the Senator's neck, using a no-slip knot. He took off the Senator's handcuffs. Senator Long ran in circles, furiously trying to loosen the noose. The Virtue man ran to the lift's control and pushed a lever. The arm inched upward. The Virtue portion of the fans cheered. Pulled to tiptoes, his hands clawed at the rope. The arm inched him off the ground, legs kicking. His hands fell away from the noose, arms and legs jerking like a spastic puppet. His face turned blue, tongue out, eyes bulged. His body arced, stiffened and then collapsed into death. The stadium filled with cheers.

Reverend John's image again filled the screen. "Next we have a sinner who defiled the Commandment, 'Thou shalt not commit adultery'! Listen and watch the evidence. And then vote!"

Karen Huntington stood in the center of her dome, pulling her hair, watching the end zone screen. The screen went dark. The audience fell silent. Then they heard a sound. Words soft and indistinct at first, building in volume, repeating itself.

"Fuck me! Oh my God, fuck me now!"

The screen filled with an image of Karen in the hotel suite, naked, in bed with men, begging for more, close ups of penetration.

The crowd silence, broken at first by a few boos, finally broke into a rhythmic chant started by the Virtue section of fans. "Stone her. Stone her!"

Karen stood in the center of her dome paralyzed by fear. She shook her head and then ran to the edge facing Ralph, who fought with the security men holding his handcuffed arms. She clawed at the glass, pleading for help.

Even before the scene ended, the vote was to kill her.

Finally, the end-zone screen faded back to Reverend John's image.

"Moses tells us in the Book that God's punishment for adultery is death by stoning. Leviticus, Chapter Twenty, Verse Ten says, '. . . and the adulteress shall surely be put to death.' Who amongst you will today act as God's hand? Go forward to punish the adulteress!"

The cameras switched to men jostling each other, rushing to the aisles, forming a mob running onto the field, hoping to be selected. Fistfights broke out as men tried to push their way to the front of the line. Ten were selected. The rest of the rabble was herded back into the stands.

The chosen men were ushered into the tunnel of her dome. Karen shrank against the glass, fingers scratching its surface. Knowing their victim could not escape, the men were in no hurry as they walked into the tunnel. They selected hurling stones, feeling their weight and shape. And then they turned on her.

She screamed. Her attackers hurled stone after stone. She ran back and forth trying to dodge the stones. There was no escape. Turning her back to her attackers, she pressed hard against the glass, as if she could transport her body through to safety. Stones pummeled her and ricocheted off the panels. Holding her palms high on the glass, her forehead pressed hard against it, she looked at Ralph. Her lips pleaded for help. Slowly, inch-by-inch, her body slid down the bloody glass panel, streaking a line of lipstick. The tips of her fingers left transparent tracks through blood covered glass.

The roaring mob overwhelmed the voice-over tape as the program censor switched his audio control to the actual sound of the crowd. Looking at the other monitors, Reverend John watched the faces of the throng. Expressions of ecstasy, pain, excitement, fear, and pious joy revealed the one thing he had counted on.

"I was right! The crowd loved watching the orgy, loved taking retribution on the adulteress, loved the killing."

The screens once again projected Reverend John's image.

"Do not be deceived: homosexuality is an abomination against God! Homosexuals will never enter the kingdom of God!"

The TV anchor Steve Brooks, a robust and masculine-looking man, stood in the middle of his dome. He watched the stadium screen reveal the fake video of him committing sodomy and then his confession before the Supreme Moral Court.

The vote was ninety-eight percent for punishment.

The camera shifted to Brooks standing in the center of his dome, unfettered by handcuffs or shackles. He ran to the edge of the tunnel and feverishly pitched stones to the opposite side of the dome. Hundreds of men flooded the field. Virtue coordinators selected ten. Unsuccessful and unhappy volunteers were herded to the sidelines so that the fans and TV audience could have a clear view of the stoning.

As Virtue coordinators lined up the volunteers outside the tunnel entrance, Brooks stood defiant in the center of the dome and then ripped off his clothes to display an athletic body.

The crowd cheered.

Reverend John said, "The damned fools can't be cheering for that homo."

Brooks stood naked, holding a rock in each fist, edging closer to the tunnel, waiting for his assailants.

The volunteers rushed the entrance of the glass cage. Only one could get through the tunnel at a time. Brooks threw a fist-sized stone at the first man entering the cage. The rock hit the man on the bridge of his nose, felling him, blocking the entrance. The other enraged assailants spilled through the narrow door into the cage one at a time, falling over their companion and each other in their haste. Brooks methodically stoned each one, crumpling them into a pile of bodies.

The crowd roared.

"I can't believe this," Reverend John said.

"If he kills them all, will you let him go free?" Oliver asked.

"Are you out of your mind?"

Brooks' punishment became a pitched battle. One assailant, holding a broken arm, cowered next to the glass, pleading to get out. Four others lay dead or unconscious near the door.

Rocks flew back and forth. One hit Brooks in the left knee, knocking him down. The remaining five men closed like a pack of jackals. Advancing, they threw stones until they stood over the Brook's inert body. They gave high five's and then they began a macabre dance around his corpse. One attacker gestured to the crowd for more and more applause. They pranced around the body like victorious gladiators.

One man pulled out a knife, held it over his head, showing it to the crowd. He kneeled over the body. The other assailants crowded close, watching.

Reverend John used a lapel mike, "I want a close-up!"

The man jumped to his feet, knife in his right hand, something in his left. A Virtue camera zoomed in for a close-up to broadcast on the stadium screen and around the world. The man held high Steve Brooks' bloody penis and testicles.

The stadium crowd cheered and stomped.

Reverend John clapped. "Yes! Better than I'd planned. Who would have thought that homo would have had the courage to be defiant? Satan is strong, but we defeated him." He watched as his program censor cut to a picture of cheering fans and then shifted back to his image on the end-zone screen.

Reverend John watched the screen as the crowd hushed to hear his next pronouncement.

"The Good Book tells us 'Thou shalt worship no God before me!' Virtue has discovered Commandment-breakers in the highest offices of our Nation. The Secretary of Interior, Michael Zeller, is a pagan! He worships false idols! Here is evidence showing him worshiping pagan gods."

The image of a wooden alter in a natural setting surrounded by trees appeared on the screen. There were burning candles, a silver chalice of water, bowls of earth and charcoal and a silver Pentacle, a five pointed star enclosed by a circle, an amulet for magical evocation and symbol of Witchcraft. There was a wand and pictures of an exotic male god and a female goddess.

Zeller, wearing a black cape, walked into the picture, and poured white powder to form a circle around the wooden alter. He stood inside, knelt and then raised his hands. He chanted, "Elements of the Spirits bring your presence into my circle." He picked up the wand and pointed it to the sky. "The circle is cast and we are between worlds, beyond the bounds of time, when night and day, birth and death, joy and sorrow meet as one." He brought the wand down to clasp it between his hands as if in Christian prayer. "I pray you will give me your power."

The camera zoomed in tight on Zeller. His face elongated beast-like, shocking the stadium audience into silence. And then his eyes changed from brown to fiery red. The audience gasped at the face of the devil. One by one, spectators began booing and jeering until the stadium shook with the roaring of the mob. The vote was unanimous.

Without taking his eyes from the screen, Reverend John said, "That was excellent! The eyes and face created just what I wanted."

"A creation you couldn't have had without me," Oliver said.

Reverend John waved him off and watched Secretary Zeller holding the bars of his cage, shaking his head, shouting something. He began hopping from foot to foot as flames crept up from the platform beneath the cage. He grabbed the top bars and pulled his feet up. The flames continued to rise. He raised his legs and jammed his feet against the sidebars. Flames rose higher. A camera focused on his face, contorted by screams. His clothes caught fire and burned off, falling piece by piece. The fat of his legs and butt caught on fire. He could no longer escape. His feet slipped off the bars, his smoking legs fell and, screaming in agony, he dropped. The flames exploded through the top of the cage. Several minutes later, the flames died. All that remained at the bottom of the cage was a blackened smoking body.

The crowd had gone quiet. The camera focused on the Virtue fan block. Even their cheers were subdued and looked contrived.

Oliver held his hand over his mouth.

Reverend John muttered, "We'll eliminate burning for the next punishments."

Reverend John scanned the monitors until he found Carol Thatcher, face shocked with grief and disbelief. She turned to the exotic looking woman next to her and whispered something with great emotional intensity.

Reverend John used his microphone again, "I want the woman sitting with Mrs. Thatcher identified!"

The cameraman zoomed in on the woman's face and then opened his field of focus to take in Senator Thatcher sitting on the bench next to his executioner, Mack Bradley. Thatcher's face was stone, showing no emotion. Bradley's lips were curled into a vicious smile and his eyes danced, taking in the scene with childlike excitement.

A screen on Reverend John's left filled with the woman's passport picture, identifying her as Jamila Meer, a diplomat from the Moroccan Embassy. He looked at the screen. "That's odd. Why would a Moroccan diplomat be sitting there? Doesn't make sense. I'll look into that later."

Physically supported by the woman, Caleb and Bob Roberts, Carol sat on the midfield sideline just feet from where Thatcher, with Bradley holding his handcuffed arm, now stood on the Astro-turf.

Reverend John had enjoyed the phone call from Caleb, listening to his pleas to allow Carol to take Thatcher's body for a private funeral immediately after The Punishments. He finally relented, reminding Caleb that the other sinners would be hung from the golden stanchions spanning Independence and Constitution. The bodies strung up to remind all what happens to those who offend Biblical Laws.

Suspended from the stanchions, crows pecking out their eyes, hung until they rotted, and then the remains scooped up and tossed in the garbage in the public landfill. Carol Thatcher should be grateful that she could bury her husband.

He watched Carol strain against Caleb and a security man as she tried to get to Thatcher. Her lips moved, mouthing, "No! I love you! I love you!"

TV cameras focused on Thatcher and Carol. Reverend John pushed the coffee table away, put his feet on the floor and leaned forward. Mack Bradley grasped Thatcher's neck and forced him to his knees. Still grasping his neck, Bradley bent low, lips close to Thatcher's ear. He whispered something. Revenge must be sweet.

Reverend John's voice rose from the opto-screen repeating verses about theft from the Book. He started a hypnotic chant that reverberated around the stadium.

"THOU SHALT NOT STEAL!
"THOU SHALT NOT STEAL!
"THOU SHALT NOT STEAL!"

He was drawn to the screen showing Carol, face contorted in agony. Reverend John flipped his hand-held control to enlarge Carol's picture. Tears ran down her cheeks. When Mack Bradley aimed his revolver at the back of Thatcher's head, she leaped forward, fighting the hands that restrained her. Her lips puckered into a scream, "No!" Her screams were overpowered by the crowd's chant. She reached for Thatcher.

Reverend John watched her. Through his peripheral vision, he saw the executioner cock the revolver's hammer. He heard the shot over the cheers of the crowd and saw Thatcher's body fall face down onto the turf. The body twitched and then lay still.

Mack Bradley knelt next to Thatcher's body and touched the back of his head. He stood up, held the bloody hand above his head and turned a full circle, a triumphant grin on his face. The crowd cheered.

Carol Thatcher collapsed.

CHAPTER 34

The Stadium

Carol

SHE WIPED TEARS WITH THE back of her hand. A Virtue man drove a cart next to Thatcher's body, and helped Mack Bradley toss the corpse onto the cart's platform. They strapped Thatcher's body down so it would not roll off. Bradley sat in the passenger seat and they drove toward the tunnel that led to the stadium's parking lot.

Reverend John's image filled the stadium screens. Eulogizing the wisdom of the Biblical Laws and the Punishments, praising the audience for their participation and urging those who had not converted to do so at once, he warned time was short and non-Christians would face even more terrible punishments at the hand of the Almighty.

"We have to go now, Carol." Caleb grasped her by the arm.

She jerked away. "Where? Where do I have to go?"

Felix said, "You need to take Thatcher to the funeral home for the cremation."

The robot crawlers moved into position, lifted the domes and retreated. Men in gray coveralls pushed cleaning machines, removing blood from the field.

A passenger cart arrived. Caleb and Bob Roberts supported Carol as they walked toward the cart. Her legs seemed paralyzed, steps faltering, muscles like rubber bands. It was as if her core strength had been hollowed out.

They followed the cart carrying Thatcher's body. As fans cheered the video champion teams' return to their positions, she watched Mack Bradley and the Virtue driver transfer Thatcher's body into a waiting ambulance.

Bob Roberts had a Moral America car waiting. Caleb helped her into the back seat and sat next to her. They followed the ambulance out of the stadium toward the funeral home.

Carol looked out the back window. "Where's Jamila?"

"She had to take care of some business. She'll meet us back at Moral America," Caleb said.

Several minutes later, Caleb asked Roberts, "Are they following?"

Roberts looked in the rear view mirror and then nodded. "Two cars."

"Who?" Carol asked.

"Virtue," Caleb said.

"Why would they care now?" She asked.

"Virtue always watches." Roberts said.

The ambulance pulled into the back delivery gate of the funeral home. Roberts parked in front. They got out and walked inside. The mortician, a short rotund man, gave Carol his condolences and then greeted Caleb like an old friend. He led them into a small room containing several easy chairs, a couch and a small desk. In a trance, Carol sat in a chair.

"Mrs. Thatcher, you can wait here until the medical examiner issues the death certificate. Once you've signed it, we can commence with the arrangements."

"Arrangements?"

"I was informed you wanted the body cremated as soon as possible. There's an extra cost involved, but we will give you his ashes within several hours."

"I want to see my husband."

The mortician and Caleb looked at each other. The funeral director cleared his throat. "I would strongly advise you to remember him the way he was."

"What? Why not? I have every right."

The mortician said. "Because the bullet . . . Looking at him would be a terrible shock, Mrs. Thatcher. You do not want to remember him that way. Please trust me in this matter."

Caleb touched her shoulder. "He's right, Carol."

Darkness overwhelmed her. She shrank deep into the chair and cried.

A half hour later, the mortician came back with a man he introduced as the medical examiner, who asked her to read and sign the death certificate. Caleb helped her to the desk and pulled out the chair for her. She collapsed into it. The mortician handed her a pen, the medical examiner pointed to the witness signature line. She stared at the form, finally focusing on the line, "Cause of Death—Gunshot". She sobbed and scribbled her signature with quick uncontrolled strokes.

The medical examiner and mortician left the room.

Carol grasped the edge of the desk. "Let's go."

"Not yet. We need to wait."

"What is there to wait for?"

"His ashes."

CHAPTER 35

Virtue Headquarters

Reverend John

HE SAT ON THE COUCH with Tim Oliver and replayed the entire Punishment broadcast again, savoring each scene.

Now, hundreds of years after the Enlightenment, that so-called Age of Reason, when intellectuals first challenged Christian ideas grounded in tradition and faith, Reverend John was using their own technological tools to return the flock back to God's mysteries. He was using their science, their so-called *logos* to promote the *truth* of the Almighty and the Church.

God would reward him. Maybe that was why he had heard the Voice telling him to come home. God wanted to thank him for all eternity. That was it! God was calling him home.

Oliver stood up. "You don't need to kill Thatcher's son. He's just an innocent kid."

"How do you know what I have planned?"

Oliver rose. "Follow me. You need to see something."

They walked into Oliver's lab. He booted up a program. The screen filled with scenes of Reverend John in his office. He selected a screen and opened it. It showed Reverend John talking to Deverence about capturing Billy at Mary Lee's and taking him to the orphanage in Manhattan. Reverend John stood, open mouthed, as Oliver pulled up other scenes: the HERF gun and the nuclear weapon, paying Felix for the real trigger, and detonating the bomb in New York tomorrow.

"I'm calling Deverence. You're going downstairs."

Oliver laughed. "No I'm not. If you take me to the dungeons, a video exposing you and your lies and murders will be broadcast around the world."

"I'll stop you."

"Too late. The program is safe, embedded in multiple places. If I'm not safe it will automatically override every broadcast, every communication device."

Reverend John slumped against the edge of a desk. "You're lying."

"You saw how I altered images of those poor bastards you murdered at The Punishments. Let me show you something else." He brought up another program. An image of Reverend John filled the screen, announcing the time and location of the Second Punishments.

"I didn't record that. That's not me."

"That's your virtual twin. Viewers can't tell the difference between the real you and the avatar. I can make it do or say anything I want."

"You couldn't get away with that. I have to make public appearances . . ."

"You're already known to be eccentric. You will develop germ phobia and announce you refuse to meet people face-to-face. Henceforth all your meetings will be on screens. They'll accept your decision with pleasure. No one wants to be in the same room with you."

"You're out of your mind."

"You've always wanted to know what I was working on in my private lab. I've got a surprise." Oliver led him across the lab to the locked door, punched in a combination and opened the door into a smaller lab. "Meet your avatar."

Reverend John stood in the doorway, mouth agape, looking at a full sized model, his identical twin, asleep in a chair.

Oliver turned to the avatar. "Wake up, Reverend John."

The avatar's eye's opened. It looked at Oliver and then Reverend John. It smiled. "Hello. You must be the real Reverend John." The voice, his voice, was pitch perfect. The avatar rose, walked over and offered to shake hands.

Reverend John shrank against the doorframe.

"Shake your own hand."

"No! I won't touch it. What? How?"

"Go sit down, Reverend," Oliver said.

The avatar nodded, turned, walked back to the chair, sat down and watched them with a curious look on its face.

"Go to sleep now," Oliver said before leading Reverend John back to his large lab.

"How . . .?"

"Even people who know you extremely well won't know the real you. Think about the freedom you'll have. You can personally ride the Rapture into the arms of your Lord. Virtue will continue its mission and no one will know the difference. You will be sitting in heaven, watching yourself carrying out your vision of Virtue here on earth."

Reverend John smiled at the thought of becoming immortal.

CHAPTER 36

Funeral Home

Carol

FOUR HOURS LATER, FEELING THE effect of two anxiety pills, she allowed Caleb and Bob Roberts to assist her from the funeral home to the back seat of their car. Roberts carried a black plastic box containing the ashes. She wondered what to do with it, where to spread him. That was the problem with life. You are so busy with the details of living day-to-day, thinking life will go on forever; you never talk about unpleasant realities. It didn't make any difference now. She would have plenty of time to decide what to do with his ashes later. Roberts put the box on the front passenger seat.

"Buckle him up," she said with slurred voice.

"Huh?" Roberts looked at her in the rear view mirror.

"Oh never mind. Nothing can hurt him now." Her laugh dissolved into sobs.

Caleb put his arm over her shoulder. "We'll take you back now."

"Back? Back where? To my house? I have nowhere to go."

"We're going back to our suite at Moral America."

"I have to get Billy."

Roberts pulled out into traffic and looked in the rear view mirror. "Virtue is following."

"Where's Billy?" Caleb asked.

"Secret." She gave in to the drug and nodded off.

She woke up when the car dipped on the ramp of Moral America's basement garage. The two men helped her to the elevator. It shot up to the executive floor, gravity pushing down her stomach. She fought throwing up. Roberts unlocked the door to the suite and they led her to a couch. She leaned back and closed her eyes, listening to someone double lock the door behind them and then heard footsteps leading into the bedroom. She slept.

Sometime later, she felt someone touch her hand. She tried to focus on the man sitting on the couch next to her. She closed her eyes, thinking she was dreaming, wondering if now she would always dream and hallucinate about Thatcher.

"Carol?"

His voice. It was a delusion. She shook her head. Opened her eyes and focused on Thatcher's image. She touched his face. Impossible. It had to be someone else. She had to be in a drug-induced coma.

He kissed her forehead. His scent.

She wrapped her arms around his neck and held on like someone drowning.

They cried and held each other.

After a few minutes, she said, "How? Why? I don't understand."

Thatcher nodded as Caleb, Roberts and Jamila walked into the room and sat in chairs across from them. "I didn't understand either. But they can tell you."

Caleb said, "It was Jamila's idea, her plan. You tell them."

Jamila leaned forward, elbows on her knees. "When we met, you told me Mack Bradley was a closet homosexual working for Virtue and he'd vowed to kill Thatcher. I had

Roberts set up a meeting with Bradley. After the introduction, Roberts left us so there would be no witnesses. I threatened to publicly expose Bradley. Then I gave him a way out: I promised a small fortune and a private jet to flee the country after faking Thatcher's execution. He lived up to his promise and I lived up to mine."

They were silent. Finally Caleb asked, "But how did he pull it off? Thatcher looked like he'd been shot."

Jamila said, "I gave Bradley a ring with a hidden needle filled with a quick-acting knockout drug. Bradley injected the needle into Thatcher's neck when he pushed him to his knees. Bradley held Thatcher's shoulder with one hand, so he could sense when Thatcher would collapse and he pulled the trigger. It was a blank cartridge.

"I'd fitted Bradley's inside upper arm with a plastic bottle full of blood matching Thatcher's type. A tube ran down his shirtsleeve. Bradley squeezed the bottle when he reached his hand down to touch Thatcher's head. Blood squirted under his palm and into Thatcher's hair."

"But we followed the ambulance to the funeral home. The medical examiner . . ." Carol said.

"We found a dead homeless man. Dressed him in identical clothes. Shot the dead body in the back of the head, so his face would not be recognizable, and put him in the ambulance. Moral America agents drove the ambulance. At The Punishments, the dead man was already in the ambulance when we put Thatcher inside. When we arrived at the funeral home, they took the homeless corpse out and they delivered Thatcher here. The funeral director and medical examiner didn't know Thatcher. They cremated the wrong man."

"Why the hell didn't you tell me?" Carol asked Jamila.

"We knew Virtue would have a camera on you at all times, watching for an anomaly in your behavior. If you had known, you would have given away the plot, because you couldn't have faked real emotional distress," Jamila said.

Carol squeezed Thatcher's hand. "I'll go get Billy . . . and then what? Where will we go? If and when Virtue discovers you are still alive, they'll try to kill you again."

Jamila held up her hand. "We have a deal, Carol. I promised to help you and you promised to help me. I saved your husband's life for you today. Tomorrow you're going to help me save my daughter. Thatcher will be well enough to pick up Billy and meet us in New York. I'll have a jet waiting and the three of you will come overseas with me. You'll be safe from Virtue."

"Carol can pick up Billy and I'll help you," Thatcher said.

"No. This is between Carol and me, not you and me."

"I don't know how I can help," Carol said.

Jamila lips formed into an enigmatic smile. "You'll be surprised. I have a plan."

CHAPTER 37

Washington

Thatcher

BOWMAN DROVE INTO ANACOSTIA PAST buildings with broken windows, street littered with garbage, past burned out cars. Thatcher sat in the front passenger seat, Roberts in back. Men, covered with ragged blankets or old coats, huddled near cardboard shelters. Teenagers ganged up on street corners, throwing them hostile looks.

"Man, I never imagined a ghetto this close to the Capitol. Kinda scary," Bowman said.

"More like disgusting. Congress has control of D.C. and hasn't provided anything for these people," Roberts said.

Thatcher pointed to a four-story brick building. "That's gotta be where Mary Lee lives. Pull over."

A gang, standing in front of the building, shot them aggressive looks before drifting away.

Thatcher glanced at Bowman, "Roberts will come with me. You stay with the car. You armed?"

Bowman patted his coat. "Yeah. Hope I don't need it."

Thatcher led Roberts up the crumbling staircase, down a hall covered with graffiti, through the smells of garbage. He noticed a different smell as they walked closer to the apartment, a scent that recalled Afghan battle scenes. He stopped next to the door. Roberts had a pistol ready. Thatcher knocked. No response. Knocked again. Nothing. Listened.

Nothing. Tried the doorknob. It turned. He pushed the door open and stepped into the scent of death.

Blood everywhere. A black woman's body, Mary Lee, sprawled on the couch, a bullet hole in her forehead. Another wound in her right shoulder. A brown streak of dried blood streaked down her arm to pool on the linoleum.

Dishes and papers scattered across the floor, the aftermath of a fight. Roberts looked in the kitchen and motioned to Thatcher. A teenager lay curled in fetal position, dead eyes starring at the stove. A switchblade knife near his hand. Blood on its blade. He'd sliced one of his attackers.

Thatcher searched the bedroom, the closet, under the bed. No Billy. He put his hands against the wall and heaved.

"We've gotta get out of here," Roberts said, taking Thatcher's arm.

On the sidewalk near the car, Thatcher spotted two teenagers leaning against the wall. He told Roberts to wait while he approached them.

"Did you guys see anything?" Thatcher asked.

They shook their heads. One started to say something.

The other boy said, "Don't, Jessie."

"I don't give a shit. Yeah, we seen something. You're too late. Other white guys like you come earlier and dragged a little whitey out of the building and put him into a car."

"Anything else?" Thatcher asked.

"Yeah. One of the guys was holding his arm. Looked like he was bleeding."

"Who? The kid's arm? Is the kid hurt?" Thatcher asked.

"Naw. One of the old guys. The kid was putting up a fight."

Back in the car, driving toward Moral America, Roberts' iCom rang. He looked at a text message. "Caleb says he got a text from someone called 'Brutus'. Virtue is taking Billy to the Save-a-Child orphanage in Manhattan."

"It's about four hours. I'll drive," said Bowman.

"I'm in," Roberts said.

"I want you here with Caleb to help relay information to me if you hear again from Brutus," Thatcher said.

"Caleb can . . ."

"I need you here for backup, in case this 'Brutus' is a false lead to distract us."

CHAPTER 38

New York

Felix

THE NEXT AFTERNOON, JAMILA SLIPPED into the role of Felix like a chameleon changes color. She drove to LaGuardia International Airport, mentally reviewing her preparations. She had spent days perfecting today's plan.

She had hired, outfitted and instructed three models that physically resembled her. Hired four bodyguards from a security agency. Walked her planned and alternative escape routes through the corridors of the airport. Spent tens of thousands in bribes for the codes to locked doors. She had a round trip ticket to Chicago in her pocket. It would allow her through security into the concourse itself either to hide or take the flight as an escape alternative.

She drove a rental car to an isolated part of the long-term parking lot. Cracking open her trunk, she removed four red maintenance cones to reserve the empty space next to hers and then transmitted the GPS coordinate to her father. She sent a blind copy to Carol Thatcher.

Her phone conversations with her father had convinced him she was unstable. She was having a mental breakdown. He had to help her; it was his last chance for the additional twenty million. Greed had forced him to agree to bring her daughter to New York to trade for the cash and the Swiss bank code. He would park at the parking space and wait for her to bring the money to exchange for Sara.

Fifteen minutes past the appointed meeting time, wearing a red wig, dressed in a black dress, pearl necklace and high heels, she walked into LaGuardia, surrounded by her four bodyguards, the meeting place a restaurant with five escape routes. A Virtue man sat at a table, a roll-on suitcase near his feet. She exhaled. The suitcase was as she had ordered them to pack the money in — a red Tumi.

The Virtue man looked like a kind person. She wondered how he had lost his forefingers. He held his right arm gingerly. The upper arm of his sport coat bulged as if his bicep was bandaged. He glanced at her but looked away, looking for a man. Everyone thought Felix was a man. She could not identify other Virtue agents in the area, but she knew they were near. Reverend John wanted the trigger, but he would also want his money back, and her as well.

Her guards positioned themselves around the restaurant as she had instructed. She walked inside, sat at a nearby table and ordered a cup of green tea. Pretending to talk on her iCom, she studied the waiters and other customers. Nothing seemed out of place. The Virtue man looked at the time on his Rolex and studied people walking past.

She left cash for the bill, stood up, walked past the agent and then turned back. She smiled. "May I join you?"

Deverence looked startled. "No."

"Don't you like women?" she asked in a flirtatious voice.

"I'm waiting for someone."

"He can't make it."

His eyes widened. "What?"

"What's the name of the man you wait for?"

"How do you know I'm waiting for a man?"

She smiled and waited.

He looked at her for a long moment. "Felix."

"Oh, I work for Felix," she said with a feminine lilt to her voice.

His forehead wrinkled. "Where is he?"

"I have absolutely no idea. I've never met the man. He calls now and then and tells me to go get this, go get that." She sat in a chair next to his suitcase. Her left hand opened the purse in her lap for fast access to the derringer. She placed the bomb's trigger in front of her on the table. "I simply can't imagine how this ball-point pen could be worth so much money."

He reached for it. She pulled it out of his reach. "May I see the cash?"

Deverence reached down and unzipped the top of the suitcase.

She looked at neat stacks of bills. "This is so exciting. May I touch it?"

He smiled. "Of course."

She probed for anything odd. She knew the suitcase and the cash contained homing devices, so Virtue could track her. "I really can't tell if there might be fake bills within those stacks."

"We should go someplace private," Deverence said.

Her right hand sought a small magnetic device the size of a quarter inside her purse. Her left hand held the trigger. "I'll just have to trust you. Who wouldn't trust Virtue? After all, Virtue is the moral guardian of our country. Weren't those Punishments wonderful?"

"Give me the pen." He reached for it.

She withdrew it and, in a simultaneous motion, slapped the magnetic device against his Rolex. A tiny red light lit up.

"What the hell?"

She dropped the trigger into her purse. No one would die. "Oh my! That mini bomb on your watch is on a thirty-minute timer. It will detonate if you take it off or break the contact. It will go off if you try to use your iCom. It also contains a cyclometer, so if you stand up within the next thirty-minutes . . ."

"You bitch!"

"Oh, by the way. See those two men standing by the door?"

Deverence spotted them easily. They were staring at him.

"Those are my men. I have more. I'm certain that within the next thirty-minutes you'll spot them all. Ta-ta." She stood up and pulled the suitcase out of the restaurant. At the door she told her men to watch Deverence closely for twenty minutes and then they could leave.

Followed by her other two guards, Felix walked briskly down the hall, turned left into the next corridor. She heard a dull thump behind her. She turned to watch one of her security guards on the floor. The other guard's fist caught her solar plexus, knocking the air out of her lungs. He ripped the purse out of her hands. She sank to her knees, dimly aware of other people fleeing, realizing one of the guards had been bought off by Virtue. He opened her purse, took out the trigger and flung the purse on the ground near her knees. Helpless, gasping for breath, unable to reach for her derringer, she watched him hurry away and melt into the crowds. She'd failed.

The guard helped her up and handed her the purse. She thanked him, looked for other Virtue agents. They would still want her. She'd be a star of the next public Punishments. She had to save Sara. She staggered away.

She turned into another corridor and slipped into a Woman's Restroom. Her guard waited outside. Two of the three models she had hired stood near the washbasin. They were dressed identically to her. They had identical red Tumi roll-ons. She knocked a code on the handicapped stall. The third model walked out. Felix entered and locked the door behind her.

A cleaning roller can, push broom and mop stood in the corner. She removed an empty duffle from the can, pulled out a cleaning woman's uniform, undressed and tossed her wig and clothes in the bottom and then slipped into the uniform and worn tennis shoes. She dumped the contents of her purse into the uniform's left pocket and then transferred her derringer to the right pocket. She pulled on a white wig. Using a small scanner, she located five tiny GPS transmitters hidden in the bundles of cash. She transferred the cash into a duffle, and tossed the GPS transmitters into the suitcase.

She unlocked the door and, without being seen, pushed the empty suitcase out. Now all the women had identical suitcases. "Go!" The three women walked out of the restroom and turned in different directions.

She looked at her watch. Twenty more minutes before the Virtue agent dared move. She was not yet in the clear. She waited another beat. And then, dressed as an old cleaning woman, she stooped over the bucket and limped out of the restroom, pushing the can and mop ahead of her down the corridor. Several men ran past, talking into lapel microphones.

She walked out of the terminal and into the covered parking lot. Hiding between two cars to avoid security cameras, she pulled out the duffle, disrobed, put on a blouse and slacks from the can and dropped the derringer into her pocket. She took off the white wig and slipped on a blond hairpiece. And then, acting like a tired tourist, she shouldered the duffle and walked toward the long-term parking lot to give her father the cash and save her daughter.

Her adrenaline rush drained like a whirlpool, replaced by the dread of confronting her father. Would he show up? Would he have brought Sara? She thought not. He would betray her to the last. He would take the money and try to kill her.

She spotted a gray minivan in the parking space she had blocked. Someone sat behind the wheel. She could see no one else. That worried her. She could not imagine her father traveling without a bodyguard. Pretending to be lost and looking for her car, she circled the van. She saw no one but the driver. She approached the van.

The driver opened the door and stepped out. Her father smiled and spread his arms wide. "Ah, my disguised Princess has come bearing gifts."

"Where's Sara?"

"In the back, sleeping peacefully with the help of a pill. May I see the cash?"

"Help yourself." She stepped away, keeping space between them while he unzipped the duffle bag. His fingers caressed the cash and he looked up at her with dilated eyes. She glanced in back of the van. Sara could be under the blankets.

He straightened up. "Well done! Now give me the code for the bank."

"Get Sara first."

"Go look at her, my Princess."

He would kill her when she stepped into the van. "I'm not getting in that van. Bring her out. Now!" Her breath became ragged, nerves frayed. She pointed the derringer at him. "Give me my daughter now!"

He smiled. "Well, my dear, we have a little problem. Sara didn't want to come with me. She put up such a fuss that I left her with Hajar. You'll have to come back with me. We'll live with all this money and be one happy family."

"You . . ." There was a movement behind him. His body-guard, the one who had groped her in Marrakesh, stepped out from behind the van. She raised the derringer and killed the man. The shot echoed across the parking lot. This had to be settled with her father now or never.

She raised the derringer and pointed it at her father's head, her finger on the trigger. She looked at his eyes. Her hand waivered.

"You really don't want to shoot me, Princess."

Her eyelids fluttered. A heavy weight seemed to crush the air out of her lungs.

"It's all over, my Princess. You've done well. You'll never need to use that gun again." He took the derringer from her. She sank to her knees and began to weep.

"I'm so sorry my dear. You really are breaking down. It's not your fault. You tried. Now, give me the bank code."

"Never."

"If you insist. Twenty million will have to be enough. I'm going to pull the trigger now and go home to our daughter."

She heard the derringer's hammer cock. She closed her eyes. A shot. She flinched. Felt nothing. The derringer fell from his hand, clattering to the pavement. Her father's face contorted with surprise. He fell against the side of the van and slid to the ground, dead.

Carol stuck her pistol in her pocket and lifted Jamila to her feet. "We've got to get out of here." Dragging the duffle and supporting Jamila, she led her to her motorcycle.

Mute, she watched Carol stuff the motorcycle's leather saddlebags with the cash before cranking the engine to life.

"You've saved Sara. Now put on that helmet and get on behind me! Thatcher texted me. Virtue captured Billy. We have to meet Thatcher to save my son."

CHAPTER 39

Save-a-Child Orphanage

Reverend John

AT THE SAVE-A-CHILD ORPHANAGE ON Green Street in lower Manhattan, Reverend John and Deverence ordered Reverend Ted Wilson to lock Billy in a detention room. Deverence left for the airport to pick up the bomb's trigger and capture Felix.

Reverend John put on his red robe and ordered Reverend Ted to gather the children. He would conduct one last service for his orphans, making certain all had converted to Christianity before tonight's Rapture.

He did not know if Billy Thatcher had been baptized. He did not care. The feisty little bastard deserved to go to Hell. Either Billy or the black kid in the apartment in Washington's ghetto had slashed Deverence's arm with a knife, wounding his ASP just when he needed him the most. The upside of the wound was that Deverence decided not to bring his damned mutt today.

After his agents had picked up the nuclear weapon in the Bahamas, he had decided to hide the bomb and HERF gun at the orphanage. The very innocence of the place pleased him. He could not think of a more unlikely place to conceal the weapons.

He decided to inspect the setting once more before the ceremony. He climbed the stairs toward the third floor, pausing to catch his breath on each landing. He should have worked at being in better shape. The room at the top was long and rectangular with high ceilings and a polished hardwood parquet floor. It had once been a ballroom. On the right side, a row of French doors overlooked a huge maple tree rising from the courtyard below, its branches forked and twisted. He held out his robe and spun across the ballroom floor as he imagined couples dancing, admiring their bodies in the mirrored wall, rubbing against each other, whispering sexual innuendoes, kissing, fingers brushing forbidden places as they stood at the French doors, pretending to gaze down at the courtyard. How ironic this sinful room would become the epicenter for the Rapture.

The HERF gun sat on the floor next to the mirrored wall, plugged into an electrical outlet. His man who took down the Internet brought the gun back here to be recharged. He noted Oliver had installed cameras in the room to record the commencement of the Rapture. The entire world would witness his devotion to God. A red satin cloth draped an altar located in the center of the room.

The nuclear weapon sat on the top of the altar secured by two stainless steel five-inch wide straps bolted to the table and then bolted to the floor. The bomb could not be moved. A two-foot long neo-cross lay on the altar. Reverend John planned for a simple, but memorable, ceremony to begin the Rapture. He felt light headed and dizzy as though he was already rising into the arms of God.

He imagined conducting the ritual. He imagined the blast. The citizens of Manhattan were totally oblivious to the danger. They were good people, living lives snuffed out by events beyond their control. That was the grand irony of life. People struggle to lead a good life, raise a family and seek happiness. They believe they control their lives, but that was a total illusion. Only God controlled one's destiny.

He looked at his watch. There was still time for him to leave, escape the blast and continue to direct Virtue to fulfill God's plan. He could count on Deverence to arm the bomb. But if he led his fellow Christians into the Rapture today, he would sit at the right hand of God for all eternity. He could direct Virtue through Tim Oliver, and his so-called avatar, from Heaven. If Oliver displeased him, he would have the power to strike him dead.

He heard an indistinct whisper, but could not make out the words. The sound seemed to drift into the ballroom from outside. He walked to the French doors and opened them one by one, pausing at each, staring at the gnarled branches of the maple tree, holding his breath and listening. At last, he heard the Voice, calling him home.

He sank to his knees and prayed, thanking God for direction. Now he knew exactly what he had to do between now and when he would detonate the bomb.

Fifteen minutes later, he stood in a small neighborhood park, wrapped in his red cloak, Bible held high, preaching to a growing crowd. They were curious to see the Director of Virtue, the man they had so often watched on their sceens, the man who conducted the Punishments. Hundreds of people gathered. He stood upon a park bench to be seen and heard. He knew the fear of death and afterlife would cause most in the crowd to convert.

Holding the Bible in both hands, he read.

"Thessalonians 4:15 states 'For the Lord Himself will descend from heaven with a shout, with the voice of an archangel, and with the trumpet of God. And the dead in Christ will rise first. Then we who are alive and remain shall be caught up together with them in the clouds to meet the Lord in the air. And thus we shall always be with the Lord.

"Matthew 24:29 teaches us that, 'Immediately after the tribulation of those days shall the sun be darkened, and the moon shall not give her light, and the stars shall fall from heaven, and the powers of the heavens shall be shaken:

"And then shall appear the sign of the Son of man in heaven: and then shall all the tribes of the earth mourn, and they shall see the Son of man coming in the clouds of heaven with power and great glory.'

"And he shall send his angels with a great sound of a trumpet, and they shall gather together his elect from the four winds, from one end of heaven to the other.'

"Ladies and gentlemen, what the Good Book is telling us is that soon, very soon, perhaps within hours, God shall begin the Rapture with an event so appalling that it shall darken the sun and the moon. And at that moment all good Christians shall be taken up into His arms and the rest, all the non-Christians, shall be left behind to endue the Tribulation of fire and brimstone.

"God's Voice whispered unto my ear that the End Times will begin within hours! This is your last chance to reaffirm your faith in Christ, your last chance to convert to Christianity so you will ride with us into the arms of the Lord!"

Standing on the park bench, Reverend John exalted in God's work and began converting hundreds to Christianity.

CHAPTER 40

Save-a-Child Orphanage

Thatcher

THATCHER AND BOWMAN PARKED A half block from the orphanage to wait for Carol and Jamila. Several minutes later, he heard the distinctive rumble of a Harley-Davidson. He spotted them in his side mirror. They parked behind him. Carol untied the saddlebags and handed them to Jamila. Carol ran to the car and slipped into the front seat. Jamila jumped in back.

Thatcher turned to Jamila. "Where's your daughter?"

"In Morocco. I called Hajar, the old woman who takes care of her. Sara is safe and unharmed."

Carol interrupted, "Where's Billy?"

"Brutus contacted Caleb. He said Reverend John took Billy to the Orphanage. He's not hurt. Brutus also said there is a bomb inside. We've been watching the building, but haven't seen any Virtue agents."

"What did Mary Lee say about Billy's kidnapping?"

Could she take more bad news? "I'm sorry. Virtue killed Mary Lee and her son."

"Oh my God! I caused it," Carol said.

"They put up a fight. There was a bloody knife next to her son. Both Mary Lee and the boy were shot, so he must have stabbed someone. There was blood all over."

"The Virtue man I met at the airport was wounded in the

right arm. He was also missing the forefinger of each hand," Jamila said.

"Deverence." Thatcher said.

"That bomb is a so-called clean nuclear tactical weapon. The trigger is set to fire at six even if it is not inserted in the bomb. They have the real trigger, but someone has to stop them from inserting it," Jamila said.

"Let's get Billy out of there. Are you armed?" Carol asked.

He touched his windbreaker jacket. "Roberts gave me a pistol."

"Let's get Billy. I have a jet waiting for us," Jamila said.

Thatcher ordered Bowman to stay in the car to act as a lookout. They split up to scout the orphanage. Jamila went around to the back of the building. Carol and Thatcher scouted the street for anything out of the ordinary. They met at the front door. He tried the handle. It was locked.

"Ring the bell, Carol. Jamila and I will step out of sight on either side of the door."

There were footsteps from inside. Carol saw an eye staring out the security peephole. An older woman opened the door a crack. "Can I help you?"

Carol, holding her pistol out of sight, placed her foot against the door so the woman could not slam it shut. "Reverend John kidnapped our son and brought him here."

"Oh my goodness! I thought something was wrong. Come in." The woman swung the door open.

Jamila and Thatcher stepped inside. Carol said, "Take us to Billy."

A man walked into the hallway. "What's going on, Linda?"

"This is Reverend Ted Wilson, the orphanage's director. These are that boy's parents. They came to get him."

"How do we know you are his parents?"

Thatcher raised his pistol and pointed it at the Reverend. "Take us to him. Now!"

Reverend Ted raised his hands. "You really don't need that. Linda and I thought something was wrong when Reverend John and Deverence brought the boy and ordered us to lock him in the detention room." He led them down a corridor.

"Detention room?" Carol asked.

"For out-of-control kids. We seldom have to use it."

Linda said, "We should hurry. They might come back at any minute."

"Do you know Reverend John has a bomb hidden here?" Jamila asked.

The Reverend Ted stopped. "A bomb? Oh my God."

Linda hugged herself. "I knew it. He's gone insane."

"They took something up to the ballroom, but they wouldn't tell me what it was," Reverend Ted said.

"Gather your kids and get away," Jamila said.

"We have a van," the Reverend said.

"Drive upwind as far and as fast as you can without being stopped," Thatcher said. "Now give me my son."

"I'll guard the hallway," Jamila said.

Reverend Ted stopped before a door, pulled a key ring from his pocket, sorted through the keys until he found the right one. He opened the door.

Billy was in bed, lying on his back. When the door opened, he looked up and then shouted, "Dad!" He jumped into Thatcher's arms. "Mom!" Carol squeezed them both tight.

"It's time to get out of here." Thatcher turned to Reverend

Ted and Linda. "That goes for you, too. Give me the key to the ballroom and then take the rest of the kids. Leave now!"

They ran out of the building, across the street and jumped into Thatcher's car. He started the engine and pulled out of the parking space. He looked at his watch. They had enough time to get to the jet and get out of danger before the bomb would go off. A half block later, Thatcher told Bowman to stop.

"What are you doing?" Carol asked.

He turned to Billy. "Your Mom and Jamila are going take you to Jamila's home. You'll be safe there. I'll come as soon as I can. I want you to know I'll always be watching. I love you."

He stepped out.

"I'm coming with you, " Bowman said, getting out.

Jamila slid behind the wheel.

"Get back in the car, Thatcher," Carol said.

"Whatever happens, know I love you and will always be watching over you."

"No-o-o-o!"

He slammed the door and ran back to the orphanage. He heard a squeal of tires and watched the car fishtail away. Carol and Billy looked at him from the back window. He gave Billy their thumbs up sign. Billy returned it.

The door to the stairs leading to the ballroom was locked. A good sign—no one was up there. He inserted the key and unlocked the door. They stepped in, closed and locked it behind him.

"You stay here, Bowman. Let me know if anyone comes. Stop them." He ran up the stairs to the ballroom.

The nuclear device squatted like a demon upon the altar. He examined it, running his fingers across the gear-shaped hole on top and looked in the shaft for the trigger. He thought he could lift the bomb and hide it somewhere, perhaps toss it out the window into the courtyard below. Do anything to delay before Deverence and Reverend John could insert the trigger. He moaned when he discovered the bomb had been strapped to the table, the table bolted to the floor. He pushed the bomb. It was solid. There was no way he could move it. It would take too long to find the tools to unbolt the table or the bomb.

He once again ran his fingers across the top of the bomb, feeling the sharp edges of the trigger shaft. The orphanage must have a playground for the kids. There had to be a sandbox in the playground below. He could fill the trigger hole with sand. That would make inserting the trigger impossible. He started for the stairs. There was a scuffling sound downstairs, then a shot. He reached for his pistol.

CHAPTER 41

Manhattan

Reverend John

HE HAD BAPTIZED HUNDREDS OF people in the park. Hundreds more waited. He looked at his watch. Time to get back to the orphanage. People trailed after him on the sidewalk. He stopped at an intersection red light and spotted the Save-a-Child van driving up the street toward him. Had they come to pick him up?

The van slowed and stopped next to him. Reverend Ted gripped the steering wheel. A woman passenger leaned toward the Reverend. He couldn't see her face, but there was something vaguely familiar about her hair. Kids jammed the van. Obviously, they had not come to pick him up. In fact, they were oblivious to his presence, such a contrast to the adoring looks of the hundreds he had just baptized. He smothered his resentment.

The woman turned from Reverend Ted and faced forward. Linda! He had always wondered why she had supported Reverend Ted's work with such passion, why she had urged him to promote Reverend Ted to the directorship of the orphanage.

Truth was bitter. When she had fled the house with Pearl, she had run to Reverend Ted. He should have known that was where she would have hidden. She had probably been living with him in the orphanage. Sleeping with him. She was nothing but a . . . a harlot! An adulteress!

The light changed and the van inched forward. Linda looked at him. A startled look crossed her face and quickly morphed into one of disgust. She turned away. He recognized the faces of his two Pearls. Obviously Linda had lied to him. She had taken the first Pearl to the orphanage, hidden her under the protection of Reverend Ted. She had lied to him. Blasphemy! A lying whore!

His old college friend, the best man at their wedding, Reverend Ted had betrayed him. Betrayed God! They drove away and he cursed them. They would be sorry. They would miss the Rapture. God would not take them into his arms. Yes He would—they were Christians. He couldn't think on that now. He was on an assignment for God Himself. He hurried toward the orphanage.

CHAPTER 42

Save-a-Child Orphanage

Thatcher

HE HEARD FOOTSTEPS. THATCHER PULLED the pistol from his coat pocket, tiptoed to the top of the stairs and snuck a quick look. Bowman's body was sprawled on the lower steps.

Deverence raised a gun in his left hand and fired. The bullet hit the wall next to Thatcher's head. He returned a wild shot. Deverence flattened against the wall, hiding behind the corner of the second landing. They shot at each other. The shots ricocheted from brick walls, whining like angry wasps.

A ricocheting bullet punched into Thatcher's right shoulder. His pistol dropped. Hope drained from him as his gun clattered down the stairs. He pressed against the wall, fingers probing his wound. It hurt like hell, but the bullet had not broken a bone or hit an artery. He heard footsteps—Deverence, emboldened by the sight of Thatcher's pistol on the stairs, began climbing toward him. Frantic, Thatcher knew he had made a terrible mistake. He should have fled with Billy and Carol rather than succumbing to a grandiose notion he could save the world. Too late now. At least they had time to get to safety. There was another sound from the stairs. Deverence had slipped, his foot hitting two steps in quick succession. Jamila said Deverence's right arm looked as if it had been injured. His spirits soared. He picked up the stainless steel neo-cross from the altar, tiptoed to the stairwell, pressed his back against the wall, raised the neo-cross like a knife and waited.

He heard Deverence pause on the top step, listening, trying to locate him. The man finally stepped into the room. Thatcher stabbed. The neo-cross sunk deep into Deverence's left arm and then twisted out of Thatcher's grip. The pistol dropped from the man's hand. Thatcher grabbed for it. Deverence kicked the gun and neo-cross down the stairs and then he spun toward him. He stopped with a startled look on his face.

"We killed you!"

"God resurrected me." Thatcher charged, using his good hand to grab Deverence by the throat.

They bumped against the altar, breathing hard into each other's face. Thatcher arced Deverence backwards over the nuclear bomb. Deverence suddenly relaxed and then kicked Thatcher's feet, causing him to stumble. The brawl carried them across the floor like dancers, spilling blood in their steps, struggling toward the French doors. Thatcher dropped low, grabbed Deverence's crotch and then lifted him off the floor, balancing him high on the railing. Deverence tried to jab him in the eyes. The blow glanced off his temple.

Thatcher pushed and stepped back. Deverence flipped over the railing in a slow backward loop, arms flailing, plunging toward the thick limbs of the maple, and crashing through the branches. His head wedged in a fork with a brittle snap. Deverence's eyes stared at Thatcher as if surprised. His body swung gently from the limb. Thatcher, wincing from the pain of his wounded shoulder, leaned against the doorframe and watched the body swing gently. His legs weakened and he slid to the floor. Time slipped out from under him. His mind flirted with the boundary between life and death.

Sometime later, he heard a sound. He opened his eyes.

"Impressive, Thatcher."

Thatcher shook his head and looked for the voice. How long had he been unconscious?

Reverend John stood behind the altar, aiming Deverence's pistol at him. Thatcher held his bleeding shoulder and staggered to his feet.

Reverend John pulled the trigger three times, bullets shattering a mirror.

How many times had Deverence shot? The slide of the semi-automatic had not locked back, so there was at least one more shot. Sooner or later a bullet would hit him if the bastard kept shooting. Thatcher moaned, staggered to the wall and sank to the floor. His wound smeared a trail of red blood on the glass. His good arm fell on top of the HERF gun. He pretended to pass out. Reverend John might walk close to finish him off. In that case, if he were lucky, he would have a chance to use his feet to trip the Reverend. If not? He would have to wait and see.

Reverend John watched him for a moment and then walked toward the stairwell and retrieved the neo-cross. He walked back to the altar, placed the pistol on top and then looked closely at the neo-cross.

"You stained my neo-cross with blood." He used the cloth covering the altar to clean the blade. "Can you hear me?"

Thatcher slurred an incoherent answer.

"What? I can't hear you."

"Trigger in Deverence's pocket. You'll never get it in time."

Reverend John laughed, reached under his red cape and pulled out the trigger. "Deverence met me earlier, before he came up here." He looked at his watch and then picked up the trigger. "Five minutes until Rapture!"

Thatcher spotted the cameras and wondered if Brutus was filming the action. "You're a genius, Reverend John. Explain to me how you made up evidence to convict the victims of the Punishments."

"God's Voice directed all my actions."

Thatcher's finger found the HERF gun's switch. He pushed it. He heard a short hiss of electrical sound, but felt nothing. Reverend John acted as if nothing had happened. The HERF gun's electromagnetic charge should have destroyed the man's pacemaker.

Reverend John looked at his watch again.

Thatcher pushed the switch again. This time, there was no sound. He had failed. That was his last chance.

"It is time!" Reverend John raised the neo-cross high with his left hand. He held the trigger in his right hand. He looked heavenward and prayed,

"Dear Lord, I present you with the trigger that will arm the 'Hammer of God', and thus I begin the Rapture in Your name. I am your faithful servant for eternity."

He placed the neo-cross on the altar and raised the trigger high as an offering and, with great ceremony, lowered it into the nuclear device's slot. He pushed the trigger down through the gear-shaped opening, and twisted the top to lock it in place.

"Praise the Lord!"

Thatcher rolled onto his knees and held on to the HERF gun case in an effort to rise.

Reverend John pointed the pistol at him. His hand shook. A puzzled look crossed his face. The pistol clattered onto the altar. His hand clawed at the pacemaker buried under his collarbone. "No! Not now. Not yet." He staggered and grasped the altar with both hands, mouth agape.

Thatcher lurched toward him.

Reverend John moaned, leaned over the bomb and then slid to the floor. He twitched and died.

Filled with desperate hope, Thatcher examined the bomb. The gear of the trigger fit flush within the opening on top of the bomb. Jamila had told him how to remove the trigger. He pushed down in the center of the gear with his forefinger. It gave.

"Yes!" He would see his family again. He pushed deeper until the top of the gear was below the bomb's stainless-steel surface. He twisted his forefinger to the right. Nothing happened.

Thatcher felt a jolt when the trigger fired.

CHAPTER 43

Thirty-five years later
Presidential Inauguration

William Thatcher III

WILLIAM THATCHER III STOOD IN front of the Chief Justice of the Supreme Court, his arm brushing the reassuring shoulder of his wife, Sara. He felt the smooth texture of the Bible under his fingertips and repeated the oath making him President of the United States of America.

In spite of his tall stature, self-confident and poised outer appearance, he was frightened by the enormity of the task of healing the nation.

The nuclear blast had destroyed a large part of lower Manhattan. Even though radiation had not been as bad as from a dirty bomb, and cleanup had begun, the economy had been devastated. Rising seawaters were another complicating factor inhibiting developers to rebuild. An enormous task lay ahead.

Twelve years after his father had died trying to disarm the bomb, Tim Oliver had a heart attack and died, triggering an automatic broadcast of Reverend John's treachery and a repudiation of Virtue's rule. Until that moment, Oliver, through his robotic avatar, had been able to keep up the façade that Reverend John was still alive and controlled Virtue.

Later, after the resulting investigations, rebellions and elections, the nation began to heal. Thatcher's name had been cleared. They finally could move back from Morocco. After graduating from Harvard, Billy entered politics and had just won a landslide Presidential victory by vowing to rebuild the nation's infrastructure, honor the Constitution, including equal rights, women's right to vote and the separation of church and state. He thought about the terrible things that had been done under the name of religion throughout the centuries. But there would always be religion. If there were no religion, man would invent it. And he wondered if, during the next four years, he could use the bully pulpit to make citizens pay attention and not get sucked into supporting candidates with hidden agendas that threaten democracy.

And now, stepping to the podium, looking at the faces of thousands of citizens, and into the cameras that would broadcast his words to the nation and throughout the world, he felt the weight that his father must have felt trying to save the country from demagogues and fundamentalists.

He wondered if his father had felt afraid.

He prayed for success in the forthcoming endeavor.

He glanced at the Presidential Inauguration Ceremony VIP Section and smiled at his mother and his mother-in-law, Jamila. They were lucky to have each other, their friendship begun in adversity and tragedy.

Billy smiled, looked high into the blue sky and gave his dad their thumbs-up signal. He knew his old man was watching.

The End

CPSIA information can be obtained
at www.ICGtesting.com
Printed in the USA
LVOW12*1610030816

498912LV00007B/25/P